Anger Ebbed
and
Another Emotion
Appeared . . .

Very slowly, the little creases about Dalton's eyelids softened, yet his sea-blue eyes took on the fiery passion she had only once imagined could be there. He gently pulled her closer to him and lowered his lips to hers.

His lips were warm and soft and tasted sweet. Jane forgot where she was, who she was, what she was doing. She gave very little thought that anyone passing by might discover them—and damned little thought to Lord Scythe. This was all she had ever wanted.

Yet one kiss was not enough . . .

Thief of Hearts

Melinda Pryce

DIAMOND BOOKS, NEW YORK

THIEF OF HEARTS

A Diamond Book / published by arrangement with
the author

PRINTING HISTORY
Diamond edition / July 1991

ISBN: 1-55773-543-3

Diamond Books are published by The Berkley Publishing Group,
200 Madison Avenue, New York, New York 10016.
The name "DIAMOND" and its logo are trademarks
belonging to Charter Communications, Inc.

PRINTED IN THE UNITED STATES OF AMERICA

10 9 8 7 6 5 4 3 2 1

To My Hero and Lover

Thief of Hearts

Chapter 1

'BUNDLED UP AND carted off like so much excess baggage,' Miss Jane Manley grumbled to herself as she stared out the window of her uncle's jolting carriage.

She pulled her fine, dark brows closer together and glowered at the Lincolnshire countryside rapidly passing by in the waning twilight. Jane dared not show her irritation to the true objects of her displeasure, who were seated across from her inside the carriage, so she directed a dagger-eyed glare at what she felt was an extraordinarily offensive hayrick.

However, the objects of her displeasure were not to be deceived by her subterfuge.

"There is no need for such dark looks, Jane," Lady Manley scolded as she adjusted her pink kid gloves over her plump fingers. She barely glanced in Jane's direction.

"We have trod this ground before. I should think even *you* would understand the situation in which your uncle and I find ourselves."

"Yes, Aunt Olive," Jane answered dutifully.

She glanced to her uncle, who was seated beside her aunt.

Sir Horace Manley's several chins lay folded up upon his rumpled cravat. Sounds of imminent strangulation issued from his throat, therefore Jane knew him to be asleep.

She was quite relieved, actually. Even though his snoring was exceptionally loud and unpleasant, it was infinitely to be preferred to the sounds Uncle Horace made when he was awake.

"Your uncle and I have incurred certain expenses in bringing Horatia out this Season," her aunt continued the explanation which Jane had heard many times before. "And, of course, we anticipate incurring many more."

Lady Manley leaned forward and patted the plump hand of her daughter, who was seated beside Jane.

Jane's cousin looked up, simpered at her mother, then lowered her head to resume her contemplation of her reticule. Either that or to doze off again, as Jane rather doubted that Horatia was possessed of the mental acuity to contemplate anything more complicated than the Yorkshire pudding of which she was so fond.

"Therefore, as we could no longer afford to have you continue in our household, there was no alternative but to see you married." Lady Manley gave Jane a cold stare. "I see no reason for injured feelings. After all. . . ."

'After all,' Jane repeated to herself in anticipation of the lines she had learned quite by heart, having heard them so often, 'you've benefited from our charity these ten years past.'

"You've benefited from our charity these eleven years past," Lady Manley reminded her.

Jane looked up, startled. "Has it been eleven years already?" she exclaimed, truly surprised. Then she could not resist adding, "I vow, I've been enjoying myself so well that I've clearly lost all account of time!"

Lady Manley snorted rather indelicately.

"Of course, 'tis a great pity that your father did not leave enough when he died for us to bring you out with Horatia, although at three and twenty, you *are* rather old to be coming out," Lady Manley added with a critical glare.

Jane merely stared silently at her own hands resting in her lap. The plain white cotton gloves which she wore contrasted sharply against the old brown bombazine cloak.

She was all too aware of her own poverty. In fact, her aunt never missed the opportunity to remind Jane that her wastrel father and extravagant mother had been thoughtless enough to die quite young and quite penniless, and to leave Jane entirely dependent upon the charity of her father's older brother.

Jane twisted around her index finger one of the dark curls which peeped out from beneath her straw bonnet. Even after eleven years, she found she still missed the love and laughter she had shared with her parents.

Before the heavy sigh could escape from her lips, Jane gave herself a mental shake. 'Twas illogical now to lapse into fond remembrances. For the present, she had much more pressing matters with which to concern herself.

"You should be exceedingly grateful to your uncle and me," Lady Manley was once again belaboring the subject. "You shall never have the slightest idea of how difficult it was for us to arrange a suitable match for you. I can scarcely credit that we were fortunate enough to marry you off to a viscount, of all things!"

The unbelievable shock of the entire situation caused Lady Manley to snap open her fan and flutter it furiously before her.

"Imagine! You, a viscountess." Lady Manley spat out a sharp, humorless little laugh. "I only hope we attract at least an earl for Horatia. It simply would not do to have you outrank her."

Jane had already decided long ago that she would be quite willing to allow Horatia to be the viscountess if she, herself, could merely be left alone.

"Of course, you may thank your lucky stars that your uncle was still able to offer some small token by way of a dowry, considering our own enormous expenses at this time."

Jane found small consolation in the fact that she had been sold off to the lowest bidder.

"You may also consider yourself extremely lucky that Lord Scythe was not overly concerned with your lack of fortune, if I may say so."

Jane could not recall a single instance where her aunt had *not* said so. She could not help but twist her lips and frown.

"You would do well to alter that unpleasant expression before we arrive in London," her aunt warned her.

Jane did not change her expression one iota.

"I am quite certain that part of the reason Lord Scythe offered for you was because you do have a certain prettiness," Lady Manley owned reluctantly. "Not quite the same prettiness as Horatia, but adequate, nonetheless. And a certain innocence."

Jane turned to resume staring out the carriage window in the hope that her aunt would leave off her ceaseless badgering. Perhaps if she did nothing to encourage her, then, with any luck, the lady might make an end of it. Luck was not on Jane's side. The boredom of the long carriage ride had given Lady Manley all the impetus necessary to continue her harangue.

"Prettiness and innocence are what gentlemen seek in their brides," Lady Manley told her. "*You* would do well to remember that—and not appear so morose. Your intended husband most assuredly does not want a sour-faced harridan."

'His lordship wanted a bride,' Jane silently corrected her aunt. 'Any bride. I am quite certain that my appearance had precious little to do with his choosing me.'

The late Lady Scythe had presented his lordship with six offspring in rapid succession and had then departed this life. It was common knowledge—indeed, one might go so far as to say it was a subject of ridicule—that her ladyship had barely had time to grow cold in her grave before his lordship was eagerly seeking a new wife and stepmother for his six obnoxious offspring.

Her ladyship had been dead now this past year and a half and his lordship was still seeking—and still being rejected by even the most desperate ape-leaders. The man had been everso determined to capture a bride—and he had caught the hapless Jane.

In truth, Jane pondered, it was not so much that she had been caught as that she had been thrown at him by her aunt and uncle, much, she supposed, as the Christians had been thrown to the lions. However, to the lions' credit, she doubted that they had been offered anything as gauche as mere monetary compensation for their foul deeds.

Jane also considered the martyred Christians to have been far luckier than she. At least they had been allowed to die and go on to their reward. She, on the other hand, would have to live, and spend the remainder of her natural life raising someone else's children.

Unless, of course, his lordship had other plans—for other children. Oh, heaven forbid!

Jane thought that she had rather steeled herself to the

idea of submitting to a stranger she did not love. However, as the time grew closer, she felt revolted by the very thought. Making love was made for lovers, she believed.

"You are quite correct, Aunt Olive," Jane began slowly in preparation for what she intended to say. She made a conscious effort to smooth her rumpled brow and direct a more placid gaze at her aunt. "I am being most illogical about this entire matter."

"There's a good girl," Lady Manley said, smiling complacently. "I knew you'd come 'round."

"After all, I shall have a home. . . ."

"A town house in Mayfair. Another at Bath. Estates in Northumberland," Lady Manley recited the inventory which she and Sir Horace had studied most assiduously.

"I shall have an allowance. . . ."

"Considering the fact that you are accustomed to living on virtually no money at all, I believe you will find Lord Scythe to be most generous," Lady Manley answered with a satisfied grin.

"I suppose becoming a viscountess is fair enough exchange for raising all those children," Jane continued to lead the conversation in the direction in which she had determined it should go. "As his lordship already has several heirs, I don't suppose he will be bothering me very much to produce one. I mean, I don't suppose that, besides my wedding night obligation. . . ."

"Jane!" Lady Manley cried, visibly agitated. Her head swung rapidly back and forth between Sir Horace and Horatia.

Sir Horace was still snoring loudly.

Jane darted a quick glance in her cousin's direction. To all intents and purposes, Horatia appeared to be sleeping. But Jane had noticed a furtive blinking of her eyes. Horatia was quite awake and listening intently, and all the while trying very hard to let no one know.

"But I have heard it said that his lordship keeps a mistress in. . . ."

"Jane! How dare you speak so in front of Horatia."

"But Horatia is sleeping." Jane glanced in her cousin's direction again, only to catch the last fleeting movement of a pair of blue eyes drawing tightly shut. "Isn't she?"

"Or me, for that matter!" Lady Manley exclaimed. "Wherever did you learn of such sordid things?"

Reluctant to reveal that gossiping with the maid was the source of her information, Jane shrugged her shoulders and replied, "I was merely curious as to what other . . . ah, arrangements had been made concerning my status as his lordship's wife."

Jane was trying to sound as calm and as logical as she could. Lady Manley was in no mood to be logical—or calm.

"Your husband will explain it to you," she cut her off with a withering glare. "'Tis not proper that an unmarried girl should have even a passing knowledge of such . . . well, such *things.* I have tried my best to keep Horatia sheltered from that information. I have no idea what went wrong with raising you."

Jane sighed audibly. Ah well, she would not have to wait long to discover what other "arrangements" had been made for her life.

Tonight they were to stay with the Hargreaves, old friends of the family. By the following evening, they should reach London, where she was to be married quickly and quietly to Lord Scythe. That would leave Uncle Horace and Aunt Olive free to bring Horatia out splendidly.

Jane truly harbored no resentment against her aunt and uncle for wishing to bring Horatia out splendidly, and without any encumbrance from an impoverished, unmarried cousin. She had never wished to be a burden upon them. Her greatest incentive to marry Lord Scythe had been the fact that she would at last be free of her aunt and uncle's oppression. Her greatest regret, however, was that she had not been able to persuade them that she wanted no marriage at all, only a quiet life alone in a simple cottage in the country.

Jane tried to think of something that Lord Scythe would find so abhorrent about her that he would be justified, and rightly so, in crying off their betrothal.

Her lack of fortune had not deterred his lordship.

If she had nurtured the slightest hope that her countenance could convince Lord Scythe of the error of his judgment, she thought she might even go so far as to cross her eyes and wear a ring through her nose. However, she realized that there was little opportunity of acquiring a nose ring along the journey.

She pondered the possibility of taking snuff. Certainly, it would be far more easily obtained than a nose ring. Jane also recalled a childhood friend's grandmother who had smoked a thin, white clay pipe. Perhaps she might take to one of those.

Then she realized that these were all very unimportant peccadillos which his lordship would certainly be more than willing to overlook in exchange for an unpaid nanny.

Jane threw a surreptitious glance at the two people who, for so many years, had scolded and belittled her, and who now so willingly and callously abandoned her to a complete stranger.

No, she shook her head and sighed. Murder was out of the question. Murder would not achieve her dream of a peaceful country cottage alone, but only a short drop at the Tyburn. And while Lord Scythe might, indeed, balk at the idea of marriage to a murderess, Jane truly could not find it in her heart to do in even her wicked aunt and uncle.

Her "certain prettiness" and "air of innocence" were all that Aunt Olive said had attracted Lord Scythe—and even they were merely "adequate."

Making herself less pretty did not appear to be the solution. If only she were not quite so innocent. Perhaps *that* would deter his lordship.

Most assuredly, that was *not* the ideal solution! A logical solution, perhaps, but not what she was seeking. In three and twenty years, she had not found the man she could truly love. There was very little chance he would appear on this journey and amend her situation.

Left without alternatives, she truly was trapped.

The carriage jolted over a deeper than usual rut in the bumpy dirt road.

"Damn your eyes, coachman!" were Sir Horace Manley's first words as he awoke.

He glared out the window at the gathering night.

"Why did you not wake me?" he snarled at Lady Manley. "What were you doing that it got to be this late and this dark and us still not arrived at the Hargreaveses'?"

"What was *I* doing?" Lady Manley arched her brows and

glared coldly at him. "What do you expect me to do? Get out and pull the carriage along?"

"Well, you've the face for it," Sir Horace grumbled.

"And *you* have the disposition for it," Lady Manley countered. "*If* we were employing mules."

With a snort, Sir Horace turned from his wife and jabbed at the ceiling of the carriage with his silver-handled cane.

"Faster, Watley, faster!" he bellowed his irritation. "Or we'll never reach the Hargreaveses' before nightfall."

The sharp crack of the whip and the increased jolting of the carriage indicated that the coachman had immediately complied with Sir Horace's orders.

"Damnable highwaymen infesting the countryside," Sir Horace complained, hugging his arms more tightly across his broad middle, as if to protect the ample purse safely stored there.

Was it the movement of the carriage, Sir Horace's volume, or the lurid subject of the conversation which finally roused Horatia?

"Highwaymen!" she gasped.

Sir Horace nodded his affirmation. "Why, only last week, Lord Grimsby was waylaid by a band of brigands along this very road."

"How horrid!" Lady Manley declared, covering her breast with her pink-gloved hand. "Was Lady Grimsby traveling with him at the time?"

"Aye, she was," Sir Horace answered. "They took Grimsby's purse, her ladyship's jewels, knocked the valet over the head, and carried off the maid!"

"Oh, the poor thing!" Lady Manley gasped at the sheer horror of it. "Surely they did not get *all* her jewels?"

Sir Horace nodded grimly.

"Whyever should they want the maid?" Horatia asked, clearly quite bewildered. "I should never have supposed that highwaymen would have much of a care for the tidiness of their houses."

Jane cast her cousin a sidelong glance and silently shook her head. 'Indeed, 'tis not *my* place to enlighten her,' she decided.

Suddenly, Jane and Horatia were slammed against the

backs of their seats while Sir Horace and Lady Manley were propelled into their laps.

Righting himself, Sir Horace beat angrily with his cane upon the ceiling of the carriage.

"Damn you for an addlepated twit, Watley!" he bellowed. "Start moving again, if you value your life and your position."

"Ah, but he does value his life, Sir," came the smooth, deep voice. "That is why he has stopped for my friends and me."

Jane snapped her head toward the door beside her. A highwayman, silhouetted in the ebbing light of nightfall, had reined his sleek, black horse to a stop and now trained the barrel of his pistol directly at her head.

Lady Manley emitted a piercing shriek. Horatia covered her face with her hands, then spread her plump little fingers apart to peer through them.

"Damn you for a rogue and a scoundrel!" Sir Horace cursed as loudly as ever. "I'll see you swing for this—the lot of you!"

"My friends have detained your coachman momentarily," the highwayman replied coolly, apparently unmoved by Sir Horace's voluble threats. "I am afraid you have no alternative but to pass the time with me. I trust you will not find me too tedious a companion."

Jane felt cold fingers of fear creep up her spine. Uncle Horace would not easily be separated from his purse, nor Aunt Olive from her jewel case. What had she of value to satisfy the highwayman? Would she perhaps suffer the same fate as the luckless Grimsby maid?

What had happened to the maid? Was the poor unfortunate even now lying murdered in an unmarked grave, unmourned and unavenged?

Jane felt her eyes begin to brim with tears and her lower lip begin to tremble in spite of her best efforts to remain calm. She had been hating her miserable life and all its gloomy prospects, but she truly had not been so desperate that she was ready to depart this earthly existence merely to escape Lord Scythe—no matter how many obnoxious children the man had.

Jane hoped the poor maid at least was still alive, yet perhaps imprisoned in some distant, deserted castle, captive of some highwayman—some darkly handsome highwayman. Jane's thoughts took on a startlingly unexpected new dimension—a highwayman who had fallen hopelessly in love with the maid, and she with him, so that she had willingly remained, and every night. . . .

The very real highwayman tossed a leather bag in through the window of the carriage. Jane drew in a great gasp of surprise as it landed squarely in her lap, destroying all her fantasies.

She watched the highwayman cautiously. His clothes were entirely black, and so ordinary that Jane could not have described them if her life had depended upon it. He had tied a black silk scarf about his head, much in the fashion of a pirate or a gypsy. He also wore a black silk mask which covered all but his fine lips and squared chin and the little hollows between his jaw and cheekbones.

"If you would be so kind as to assist me, Miss," he inquired softly of Jane.

His voice held nothing but the utmost courtesy, yet Jane sensed that his polite request would brook no refusal. She slowly picked up the leather bag and opened it.

"Sir. Ladies." The rich volume of his voice again filled the carriage. "You will kindly unburden yourselves of your valuables and place them in the bag which this obliging lady will hold open for your convenience."

He waved his pistol at Jane. When she hesitated, his eyes held hers intently and he said, "I would warn you not to dawdle, Miss, as any delay makes the finger which I hold upon the trigger extremely fatigued and prone to sudden muscular contractions."

Jane hated the man for his cold and calculating thievery. She hated herself for being unable to resist his callous demands. Yet she held the bag open as Sir Horace dropped in his heavy purse and Lady Manley poured in the contents of her jewel case.

"I would like to express to each of you my deepest appreciation for the munificence you have displayed this evening," the highwayman said.

He inclined his head slightly. Short strands of hair slipped out from under the black silk scarf and curled gently about the small lobes of his ears. Did his brown hair have a reddish hue or was it a mere trick of the twilight?

The highwayman swung his restless horse about, turning to Jane. The last glimmer of light illuminated his face. He nodded to her and said, "My thanks to you as well for your invaluable assistance."

Jane watched his lips as he spoke. Try as she might, she could not help but stare at the man as if she were quite bird-witted.

Then the highwayman smiled at her. For a moment, Jane felt as if she had entirely forgotten how to breathe.

It was no ordinary smile. At first only the corners of his lips turned up, impressing tiny crescent-shaped dimples above the corners of his mouth. The cleft in his chin had not been noticeable until he smiled.

"Pass me the bag—slowly," the highwayman instructed her.

Bit by bit, Jane returned to an awareness of her surroundings. She drew in a deep, much-needed breath.

Another man's voice suddenly cried, "Quickly, back there! Another carriage comes!"

The highwayman drew his horse closer to retrieve his booty.

Jane looked directly into the eyes of the man who was now so close to her. The dim twilight could not disguise the color of his eyes—soft blue-green, like two pools of clear sea-water remaining in the hollows of the sand after the rest of the tide has gone out. The silken mask could not cover the soft eyelids, half-lowered over his gaze, nor the gentle creases under the fullness of his lower lids. Nor did it hide the faint touch of amusement behind his intense concentration.

Jane was suddenly seized with the conviction that a man—even a highwayman—who had eyes like those could perhaps be dangerous but never truly evil.

She realized that she was about to commit the most illogical act of her life. Yet she also knew that rather than spend the rest of her life with Lord Scythe and all his tedious certainties, she would take her chances with the man possessing that smile and those eyes.

Cautiously, she rose from her seat, ducking her head to

avoid striking the carriage ceiling. Very slowly, she pushed
open the carriage door and stood at the edge of the step.

Suddenly seizing the highwayman's arm for support, she
flung herself from the doorway of the carriage to land side-
saddle behind him on the horse. She clasped her arms about
his waist in a veritable death grip to prevent herself from
falling off the other side.

"What the deuce!" the highwayman exclaimed. He tightened the reins to maintain control as his horse whinnied and
shied and pranced about uneasily. "Release me this instant!"

Jane clung to him all the more tightly.

The other man's voice called out again, but this time in
a much more agitated tone, "I say, are you quite done yet
back there? We'll never get away if we don't go now!"

"Release me!" the highwayman demanded, spinning the
still frightened horse about in an attempt to unseat Jane.

"I'm coming with you," she informed him determinedly,
her arms clasping his waist frantically.

The two accomplices who had been detaining the coachman suddenly galloped past. The sound of a carriage approaching from the opposite direction could be heard
through the darkness.

The highwayman shrugged his shoulders, dug his heels
into the flanks of the sleek, black horse, and galloped away,
with Jane clinging desperately behind.

Chapter 2

HORATIA BLINKED IN bewilderment. She stared after Jane, who was seated behind the man on the dark horse and rapidly diminishing into the distance. She looked down at the place beside her in the coach which her cousin had so recently occupied. Then, once more, just to be certain that she truly had seen the astonishing incident, she looked back up to see that Jane had indeed completely disappeared into the night—with a highwayman, of all people!

"Well, there she goes," Lady Manley stated quite bluntly as she peered out the carriage window.

"Bah! Let her go," Sir Horace declared, waving his fleshy hand in a gesture of disdain.

"Indeed," Lady Manley agreed. She turned from the window, snorting and slapping her hands down into her lap in a gesture of finality. "Good riddance to bad rubbish, I always say."

"Bloody hell!" Sir Horace suddenly exclaimed. "The shameless chit made off with my money!"

"And my jewels! Who would have imagined such a thing from quiet little Jane?" Lady Manley shook her head. "I did my very best to raise the girl properly."

"So you did, my dear," Sir Horace reassured her.

"I thought she was becoming quite sensible, actually," Lady Manley lamented.

"'Tis not your fault that she reverted to whatever damnable habits she learned from my brother's extravagant wife." Sir Horace leaned closer to Lady Manley and muttered confidentially, "Heard the wife had gypsy blood in her, if you take my meaning."

"Please, Horace. Not in front of Horatia," Lady Manley reminded him.

"Oh," Sir Horace mumbled.

"Indeed, Jane must have got that wild behavior from her mother's side," Lady Manley decided. "Certainly no one on *your* side of the family has ever comported himself in such a disgustingly wanton manner."

"Never!" Sir Horace declared.

"Except perhaps your brother."

"Quite."

Horatia was feeling frightened and quite alone in the dark carriage. Jane was six years older than she. In the eleven years since her cousin had come to live with them, Horatia had grown rather fond of her. Jane had become like a very sensible older sister. Whatever would she do without her?

"Why should Jane want to leave us like this?" Horatia pouted.

Sir Horace and Lady Manley exchanged furtive glances.

When she received no answer, Horatia continued, "I really would not have thought it of Jane." She shook her head, the ribbons of the stylish bonnet fluttering gracefully about her rounded little cheeks. "Perhaps it was all that talk of the Grimsby maid. Imagine Jane being so concerned as well with the cleanliness of a bandit's lodgings."

Lady Manley leaned forward and patted Horatia's hand.

"Never you mind, my dear." She glanced back to Sir Horace with a knowing look. "I'm certain Jane was concerned with other things as well."

The coachman's quavering voice interrupted them. "Sir, are you and the ladies quite all right?"

"Watley! Are you just now coming to your senses?" Sir Horace demanded.

"Well, Sir, it did take a while to compose meself," he admitted.

"Too long. Too long," Sir Horace grumbled.

"You and the ladies have suffered no harm, I trust, Sir," Watley asked.

"Of course not! No thanks to you." Sir Horace swung his silver-handled cane at his coachman's head.

Fortunately, Watley had been in Sir Horace's service long enough to have learned when to duck.

"Damn you for a walleyed oaf! Why did you stop for those highwaymen?" Sir Horace demanded.

"Well, they had pistols, Sir," Watley tried to explain. "Trained at me very head, they did. They'd have shot me nose off if I'd have moved one hair, they would have, Sir."

"'Tis no excuse for bad driving," Sir Horace snorted and again swatted in vain at the coachman.

He poked the cane forward and demanded, "Back to your task, man. See if you can get us to the Hargreaveses' before dawn, you snail-paced lackey!"

Sir Horace took one more swipe at Watley, but the man was already clambering up onto his box. Sir Horace and Lady Manley were flung back against their seats as the carriage took off with a lurch.

"The Hargreaveses!" Lady Manley gasped. "Whatever on earth shall we tell them? They *are* expecting a party of four. Although," she mused, "I do suppose it is better form to arrive with one less guest than one extra."

Sir Horace was unusually silent for a moment.

"Well, Horace, what shall we tell them?" Lady Manley demanded, becoming increasingly impatient for a solution as the carriage rolled inexorably closer to the Hargreaves.

Sir Horace frowned and began to grumble to himself to relieve the great strain which thinking imposed upon him.

"Don't suppose we could tell them that we left her at home?" Sir Horace offered weakly.

"Not when everyone knows that we were taking her to London to be married!"

"Hmmph, well. . . ." Sir Horace resumed his contemplation. "Can't hardly tell them that the silly chit ran off with a highwayman," he said at last. "Does make her look like a bit of a lightskirt, don't it?"

"Please, Horace! Not in front of Horatia."

"Hmmph," Sir Horace conceded with a nod. "Wouldn't reflect so well as to how we've raised the girl either, would it?"

Lady Manley shook her head and snorted. "Isn't it just like Jane to make *us* appear in a bad light?"

"Don't suppose it would look too well for Horatia either," Sir Horace offered.

Lady Manley gasped in alarm. "Should news of Jane's

indiscretion become common knowledge, why, the damage it would do to Horatia's prospects of making an exceptionally brilliant match—I shudder to think!"

There was a great gap of silence as the Manleys brooded over their predicament.

"Mama?" Horatia ventured.

"Don't bother Papa and me now, my dear," Lady Manley replied. "We are having everso much trouble trying to think."

"But, Mama, do you suppose we could tell them that Jane had been kidnapped by the highwaymen?"

"Kidnapped?" Lady Manley repeated skeptically.

"Just like the Grimsby maid," Horatia suggested.

"Precisely!" Lady Manley exclaimed, clapping her hands together. "After all, who else is to know the truth?"

Lady Manley dug her elbow into Sir Horace's rounded side. "Why, Horace, how could you have missed such a perfectly simple explanation?"

Sir Horace snorted. "I notice *you* were not the one who thought of it, either," he replied glumly.

"Nevertheless, it is the perfect solution."

Horatia beamed. She was exceedingly proud of having thought of such a lovely excuse—and all by herself, too.

"It certainly is not *our* fault that we were stopped by highwaymen. Therefore, we are spared a great deal of embarrassment," Lady Manley expanded upon Horatia's tale. "Nor could anyone misconstrue the kidnapping as improper behavior on Jane's part. Therefore, we are again spared a scandal and any damage which it might do to Horatia's prospects."

Lady Manley smiled smugly to herself.

But Sir Horace was frowning. "We should have to notify the constable," he complained. "I mean. they might even expect us to contact the Bow Street Runners to search for the worthless chit."

"Then we shall do precisely that," Lady Manley answered.

"But suppose they find her?"

"Pish-tosh," Lady Manley exclaimed, waving the very idea away. "They haven't found the Grimsby maid yet. And anyway, Jane is an orphan. After the initial round of gossip, no one will ever bother about what happened to her."

"But what happens when no ransom note arrives from the kidnappers?" Sir Horace asked.

Lady Manley shrugged her shoulders. "That is still no cause for alarm. 'Tis a well-known fact that highwaymen are notoriously poor correspondents."

Sir Horace snorted and nodded his agreement.

Horatia sighed wistfully and commented, "Still, I shall miss Jane."

"But not for long, dear," Lady Manley offered by way of consolation.

Horatia's full, pink lips pulled into a pout. "Most of all, I shall miss the lovely wedding we had planned."

"Ah, well, my dear, I shouldn't worry about that too much, as it really was nothing compared to what *your* . . . . Oh, horrors!" Lady Manley suddenly screeched. "What shall we tell Lord Scythe?"

Sir Horace snorted. "If the man wants Jane, he will simply have to go looking for her himself."

"Rightly so," Lady Manley agreed, heaving a huge sigh of relief.

Sir Horace grumbled, "Just hope his lordship realizes he has to return the dowry if he don't find her."

Without the protection of a saddle, the back of the horse was becoming increasingly hard as Jane's bottom bumped up and down as they fled across the furrowed field toward the distant woods.

The damp air of the early spring night whipped furiously about her face and whistled in her ears. She needed to keep blinking as the sharp air drew tears from her eyes.

The night was growing colder. Jane's body shuddered involuntarily in an effort to warm her. She wished she could pull her cloak more closely about her but feared even the slightest loosening of her grasp on the highwayman would allow him to shed her unwanted company by knocking her off the horse. Then, alone in a strange woods and quite possibly injured, what would she do?

And merciful heavens! She still carried the highwayman's leather bag clutched tightly in her hand. Her fingers were beginning to cramp about it. In full possession of the highwayman's plunder, she truly was his accomplice!

Cold, uncomfortable, and certainly in deep trouble with the law, not to mention with her aunt and uncle, Jane was suddenly beginning to have serious doubts concerning the wisdom of running off with the highwayman. Perhaps if she could escape now and return with the stolen property, all might be forgiven—or at least she might be sent off in disgrace to live out her days peacefully and quietly in the country, just as she had always wanted.

Of course, there was always the possibility that her aunt and uncle would not be so forgiving. She had heard that Newgate offered horrendous accommodations. She supposed hanging could be rather uncomfortable, too.

Or perhaps her aunt would consider it a more fitting punishment to make her marry Lord Scythe! Her greatest fear was that his lordship might still be willing to marry her in spite of all the trouble she had taken to become disgraced.

As they entered the woods at a gallop, the lowest branches of the enclosing trees stung as they slapped against her face and shoulder. Jane ducked her head behind the protection of the highwayman's broad back.

His body was warm with the tension of the robbery and the exertion of riding. He felt good against her icy cheeks.

She pressed her face closer to him, the better to keep warm. She heard a crunch and winced. She knew the brim of her old straw bonnet would never again be quite the same.

Then, suddenly, she decided that she really didn't give a tinker's dam! Not about her bonnet, not about her discomfort, not about what Aunt Olive or Lord Scythe—or anyone else for that matter—might think of her.

The man she had run away with felt good. With her arms wrapped tightly about his slim waist, she could feel each firmly corded muscle of his stomach moving against her forearms and the sinewy muscles of his back rippling against her breasts as she and the highwayman moved in synchronization with the horse's pounding stride.

He even smelled good. As her nose pressed closely into the soft black wool of his jacket, the scent of vetiver—exotic grass and green earth—drifted up to her.

And, merciful heavens, he was handsome! She eagerly anticipated the moment when they would finally stop . . . and he would turn around . . . and take off that blasted mask! . . . and look at her with those pale sea-blue eyes and smile his crooked smile at her once more.

Yet the highwayman remained totally disinterested in her presence as he guided his galloping horse over the narrow, rutted path through the woods.

The pace began to slow. The highwayman, followed by his two accomplices, reined his mount to a halt.

The night was dark. The few tiny stars which had ventured out gave no helpful light. The moon was only an arched silver sliver in the sky. Jane had no idea where they were or why they were stopping.

The highwayman swiveled in the saddle as best he could with Jane's arms still locked about him.

"Release me and dismount," he ordered.

Out of the darkness, his deep voice poured over her like honey. She almost obeyed him unquestioningly, just as she had done in the carriage.

Suddenly, she squeezed her arms more tightly about him so that no one should be able to pry them apart.

"No!"

Jane hardly had expected it of herself, to be so blunt and so disobedient. It truly was not like her.

Apparently the highwayman was equally unused to such a response to his orders. He sat silent for only a moment.

He drew in a deep breath. Jane's arms ached as the muscles of his expanding chest pulled against her joints, but she had no intention of releasing him yet.

The highwayman repeated more firmly, "Release me and dismount."

"No!" Jane, too, repeated her response with stubborn defiance. Then she cautiously suggested, "You dismount first."

"No." There was a stern refusal in his reply. Yet, at the same time, Jane thought she detected the slightest sound of the same amusement that she had seen dancing in his eyes in the twilight.

Jane swallowed hard and tried to explain. "If I release you, you will knock me off the horse and leave me here— alone. I have no intention of allowing you to do that."

"I have no intention of leaving you alone," he told her softly.

There was silence between the two.

"How do I know I can trust you?" she finally was able to ask. Cautiously, she added, "After all, you did rob my aunt and uncle."

Much to her surprise, the highwayman chuckled.

"How do I know *I* can trust *you?*" he countered. "After all, you showed rather a natural talent for becoming a highwayman yourself."

She felt him reach to his waist and pat the leather bag which she still clutched. The coins and jewelry inside clinked against each other.

"If I dismount first," he continued, "perhaps you will jump into my saddle and steal my horse as well as my booty."

"I am no thief!" Jane reminded him sharply.

"Perhaps," he conceded with a shrug. "You know, they say there is a certain honor even among thieves. I suppose we must begin to learn to trust each other some time."

Before Jane could agree, the highwayman had swung one long, muscular leg over the pommel of the saddle. If she had continued to hold him, she would have gone headfirst off the horse. Quickly, she unloosed her grasp. The highwayman deftly dismounted.

He stood back, his hands on his hips. Was he waiting for her to ride off on a purloined steed?

Well, she would certainly show him *she* was not the thief here. Jane remained on the horse, quietly waiting.

From out of the darkness, his strong arms reached up to her. He grasped her about the waist. To steady herself, she placed her hand upon his chest. He gently lowered her to stand before him.

His breath was warm on her cheek. His hands remained softly encircling her waist. One more step and she knew she should feel his lean body pressing against hers.

Once again she felt that she had quite forgotten what breathing even was, much less how one went about performing the mysterious process.

Light suddenly flooded the area about them. The sounds of laughter and yapping dogs filled the air.

She peeked around the highwayman's shoulder to try to determine where she was. They had stopped in the courtyard of an ancient inn. She studied what little she could discern in the dim light emerging from the doorway.

Curiously, the courtyard appeared to be at once busy and deserted. Farm implements lay scattered about along with old harnesses and trappings, yet nothing appeared to be in usable condition.

She could find no sign to indicate what this place might be called. Propped against the wall of a shed was the crudely rendered picture of a horse, yet the board on which it was painted was so badly weathered that the horse was headless—and the paint had turned the strangest shade of green. All in all, Jane knew no more now than when she first arrived.

A group of rather disreputable-looking men had emerged from the inn and were making their way toward them. Jane involuntarily pulled herself closer to the highwayman. She was not certain she could trust him, but he was the only protection she had in this strange place.

The highwayman turned his back to her and faced the crowd. Feeling more alone and helpless than ever, Jane cowered behind him.

The highwayman quickly summoned one of his masked companions to his side.

"Ale for all," he called his invitation to the ragged group as he slipped a few coins into his friend's palm.

Readily, the men then returned to the taproom for the promised drinks. The door closed tightly behind them.

Jane was left in the dark courtyard completely alone with the highwayman.

He turned to her.

"Those fellows were too preoccupied with ale tonight to notice you," he remarked. He slowly ran his finger up and down the section of cloak covering her arm. Was it the cool night air or his unexpectedly gentle touch which made her shiver? "You can be thankful this dark cloak rendered you invisible in the shadows between me and the horse."

Jane grimaced. She knew—indeed, she had been told for the greater part of her life—that she was plain. Aunt Olive and Uncle Horace had done their best to ensure her being "inconspicuous" beside the lovely Horatia. But never in her life had she been accused of being "invisible." She found she did not like it one bit.

Then she recalled the rough-looking group of men who had returned to the taproom. Jane shivered. Perhaps being invisible was not so bad after all.

"'Tis a certainty you can't walk through the taproom bold as brass, although that doesn't seem to stop you from pursuing other adventures in the same manner," the highwayman remarked sarcastically.

Jane drew back, affronted. Then, in the dim light, she saw the corners of his mouth turn up into a teasing smile. Slowly, she smiled in return.

"Then what am I to do?" she asked.

"I needn't remind you that this escapade was your own doing. 'Twould serve you right if I made you stay out here and sleep with the horses tonight," he threatened with the same bantering tone.

Jane was not about to admit that he was quite correct—at least about where lay the blame for her escapade.

"Come," he said more softly. "I shall get you inside without being seen."

He seized her wrist. His grasp was strong—there would be no escaping him—yet he held her almost tenderly, never bruising her delicate skin. He began to lead her across the dark courtyard.

She had no idea where he was taking her. It could be to shelter or to her certain doom. Yet she followed him. The fact that she could not release herself from his grip made not the slightest difference. She truly was not certain that she wanted to be released.

"Is there no private entrance?" she asked timidly as they traversed the dark courtyard.

He gave a brief, derisive laugh.

"Do you actually think this inn is equipped to entertain such an elite class of patrons?" he countered, casting his arm about to indicate the dilapidated buildings, part rotting timber, part crumbling brick, part disintegrating wattle and daub.

Jane pressed her lips together and made no reply.

"Actually, there was one. Once, long ago," he told her,

a faint note of sadness discernible in his deep voice. "That section of the inn is no longer habitable, like so much else about here."

The highwayman quickly pulled her to the rear of the inn. Slowly, he pushed open the heavy, weathered door.

A fat man wearing a white apron leaned over the large black kettle which simmered in the fireplace. Jane assumed he was the innkeeper.

The man merely nodded to the highwayman as he entered the room.

Jane paused with surprise.

'I know *I* should be extremely startled to see a masked man enter my inn if I were not quite accustomed to it,' she decided. 'The highwayman must come here often.'

When the innkeeper saw Jane enter behind the highwayman, he did indeed startle.

"We'll take the back stairs to my room," the highwayman said to the innkeeper.

The fat man nodded.

Jane swallowed hard. His room! Her heart gave a jump. She knew perfectly well what fate awaited her in the highwayman's room. She drew in a deep breath of resignation. She also knew perfectly well, she told herself, that this was one of the consequences of running off with the highwayman.

"I'm aware of the lateness of the hour, but send up a tray, please," the highwayman requested.

"'Twill be about a half of an hour, sir," the innkeeper said apologetically.

The highwayman nodded his approval.

Merciful heavens! The highwayman intended to eat in a mere half an hour. The man surely did not believe in wasting time, did he?

As the highwayman had yet to release her hand, Jane had no choice but to follow him up the narrow servants' stairs and down the dimly lit hall until they reached a closed door.

Without releasing her wrist, the highwayman pulled a large iron key from the pocket of his black jacket. He unlocked the door and flung it open.

Jane found herself pulled into the low-ceilinged bedchamber with such momentum that she could not stop herself until she had fallen upon the large, lumpy bed in the center of the room.

She landed facedown in the dusty feather ticking. Slowly, she turned and propped herself up on her elbows. In the smoky firelight, she saw the highwayman lock the door and replace the key in his pocket.

What had initially appeared to her to be a logical action on her part now caused her stomach to churn and her toes to turn to ice. Still, in spite of her growing trepidation, she had to own, when she looked at the highwayman, that she felt a certain excitement.

What a terribly wicked, wanton—and wonderful—way to feel!

She drew in a deep breath and raised her chin in an effort to appear imperturbable and perhaps just a bit disdainful. In truth, she felt nothing of the haughtiness she sought to convey.

'Very well now, Jane,' she tried to tell herself as the highwayman turned and took a step toward her. 'Do try to remain calm. After all, you *are* a gentlewoman.'

Falling back upon the bed, she raised her eyes to the ceiling and threw one trembling hand over her face, steeling herself for the fatal moment.

"I am prepared, sir," she managed at last to say in a very, very tiny voice. "Do your worst."

The highwayman began to chuckle.

Chapter 3

THE HIGHWAYMAN STOOD there chuckling for so long that Jane, at length, began to doubt the man's sanity.

At last she lowered her arm and raised herself on her elbows to view the lunatic who had dragged her here merely to lock her in his room and laugh at her.

But she saw no raving madman, merely the highwayman. He leaned against the door frame. His arms were crossed over his muscular chest. His fine lips were drawn back over even white teeth in that familiar crooked smile. Laughter deepened the creases around his eyes, but the same look of amusement sparkled in their blue-green pools.

Between deep chuckles, the highwayman finally asked, "My worst what?"

"What an absurd question," she said, sitting upright upon the bed. She frowned at him. "I . . . I know you've brought me here to ravish me."

"Why should you think that of me?" he asked, frowning back at her.

"That's what all highwaymen do, don't they? I mean, that's what the novels I've read would seem to indicate."

"Ah, well, if I were your guardian, I should take care that you read more accurate novels." The smile returned to his lips, the laughter to his eyes.

"Surely you know about these things better than I," Jane said, rather amazed that he seemed not to. "You really must."

"Must know about highwaymen?"

"No, no," Jane corrected. "You must. . . ." Her courage fled in midsentence.

25

He frowned, but there was still a hint of laughter hidden behind the black silken mask. "Aside from the fact that you seem to think ravishing beautiful women an age-old tradition much revered among highwaymen, please take this opportunity to explain why I 'must.' "

"Well," Jane hesitated. "The explanation is not so simple."

The highwayman nodded and grinned at her. "Coming from you, miss, I am not surprised."

She shyly returned his grin, then drew in a deep breath in preparation for her explanation. "You see, I was on my way to London to be married."

"Ah, of course," he said, spreading his long, muscular arms in a gesture of total comprehension. "That explains it all."

"No, it doesn't. It doesn't even begin," she said, fidgeting with the little leather bag she still held in her hand. "You see, I do not love the man I am to marry."

The highwayman shifted his weight from one foot to the other and crossed his arms again. "I understand that to marry someone for their fortune or position—or if one's luck holds, for both—is not an uncommon occurrence among the *ton.*"

"What would *you* know of the *ton?*" she demanded crossly. Her demand turned into a frustrated wail. "Oh, what do *I* know, for that matter? All I know is that I do not want to marry him. All I ever wanted was a quiet life in the country. But my only choices were to live the rest of my days being constantly reminded that I was merely a poor relation or to marry a man I barely know and certainly do not love."

The highwayman leaned back against the wall, nodding. "You do seem to find yourself in quite a predicament."

Jane sighed with relief. "I am so glad you understand my situation." For some unaccountable reason, she was beginning to feel quite at ease unburdening herself to this man. "I had tried my best to think of something which would cause this marriage not to take place."

"Quite a dilemma, I should think," he observed, thoughtfully stroking his squared chin.

"He doesn't seem to mind that I am without fortune."

The highwayman waved his hand with a mocking air of disdain. "A mere trifle."

In spite of herself, Jane smiled. "He didn't even seem to mind that I . . . well, that I am rather plain looking."

The highwayman's sea-blue eyes swept over her body, then returned to gaze intently into her eyes.

"I should not have described you in precisely that fashion," he said. Then he shook his head and smiled. "But, 'tis your tale, miss. Proceed."

"Then it came to me! I thought the solution quite logical, actually," she added modestly, then continued, "I thought perhaps if I were not a virgin. . . ."

The smile was gone from the highwayman's lips and the laughter from his eyes.

With a brave effort, Jane tried to finish her explanation, in spite of the apparent anger suffusing the highwayman's face. "Perhaps the man I am to marry will not want me, and my aunt and uncle will send me away. . . ."

Her words rushed out, hurrying to finish before her courage left her completely. "So you see, you really must, or all this will have been for naught."

Suddenly, he pushed his lean frame from the doorway and, with two long strides, stood directly before her.

'Merciful heavens!' Jane thought. 'I never *dreamed* he would be so willing to cooperate!' Her body was tense with a strange mixture of fear and anticipation.

But he merely stood there, staring down upon her.

"All this for naught?" he repeated incredulously. "You mean to say that you deliberately ran away with me so that you could . . . so that I would . . . Oh, come now, miss. I mean, if you were that desperate, surely there were other, ah," he hesitated, ". . . opportunities."

Jane shook her lowered head. "No others seemed to present themselves," she admitted.

"You caused me all this trouble just so you. . . ." The man strangled what he was going to say deep in his throat. His face was growing red with the words—and perhaps, Jane feared, even with the curses—which he wanted to speak but held back.

Well, really! *She* was the one who had got herself into this troublesome situation. *She* was the one who would eventu-

ally have to answer to Uncle Horace and Aunt Olive and
Lord Scythe, and perhaps even to the magistrate, while the
highwayman disappeared into the night, never giving her
a second thought. What on earth had this fellow to be angry
about?

"You little fool!" he declared. "You haven't the least idea
of what you might have got yourself into, have you? Suppose
I were not the honorable thief that I am? Suppose I were
the type of man who would indeed abduct and ravish you,
and then murder you—or perhaps consign you over to a life
worse than death?"

Jane dropped her gaze to her hands, clenched tightly
about the little bag in her lap. She tried to think. How could
she tell him that, mask or no mask, he had, quite frankly,
the handsomest face she had ever seen—even if only in
parts? How could she admit to him that from the first moment she saw him, she knew with certainty, deep inside, that
she could trust him with her very life?

"You never considered that danger, did you?" he demanded.

"Well," she answered, shrugging her shoulders. "One
way or the other, at least I should not have to marry."

The highwayman was shaking his head. "I must own,
your logic is impeccable. Convoluted, but impeccable."

"Thank you."

"Of course, your aunt and uncle have by now alerted the
authorities, who are already upon my trail, searching for
you," he reminded her.

Jane winced, more because of her own thoughts than anything the highwayman had said. She greatly doubted that
Aunt Olive and Uncle Horace would be eager enough to
have her returned to go to all that inconvenience.

"Did you ever stop to consider the danger in which this
escapade of yours has placed my men and myself?" he demanded angrily.

Jane drew back, extremely surprised. "Why, you live for
danger. You're highwaymen."

He grasped her chin in his hand and lifted her face to his.

"I may be a highwayman, a brigand, a thief—whatever
epithets you may wish to heap upon my head—I *am* all
that," he told her, his voice low and deep. Then he released

her chin. He dropped his gaze and turned away. "God help me, the more is my shame. But that is *all* I have been—until now."

Jane felt the sodden lump in her throat growing heavier.

The volume of his voice grew as his anger intensified. "Thanks to your quite mad leap this evening, you have also turned me into an abductor of young women."

The highwayman spun and struck the bedpost with the heel of his hand so hard that Jane felt the bed shake and heard the hard mahogany crack.

"But there is one thing that I certainly am *not*. And no madcap scheme from some coy, reluctant bride will ever turn me into *that!* I have *never* taken an unwilling woman," he told her hoarsely. "I do not intend to take you."

Jane decided that now was not the right moment to remind him that she was not exactly unwilling. Perhaps after he calmed a bit he would listen to reason.

Without glancing back at her, the highwayman strode toward the door. Withdrawing the key from his waistcoat pocket, he reached out and unlocked the door. As he began to twist the knob, the door was pushed opened by a sizable, rounded bottom. A buxom redheaded wench carrying a heavy tray entered the room backward.

As the maid turned round, her dark eyes immediately sought the highwayman's.

"Well, hello, love," she crooned, casting an appreciative smile at him.

Jane watched the highwayman's brow smooth as the anger dissolved from his face. His fine lips spread into the familiar crooked, teasing smile.

"How nice to see you again, too, Nell," he responded.

Jane watched this Nell person with piqued curiosity.

The serving maid's bare arms were round and white. Her full breasts jostled back and forth as she carried the heavy tray into the room. They strained against her bodice as she set the tray upon the small table by the window. As the maid stood, she raised her arm to brush back the flaming red hair that had fallen into her face. Jane marveled that the maid did not spill out of her dress.

"I see you've picked up something extra this trip," Nell

remarked to the highwayman. Her lips curled and her eyes hardened as she appraised Jane.

Jane returned the maid's sneer with a disdainful glare.

How *dare* that trollop believe that *she,* Miss Jane Manley, niece of Sir Horace Manley, Baronet, would ever stoop to . . . then the glare faded from Jane's eyes. That *was* precisely why she had run away with the highwayman. Ashamed that her motives were so transparent to others, Jane lowered her gaze to the bare wooden floor.

The highwayman made no reply, but Nell needed none.

"Appears as if you've no idea what to do with her now that you have her," Nell offered, cocking her head at him. "So much for the wellborn ones." She sneered at Jane again.

"Oh, I've several very good ideas of what to do with her," the highwayman replied, turning to Jane to emphasize his point.

From the expression he wore, Jane was quite certain that his ideas included a sound thrashing, a severe throttling, and perhaps a quick trip to the bottom of the Thames with an anvil fastened securely about each ankle.

"Looks like you might be needing me tonight after all." Nell smiled warmly at the highwayman. As she passed through the doorway, she deliberately brushed her more than ample breasts against his arm.

"No. I have business to which I must yet attend tonight, Nell," he told her, giving her a pat on her exceptionally rounded bottom. "But you know your offers are always appreciated."

After the pouting Nell had disappeared through the doorway, the highwayman turned back to Jane.

"Eat," he commanded, nodding in the direction of the recently delivered tray. "Perhaps food will restore some sense to your head."

Jane was surprised that the man could converse civilly after his recent livid rage.

"I shall lock you in—for your own safety," he told her. "The fellows downstairs can be rather unpredictable at times. Unless, of course, you think that my leaving it unlocked might enable you to achieve. . . ."

Jane hurled the leather bag at his head. She also called him a name she had heard the stableboys use frequently, although she herself had never before uttered it in her entire life. However, all things considered, she thought it fit this man quite well.

As accurate as her language had been, she wished her aim had been better. The bag dashed against the door beside the highwayman's head, missing him completely. Sir Horace's coins and Lady Manley's jewelry exploded over the room. Jane sniffed with exasperation.

"Perhaps I shall lock the door for safety's sake after all," the highwayman commented as he backed out of the room. "I do not believe the men would be safe with you running about loose."

He pulled the door closed after him. Jane heard the key turn firmly in the lock.

She clenched her fists and sat on the edge of the bed, thinking. At length she decided that since she was stuck here for the night, she might as well make the best of it.

Wistfully, she glanced back at the doorway. She supposed the highwayman would not be back—not tonight, perhaps not ever. He certainly had acted as if he never wanted to set eyes upon her again.

Jane grimaced and rose to remove her cloak and bonnet. She viewed her image, like a tiny ghost set against the dark night sky, reflected in the small panes of glass in the little window across the room.

She removed her bonnet and loosened her hair. Dark brown tresses tumbled over her plain brown cloak.

'I look like a little sparrow,' she thought. 'Small and colorless and totally insignificant. I am well-named—Plain Jane.'

Beneath the large brown cloak, her slim figure in its gray wool traveling dress appeared rather inadequate—especially when she compared herself to Nell. Merciful heavens! Nell was twice the woman she was.

Is that what the highwayman preferred? She supposed he did, since she had seen him openly admiring the maid's expansive figure.

'Is that why he didn't want me?' she thought with regret as she visualized the lush Nell.

She turned again to study her image in the imperfect

glass. She frowned and pressed her lips together. Plain she might be, but there was nothing grotesquely wrong with her.

'A pox upon the man!' she decided. 'I placed myself before him as a sacrifice to love . . . and he shoved me off the altar.'

Dalton St. Clair twisted the key sharply in the lock. He hefted it several times, then jammed it back into his pocket.

"Best to lock that lunatic girl in," he muttered angrily to himself. "And keep her there!"

He reached up and pulled off both mask and scarf with one decisive gesture. He rubbed his hand wearily over his eyes. Then he ran his long, lean fingers through his hair, disarranging the reddish-brown waves which the scarf had flattened to his head.

He breathed a deep sigh of relief. That mask and scarf could be deucedly hot! The strange girl was locked securely in his room, and he was in the company of those few who knew him and were sworn to secrecy. It was safe to remove his disguise.

Dalton shoved the mask and scarf into his pocket. He chuckled. Thompson would have a fit of the apoplexy if he could see the way this ruined the line of his jacket. He was thankful his valet was safely home at Milbury Hall and would never witness the offense against Weston's sartorial skills.

Dalton patted his other pocket, as if searching. He grimaced. Then the grimace mellowed and grew into a crooked grin. How could he so soon have forgotten the location of the leather bag? After all, he had just recently seen it go flying past his very own head.

One thing was certain, however. He was not going to go back in that room and retrieve it. Not yet, anyway. Not until some of his anger toward that foolish girl had cooled a bit—and, Dalton added to himself with a grin, some of hers had cooled as well. On the other hand, Dalton's grin widened, perhaps if she were less angry, her aim would improve.

He kicked at an imaginary dustball floating across the floor. "Damned lunatic chit!" he muttered.

"Can't imagine you having difficulties with a lady, old boy," said the tall young man who came up behind Dalton.

The man stretched out a long, thin arm and clapped him heartily on the shoulder. "Especially since this one quite literally threw herself at you."

"Ah, Tony." Dalton grinned at his friend, even though he did not feel the least bit humorous. He feared that his difficulties with this lady would not be so easily sorted out. "I merely left the moneybag in there with her."

Tony nodded toward the door. "What do you intend to do with the little runaway?"

Dalton shrugged, then answered, "I intend to leave her there until I determine how to return her to where she rightly belongs."

A wide smirk spread across Tony's lean face. "You're too nice for your own good, Dalton. That's what put you in this soup in the first place."

Dalton shrugged his broad shoulders as he and his friend descended the smooth wooden stairs, worn by the usage of more than two centuries.

"This Robin Hood game we chose to play shows signs of turning dangerous," Tony warned him as they took their seats at the small table in the far corner of the low-ceilinged, smoky taproom. "Doesn't it, Clive?" Tony sought affirmation from the other young man already seated at the table.

Clive put the half-eaten meat pasty on the pewter plate. He chewed quickly, then swallowed down a large gulp of ale. He wiped a soft, white hand nervously over his equally white brow, pushing his blond curls out of his eyes.

"I say, could have sworn that coachman was going for a pistol of his own," Clive said breathlessly. "Fortunately, Tony had already drawn his pistol and the fellow reconsidered."

"I've heard tales of another highwayman working near here," Tony informed them. "Not quite as gentlemanly as we are, unfortunately. It seems he likes to thrash valets and carry off ladies' maids."

"People are accustomed to traveling well-armed," Clive observed, "but this other fellow is making them too apprehensive by half."

Dalton nodded. "When armed people grow too nervous, sooner or later, something more valuable than mere money is bound to be lost."

Clive washed down another mouthful of meat pasty with a gulp of ale. "I say, sometimes I fear I haven't the stomach for this line of endeavor, Dalton."

"I told you when we began that you could cry off at any time and no one would ever blame you," Dalton solemnly told his friend. "You two were never under any obligation. These are my lands and my people. . . ." He hesitated. "Well, they will be some day."

Tony snorted. "If your uncle doesn't manage to lose the estate playing at hazard, or else drink it all away."

"The Marquess of Milburton may do as he damned well pleases," Clive remarked sarcastically.

"He may do as he pleases with his own fortune," Dalton corrected. "He may even squander what meager inheritance he might consider bequeathing me. I shall succeed on my own."

Then he slammed his fist upon the table, making the pewter plate clatter against the rough-hewn wood.

"But regardless of what he may think, my uncle has no right to ruin the lives of his tenants and the tradesmen who depend upon him for their livelihood!"

Dalton shook his head, angered by the futility of the task he had chosen for himself. "My grandfather knew what a scapegrace his elder son was. That is why I vowed to him on his deathbed that I'd care for our people as best I could. My uncle allots me no resources to accomplish that end; therefore, he leaves me no alternative but to find my own means."

"We're always quite careful to make certain that the people we stop are not exactly destitute," Tony interjected.

"Quite," Clive agreed, popping the last of the meat pasty into his mouth.

The conversation paused as Nell, carrying a tray laden with mugs of ale, swayed over to their table. She artfully leaned forward in front of Dalton as she set the mugs on the table.

Tony nudged Dalton and whispered in his ear, "Good old Nell. She never stops trying."

"Thought you'd be upstairs," Nell remarked petulantly to Dalton. "Not down here drinking."

Dalton merely shook his head and raised the mug to his

lips. He took a longer swallow than usual. Nell eventually grew tired of waiting for a reply and slowly swayed away.

Tony shook his head and chuckled. "So you'll be sleeping in the taproom tonight, eh? Deucedly uncomfortable, ain't it?"

"Can't I persuade one of you to be so kind as to share your accommodations?" Dalton glanced from one to the other, his brows raised questioningly.

"So sorry, old boy," Tony quickly answered. "Clive and I both have already made arrangements for companionship tonight."

"Of course, there's always Nell," Clive suggested.

Dalton merely shrugged.

"Come now, don't be so fastidious," Tony chided. "You know perfectly well Nell has been hanging out for you since we first started coming here almost a year ago. And you, hard-hearted lout that you are, won't give the lass a tumble."

Dalton shook his head.

Tony leaned closer to Dalton's ear. "Both Clive and I can assure you, the lass is a rare treat."

"I'm sure she is," Dalton replied. "But not tonight."

Dalton was at quite a loss to explain why the overripe Nell had never actually attracted him. He was willing to believe that Clive and Tony's evaluation of her skills were accurate. She most probably was quite an armful in bed.

He tried to picture Nell's enormous breasts cradled in his arms, but the only image his contrary brain would conjure was that of the strange young woman upstairs, with her firm breasts pressed tightly against his back and her slim arms clasped determinedly about his waist as they rode off together into the night.

He seized his mug and drank deeply.

Damn the girl! How could she be so stupid? Her one rash leap for adventure had jeopardized his entire operation here.

He was not so much concerned for his own safety—he had escaped more than a few traps laid for him. And if he were ever caught . . . well, 'twas a brief dance for a highwayman.

He was more concerned for Tony and Clive, brave men each, who had volunteered to assist him in his work. And he was very concerned for the families he supported with the money he appropriated from wealthy travelers.

He was concerned for the safety of that silly girl upstairs, too.

Dalton frowned as he pondered her immeasurable stupidity. What lady in full possession of her faculties would do what she had done simply to avoid marriage?

On second thought, *she* believed her reasons to be quite logical. Dalton grinned to himself as he recalled the quiet pleasure she had taken from his remark regarding her convoluted, impeccable logic.

Dalton pressed his lips tightly together. What kind of marriage was in store for her that she should resort to so desperate an act?

She had looked so fragile, and so deucedly pretty sitting demurely on the edge of the bed! Her gray-blue eyes gazed at him with an expression of concern, yet not quite fear. And there had been something else in her eyes that he was loathe to name because it was so unfamiliar. Had it been admiration?

Dalton set his jaw more firmly. The silly, headstrong girl had presented him with more problems than he had at first realized. He had never wanted her. What the devil was he to do with her now that he had her? This inn was no place for a young woman gently bred. He certainly could not leave her here. And he most certainly had no intention of keeping her!

Of course, it would have been so easy to have taken her. Dalton permitted his thoughts to wander. Her poor crushed bonnet would have fallen to the floor, releasing the soft curls of her dark brown hair. The violet-shaded eyelids would have closed over her gray-blue eyes as he raised her chin to kiss the soft, full lips. The bombazine cloak would have opened to reveal the gentle curves of her slim figure, her tiny waist, her rounded breasts. Just a handful—that's all any man could ask. Her gown would have fallen away to expose. . . .

Dalton mentally rebuked himself for being such an honorable man.

Chapter 4

BARELY EMERGED FROM his deep sleep, Dalton rolled his face across the strange arm beneath him. He caught his breath. Had he actually gone back up to the delightful, if somewhat peculiar, young lady upstairs? Had he actually. . . ? He groaned with remorse. How could he have been such a cad? He could not possibly have been that deep in his cups.

But the arm was too large to belong to such a fragile figure as hers. Oh, no! Never in his life could he have been so drunk as to have visited Nell! Impossible, he reassured himself—wasn't it?

With even greater alarm, he pushed his face up from the fine lawn fabric. The feel of the rough wood of the tabletop beneath his fingers returned his errant reason. The motion of his body sent his blood again coursing through the arm on which he had slept last night at this same table where he had been drinking—rather heavily, too, as he was now able to recall.

Dalton winced in pain as a thousand tiny pinpricks protested his arm's mistreatment as a pillow. He flexed his aching fingers and elbow, and kneaded his sore muscles until the pain subsided and normal sensation returned.

He sat erect and looked about him. The taproom was dark now. The fire which had blazed in the hearth earlier that evening when the inn was full had subsided to glowing embers that now cast only faint illumination through hazy smoke. The only other light in the room was a single taper, burning upon the table closest to the fireplace.

At either side of the rough-hewn table, an elderly man

and woman, plainly dressed in austere black broadcloth, were seated.

Dalton frowned. Seated was not quite the correct term. Propped up would seem more accurate. Their heads were bent over, their chins resting upon their chests, their hands folded before them. Their translucent skin lined with a tracery of fine wrinkles appeared so pale in the flickering yellow candlelight that Dalton began to fear they were no longer alive.

Dalton slowly shook his head. Tony and Clive were inveterate tricksters, yet he could not believe that even they would go so far as to dig up two fresh corpses and prop them at table merely to play an extraordinarily bizarre jest on him.

At least, he certainly hoped they would not. The innkeeper might be accustomed to Dalton and his friends' exploits as highwaymen, but *this* was going to be deucedly hard to explain.

A low, mumbling sound distracted Dalton from his pondering. The elderly couple unfolded their hands, raised their heads, opened their eyes, and began to eat.

Dalton sighed with immeasurable relief. Now that his senses had cleared, it was clear from the elderly man's garb that he was a clergyman of some sort. The lady was his wife, or perhaps his sister. Their heads had been bowed in silent grace. Of course, all very easily and sensibly explained.

Dalton frowned. What were such a pair doing in this remote inn and at such a late hour? Clearly, they were traveling, whether south to London or north to Cambridge, Dalton could not know.

Then his eyes narrowed with speculation and one corner of his mouth turned up in a smile. Their purpose in being here and their destination were immaterial. What was important was that such a respectable-looking couple could just possibly be the solution he was seeking to his predicament.

Dalton quickly began to inspect his clothing in the dim light. He readjusted his crumpled cravat and did his best to smooth the wrinkles from the sleeve of his shirt. He made quite certain that his waistcoat was fastened evenly, so that no mismatched button and buttonhole stood out at opposite ends of the line.

He ran his fingers through his disheveled hair and rubbed his hand over his cheek to erase any creases sleeping on his own sleeve might have left there.

He drew in a deep breath. Now he was ready to face these people.

"Good evening to you, sir, madam," he said, bowing low to them both as he stopped at their tableside. "I trust you are enjoying your meal."

Fork poised in midair, the elderly gentleman smiled benevolently at Dalton and answered, "My wife and I are grateful for all which the Lord provides."

The lady nodded vigorously in agreement, yet all the while she never ceased eating.

"Might I see that you are provided with more?" Dalton offered.

"Thank you, no. We have quite sufficient for our needs," the gentleman answered. "Are you employed here?"

"Not precisely, sir," Dalton replied.

"As I understand, there are many men who are 'not precisely' employed at the moment." Reaching into his waist-coat pocket, the gentleman withdrew a shilling and offered it to Dalton. "Take it with the Lord's blessing, Son, and use it to better your lot."

The lady smiled her encouragement to Dalton.

For a moment, Dalton stared with just the slightest bit of irritation. He thought he had made himself as presentable as possible after sleeping half the night face down on the table of an inn. Did he indeed look so disreputable that they took him for a beggar?

Then he noted the frayed wrists and the shiny elbows of the gentleman's jacket. He realized what a sacrifice these people were making. Dalton was more accustomed to giving to such people than to taking from them.

"No, sir," Dalton declined. "You misunderstand. I *am* employed."

"I am so gratified. Might I inquire as to what line of employment you are engaged in, sir?"

Dalton drew a deep breath before responding. If he was not already bound for hell for being a thief, would lying to a clergyman be the deciding factor in his eventual destination? On the other hand, he truly did not think the kindly old couple was quite prepared to learn that they were conversing with a highwayman.

"I transport goods and wares," Dalton replied, and comforted himself with the knowledge that he was not actually lying, in a manner of speaking.

Quickly, he diverted the elderly man's questioning. "And yourself, sir?"

"I am the Reverend Mr. James Willoughby. My wife and I are traveling to London, to visit with her relatives."

The lady beamed at Dalton.

"Then we proceed to Canterbury to visit my relatives," her husband continued.

The lady's smile was not quite so enthusiastic.

Dalton rubbed his chin to hide his grin of amusement at her reaction. He was furiously searching through his mind for further pleasantries to exchange before he plunged into his purpose for approaching them.

"Has your journey been comfortable?" Dalton at length inquired.

"Comfortable enough," the Reverend Mr. Willoughby replied. "Notwithstanding that we were delayed upon the road for hours with a broken wheel, a lame horse, and an inebriated coachman who persisted in falling off the box and eventually succeeded in becoming so lost that we were forced to stop here. Of course, we should be grateful that such minor incidents were our only inconveniences. I hear that there is a particularly ruthless highwayman operating in this area, may the Lord deliver us from his depredations."

"Indeed. I had heard the same, sir," Dalton began. How fortunate that the conversation had taken the precise turn which he was seeking. "That brings me to my purpose in seeking your assistance."

"You are in need of assistance?" Mrs. Willoughby finally stopped eating long enough to say something.

"My . . . my sister . . . yes, my sister and I also were traveling to London," Dalton explained slowly, adding bits and pieces to his story as he went along. "To visit a relative . . . of our mother—yes—our mother's relative, who is an invalid."

If his tiny lie to the Reverend Mr. Willoughby regarding his means of livelihood had not doomed Dalton straight to hell, he was certain this gargantuan falsehood would surely land him there!

"My sister . . . suddenly took ill—yes, and we were forced to stop here for the night."

Seeing the look of grave concern which altered Mrs. Willoughby's countenance, Dalton quickly reassured her. "'Tis nothing serious. Merely a slight indisposition from a day spent traveling."

Then he continued to embellish his tale. "However, I have just received word that . . . our relative has taken a sudden turn for the worse, yes. My sister is still not completely recovered and I am loathe to leave her alone in such a place. . . ."

"The Lord watches over his little ones," the Reverend Mr. Willoughby reassured Dalton.

"Quite so, sir," Dalton agreed. "However, I am loathe to leave her to travel alone. . . ."

"That is why the Lord sends us each other," Mrs. Willoughby told him. "We'll be most pleased to care for your sister while you travel on, and then escort her the rest of the way to London. Won't we, Mr. Willoughby?"

"Oh, my goodness," the Reverend Mr. Willoughby replied, as if startled by the very thought. Then he confirmed, "Well, yes . . . yes, my dear, most assuredly."

The crooked grin spread across Dalton's face.

"Mr. and Mrs. Willoughby, you are too kind by half."

Dalton withdrew a small leather pouch from the pocket of his breeches and held it out to the Reverend Mr. Willoughby. In his mind, he tallied what he knew remained in the pouch. Another reason to curse that featherbrained chit upstairs! If she could only know that what it was costing him to send her back to where she rightly belonged would feed four cottagers for a week!

"I shall leave with you enough money for my sister's fare and lodgings," Dalton told the kindly pair. "The remainder is yours for your most greatly appreciated assistance."

The Reverend Mr. Willoughby shook his hand before the little bag. "Oh, we could not possibly take. . . ."

"Thank you, sir," Mrs. Willoughby interrupted, gracefully yet most assuredly snatching the pouch from Dalton's hand. "You are most generous."

This time Dalton could not resist grinning outright.

"I felt compelled to lock my sister's door . . . for safety's sake," he continued. He suppressed the grin which threatened to appear, this time for reasons best kept to himself. He withdrew the heavy iron key from his pocket and handed it to Mrs. Willoughby. "I shall leave this with you. My sister will supply you with the direction of our relative. I bid you good evening."

The Reverend and Mrs. Willoughby nodded politely. As soon as Dalton had turned his back upon them, the sound of their forks attacking the remainder of the pie began to clatter through the still taproom.

Dalton retrieved his jacket from the bench he had occupied. Thrusting his long arms through its sleeves, he headed for the door.

The Lord must indeed work in mysterious ways, Dalton mused as he made his way across the dark, deserted courtyard to the stables. How providential to encounter the Reverend Mr. and Mrs. Willoughby. What an unbelievable stroke of luck that they had been so willing to watch over the girl.

Dalton chuckled. If the placid Willoughbys could know what a time they were in for with that silly, headstrong hoyden, perhaps they would not be quite so willing! He laughed outright when he imagined her flinging the leather bag at Mrs. Willoughby's head as well when she found out they were taking her to London, even after all her machinations to the contrary.

The smile slowly slipped from Dalton's face. The girl had gone to so much trouble to avoid London and her intended marriage. Would anger be her reaction when she discovered her clever plan had been thwarted—or would she resort to something even more rash? Had he done the right thing in sending her back to the fate which she was so desperately fleeing?

Of course he had! he firmly reassured himself. The little goose needed *someone* to care for her. But he surely was not the one—not now. Not with this other highwayman newly opening business—and dirty business at that—in his territory.

Perhaps in a few days, he would make inquiries of some of his friends residing in London, just to see if the Willoughbys and the girl had arrived safely.

Dalton drew his dark brows together. A strange twinge twisted his insides. He was surprised to realize the unusual pain was regret. He regretted many things about the lady, among them the fact that he had never even learned her name.

The rapping on the wood startled Jane from her sleep. *Now* what had she done to anger the highwayman so that he again felt compelled to abuse the bedpost? Then she realized that it was not her bed but the door to her room which was being mauled.

The highwayman *had* returned to her. Apparently he had reconsidered and had not found her or her proposition quite so abhorrent. Merciful heavens, the man was insistent! Extraordinarily polite as well. He had his own key—it was his room. He could have simply unlocked the door. Yet he chose to knock.

She now rather regretted having thrown such a temper tantrum last night. Perhaps he did not deserve to be called that extremely rude name after all. Nor did he deserve being assaulted with a leather bag filled with loot. Perhaps, she thought magnanimously, if the moment were right, she might even apologize to him for her boorish behavior.

Perhaps he would apologize to her for his own. She could well remember his sea-blue eyes and his fine lips. She tried to imagine the curved corners of his mouth drawn into a repentant frown and the softly lidded eyes tender with remorse. Shockingly, she found it much easier to imagine his lips drawn back in that crooked, teasing smile, and his eyes fiery with passion.

Yet, that blasted mask would persist in getting in her way! Surely this morning he would have removed it. Her breath came faster as she anticipated at last seeing his entire face.

Suddenly, the rapping ceased. With sharp dismay Jane realized that she had wasted so much time anticipating his return that she had quite forgotten to open the door for him.

Then she heard the sound of the iron key grating in the ancient lock. In her agitation, she had even forgotten that she could not open the door from her side no matter how much she might want to.

She drew in a deep breath. She quickly sat upright, clutching the worn, patched sheet to her breast. Nervously she reached up to smooth her disheveled brown hair.

Drat old locks, she thought impatiently, as it seemed to take forever for him to jiggle the lock open. How strange. He had accomplished the feat easily enough yesterday evening—with one hand, too.

Then the rattling of metal against metal ceased and the door began to open. She was watching the doorway, grinning like a blithering idiot, she suddenly realized. She struggled for control of her features. It simply would not do to have him think her over-eager!

Yet she had no control whatsoever over her countenance as her gaze was met not by the handsome highwayman, but by a rather short, plump elderly lady dressed in a frock of the plainest black broadcloth. Jane's eyes widened and her jaw dropped open.

"Oh dear," the lady murmured, opening the door wider. "I have startled you, and you being ill and all."

"No, no. I'm quite well, thank you," Jane hastened to reassure her visitor.

"Well, I'm relieved to hear you've recovered." The lady began to bustle over to the bed. Her sturdy black shoes sent Sir Horace's fallen coins and Lady Manley's jewelry scattering even more widely across the floor. She paused to look at the mess about her.

Jane's rumpled brown cloak lay on the floor at the foot of the bed where she had let it fall. Her crumpled bonnet still rested in the corner where she had flung it in frustration. Her gray traveling dress was draped carelessly over the edge of the bed.

Jane grimaced with embarrassment. She had been so angry, and so disappointed, yesterday evening that she had not even bothered to tidy the mess which that exasperating highwayman had caused her to make.

The lady looked from the money-strewn floor back to

Jane. "Your brother told us you were rather ill. He neglected to inform us that your illness entailed fits."

"My *brother* told you?" Jane repeated, frowning. Someone at this inn was extraordinarily confused. "Who are you? Who is 'us'?"

The lady reached out to place her palm upon Jane's brow. She shook her head as she removed her hand.

"You're not feverish, thank the Lord," she observed. "Then why such confusion, my dear? Of course your brother told us you had taken ill while traveling to London to visit your mother's invalid relative."

Jane's eyes lit with realization. "My brother," she repeated. "Yes, my brother. You *saw* my brother—his face?"

"Why, certainly, dear," the lady answered. "One usually does see the face of the person with whom one is conversing."

Jane refrained from replying that this was not necessarily true around here. She merely asked, "What did he look like?"

The lady blinked in surprise. "Why, he's *your* brother, my dear. Surely you of all people should be able to recall quite clearly his appearance. You *have* been exceptionally ill, haven't you?"

Well, perhaps it had been a stupid question, Jane mentally chided herself. But she *was* curious regarding her highwayman's appearance.

"Where is my brother?" she finally managed to ask. "And who are you?"

"Oh dear. I do so hate to be the bearer of bad tidings," the lady in black fretted. "Your mother's invalid relative has taken a sudden turn for the worse."

"How unfortunate," Jane felt compelled to make some suitable reply of regret regarding the well-being of a relative who did not even exist. "Where is my brother?"

"He made most urgently for London," the lady answered, "leaving you in our care. The Reverend Mr. Willoughby and I agreed to escort you the remainder of the journey."

"How kind of you," Jane replied listlessly.

So her "brother" had left her. He had not reconsidered her proposal. In fact, the highwayman had so thoroughly rejected her that he had departed without so much as a by-your-leave, and after relinquishing her to the care of complete strangers—as quickly and as callously as her aunt and uncle had sacrificed her to Lord Scythe.

Jane sat upright in the large bed, staring ahead of her at the window across the room. It was the same window in which she had inspected her figure last night, yet now the bright spring sunlight streaming in blotted out her very tiny, very plain, very undesirable image.

She pressed her lips tightly together to keep them from quivering. She held her breath, hoping that she could keep back the tears which threatened to overspill her eyes. When at last she was forced to take a breath, it came out in a jagged sigh.

"Come now, dear. I understand your concern for your relative." Mrs. Willoughby patted Jane's shoulder, then said more cheerily, "But, up, up! A hearty breakfast and we're off. By dinner time, Lord willing, you shall be reunited with your family in London and all shall be well." With that, Mrs. Willoughby bustled out the door.

Jane slowly rose from the bed and donned her gray traveling dress, nodding a tacit concession to fate. After all her efforts to the contrary, she would indeed be returning to face Aunt Olive and Uncle Horace—and Lord Scythe.

She bent down and began to retrieve the scattered coins and jewelry. She sniffed loudly as the futility of all her efforts pricked at her more sharply. The great adventure she had envisioned for herself was over before it had barely begun.

'Ah well,' she tried to console herself. 'At least I shall have the memory of a short and sadly disappointing adventure.'

The recollection of the highwayman's smooth, deep voice telling her what convoluted but impeccable logic she had almost caused her to grin in spite of her tears. The feel of his firmly muscled body still burned her breasts and the insides of her arms where she had held him so tightly. His crooked smile and clear, blue-green eyes swam before her tear-blurred vision. Her heart twisted when she realized that she would never see him again. Worse yet, she had never even learned the highwayman's name.

Chapter 5

THE LIGHT OF the early spring dawn filtered through the budding branches of the trees as Dalton guided Paladin over the narrow path in the woods. As they emerged into the furrowed field, the large black stallion, restless after a night confined in his stall, stretched his neck, eager to be given his head.

Dalton chuckled at his horse's contagious enthusiasm. After all, it *was* spring. He pressed his heels into the sleek black sides. Paladin took off at a gallop.

As they traveled over the newly ploughed fields, Dalton relished the brisk breeze that whipped about his face and hair, now freed from the constraints of the mask and scarf. He only slowed his horse's pace when at last they approached the drive of Milbury Hall.

In spite of the problems the estate presented to him, after the night he had just passed, Dalton was eager to return to the modest comforts which his home afforded—a hot bath, a hot meal, and a cool glass of wine.

Still, he forced Paladin to walk slowly up the long, rutted drive. He wanted to see, in the harshly truthful light of day, the complete state of disrepair into which his uncle, since his succession to the marquisate three years ago, had allowed the estate to fall. He needed to remind himself of precisely why he went out disguised as a highwayman every evening—and risked his life as he did.

Dalton felt compelled to see the desolate gatehouse with its crumbling roof and broken panes of glass. He reminded himself that there was no longer a gatekeeper and his plump wife and their happy brood of grubby little children, as there

47

had been in his grandfather's day, greeting guests as they entered the estate.

There was no stableboy, eagerly running to take charge of Paladin the way Dalton recalled other stableboys running for the magnificent horses which had carried so many impressive guests to visit his grandfather.

Dalton himself took Paladin into the empty stable, where he unsaddled him, rubbed him down, and turned him loose in the pasture. He then proceeded up the rutted gravel walk to the front entrance of Milbury Hall, deserted now but for Dalton and Thompson, his valet.

"Thompson," Dalton called as he entered. Receiving no answer, he repeated, "Thompson?"

" . . . What envious streaks do lace the severing clouds in yonder East; Night's candles are burnt out, and jocund day stands tiptoe on the misty mountain tops."

"Thompson," Dalton stated, shaking his head in mock dismay at the thin little man who emerged from the library with such an outlandish greeting.

"At last, our highwayman arrives, our 'gentleman of the shade, minion of the moon,'" the valet continued.

"Thompson, you've been in the Shakespeare again!" Dalton accused. "From *Hamlet?*"

"*Henry the Fourth,* sir," the little man corrected as he grinned apologetically at Dalton from over the spectacles perched at the end of his long, thin nose. He pushed them back and, the better to keep his place, closed his thumb in the weighty tome he carried.

"I really must find something else to occupy you around here while I am gone," Dalton lamented, the teasing light in his eyes brightening his face. "Else you fall into all manner of disreputable habits."

"The fault, dear sir, is not in our stars, but in ourselves."

"From *Hamlet?*" Dalton proposed again, hopefully.

"*Julius Caesar.*" Thompson shook his head with despair. "If I may be so bold, sir, *you* might derive some benefit from delving into the Shakespeare."

Dalton shrugged. How he wished he had the time.

He turned and sniffed the air questioningly. "Do I smell breakfast cooking, all the way from the kitchen? I'd fancy a joint of beef just now."

"Tell me where is fancy bred," Thompson asked. "Or in the heart, or in the head?"

"At this moment, mine is in my stomach," Dalton interrupted his valet. "Come, man. Leave off the Shakespeare. I'm famished!"

"I fear there's nothing prepared, sir," Thompson apologized. Then he frowned censoriously. "And you've only yourself to blame for that. How can I be ready when I never can tell when you'll return—or if you'll return at all?"

Dalton nodded at the truth of his valet's complaint as he followed the man through the hall and into the dining room. They passed through the faded green baize door and down into the kitchen. Dalton had long ago decided to forego the luxury of taking his meals in the dining room for the frugality of eating in the kitchen.

"I'll have something for you in a moment, sir," Thompson told him, reluctantly relinquishing his cherished volume of Shakespeare for a large black iron frying pan and a long wooden spoon.

"I've been exceedingly distraught over your well-being, sir," Thompson scolded, slapping a chunk of fresh butter into the black pan he set near the coals. He cracked several eggs into a large bowl, mixed them thoroughly, and poured them into the melting butter.

"You are always exceedingly distraught about everything, Thompson," Dalton replied as he cut a slice from the last remaining loaf of bread.

"Perhaps," Thompson conceded hesitantly. "However, even you will allow that I have good reason to be concerned this time."

Dalton skewered the bread onto a long-handled fork and held it close to the fire. "You believe yourself to have good reason to be concerned *every* time."

Thompson rested the wooden spoon against the handle of the frying pan. His beady blue eyes peered intently at Dalton over his spectacles. "Last night, a highwayman was killed."

Dalton pressed his lips tightly together and stared into the blazing fire. He shook his head grimly. What had he just been saying to Tony and Clive this very night? When people become too apprehensive, sooner or later something more valuable than mere money was bound to be lost. How he hated to be proven correct.

The valet picked up the spoon again and began to push the congealing eggs about in the pan.

"Late last night, Hodge Brackley came by, all in a lather. Seems a band of highwaymen stopped the Mail. One of the passengers drew a pistol and shot a highwayman dead, straightaway. Then another highwayman fired his own pistol, wounding that selfsame passenger. 'Twon't end until they've all killed each other," he pronounced sagely as he slid the eggs onto a plate and set it before Dalton.

"Oh, please, sir," he pleaded. "Do give up this mad mission of yours before you end up just like that highwayman— and you trying to do good, not deserving such a horrendous fate as those that rob for selfish gain! I just know one day 'twill be you Hodge Brackley comes to tell me is dead. I thought for certain 'twas you this time."

"In the first place, you know perfectly well that I would never detain the Mail. Those passengers are not wealthy people." Dalton raised one brow to a supercilious angle and stated with a half-suppressed grin, "Simply not the class of people I would rob."

Thompson returned the grin and replied, "Of course not, sir."

"Secondly, such a thing could not possibly happen to me," Dalton declared confidently as he began to tuck away the eggs and toasted bread. "I have far too much to do to take the time to be shot."

"Indeed, sir," Thompson repeated. However, the look in his valet's eyes let Dalton know with no uncertainty that the man did not believe for one second that this guaranteed immunity.

"Still and all, have a care, sir," Thompson pleaded. He handed Dalton several sheets of paper upon which were scribbled a very long list. "After all, without you, how would any of these repairs be financed? How could any of our people manage to live?"

Seeing the look of distress on his valet's narrow face, Dalton dropped his bantering manner. "I shall be careful," he promised.

He perused the list Thompson had given him. So many

bills, so many repairs, and such meager funds with which to accomplish it all.

What good use he could have made of the money that had been squandered on returning that silly girl to her family—not to mention the money and jewelry from the robbery which had saddled him with the chit in the first place! In his hurry to quit the inn and be rid of the little goose, he had left his booty with her!

He grimaced with regret. It was too late now to go back and get it. Even if he went back, it wouldn't matter so much where the money was. . . . Dalton stopped his mind in mid-thought and slowly laid his fork upon the table beside his plate. Whatever was he thinking of? He had been upon the verge of asking himself what would be the good of going back for the money when the girl would already be gone?

Dalton shook the paper he held, as if that action would also shake all thoughts of her from his head. Indeed, she *had* rattled his senses.

Horatia blinked, then stared in awe as the carriage drew to a halt before a seemingly unending row of tall, white town houses. Which one was theirs? They all looked quite alike.

She shrugged. It did not signify. Her parents would tell her which town house they had let for the Season. They were always telling her precisely what she ought to do. But they always had such marvelous things planned for her. Why should she complain?

She glanced questioningly to her mother, then blinked in surprise. Lady Manley was glaring darkly from the town house to Sir Horace and then back again.

"'Tis quite as I always expect of you, Horace," Lady Manley complained as she alighted from the carriage. "Not quite large enough."

Sir Horace muttered as he, too, descended. "For the ungodly sum I had to spend on this place, it should look like bloody Whitehall!"

Horatia looked back at the town house which her mother was approaching. She did not think it was so dreadfully small, but if Mama thought it was, well then. . . .

As she exited the carriage, Horatia confronted her father's thick finger directly under her nose.

"I'll warn you now, my girl," he said. "To make all this outlay worthwhile, you'd best land yourself a bloody duke!"

Horatia blinked her wide blue eyes and nodded agreeably. "Oh, I'm sure I shall, Papa."

She had not the least doubt that she should marry exceedingly well! Did not all the young men at the country assemblies tell her she was the loveliest, the most charming, the most captivating lady there?

The front door was opened by an extremely disdainful looking butler. One of his extraordinarily bushy eyebrows was arched at a skeptical angle and his thin lips appeared to be drawn back in a perpetual sneer.

"Perhaps the exterior is deceptive," Lady Manley said hopefully as she ascended the three white marble steps. "It must be spacious enough to accommodate all the *haut ton* who will attend the splendid affairs we have planned for Horatia."

Horatia merely smiled as she followed her mother into the town house. She was so gratified that her parents took care of all these bewildering plans and that she had nothing more taxing to do than to look pretty and smile pleasantly.

"More money spent," Sir Horace grumbled as he shoved his hands into his pockets and followed his wife.

"You must choose your suitor with care, you know." Lady Manley turned to pat her daughter's plump little hand.

"If you say so, Mama," Horatia answered, smiling.

Lady Manley leafed through the assortment of cards and invitations lying on the tray on the table in the hall. She snorted with disgust and threw down the entire pile.

"How will Horatia ever find anyone suitable if we don't receive invitations to better affairs than these?" She rummaged through the pile once again, as if she had missed something the first time. "We must receive our vouchers to Almack's. Why, the entire Season will be a waste if we are not admitted to Almack's!"

"Don't think even Almack's will help the gel," the rasping voice behind Horatia derided.

Taken by surprise, Horatia pivoted to the source of that unusual sound. Her detractor's immense turquoise turban came no higher than her nose.

Lowering her gaze, Horatia still stared open-mouthed at the exceedingly short, elderly woman.

This lady reached out, seized Horatia's chin, and pushed her mouth shut.

"Don't stare at me bug-eyed, either, gell!" the lady commanded. "'Tis quite unsettling and won't get you a husband at all, unless you can find one who's fond of frogs."

"Why, Aunt Georgina," Lady Manley declared, her disgruntled frown suddenly transformed into an expression of the utmost joy at the mere sight of her visitor.

Horatia continued to stare. So this was she—Georgina Louise Manley Tipton, the second wife of the late Archibald Tipton, fifth Earl of Balford—the lady of whom even her quite forceful parents stood in awe—her great-aunt!

"How good of you to come calling," Lady Manley continued in an exceedingly musical tone. Horatia rarely heard her mother use such a voice at home.

"Indeed it is," Lady Balford agreed. Her piercing gray-blue eyes disdainfully surveyed her surroundings.

Horatia displayed to the formidable Dowager Countess Balford what she had often been told by the young men at the country assemblies was her most engaging smile.

"Come, John," Lady Balford commanded the tall young man standing behind her. She swept past Horatia without so much as a backward glance.

John obeyed unquestioningly. As he passed Horatia, he bowed slightly and bestowed upon her the tiniest of smiles. He was then drawn on in Lady Balford's irresistible wake.

Horatia was quite taken aback. All the young men at the country assemblies turned into gawking, babbling fools in her presence. This John merely smiled and bowed—quite coolly, too. Clearly, John was an extraordinary man, a man who warranted further attention.

"Can't stay but a moment," Lady Balford informed them as she seated herself upon the maroon and white striped sofa in the center of the drawing room. "You should be exceedingly glad I've bothered to take even this much time from my busy schedule to come calling."

"Oh, we're always glad to see you, Aunt Georgina," Lady Manley gushed as she trailed behind her husband's aunt.

Turning about, she motioned furiously for Horatia to follow her.

Horatia entered the drawing room, attempting once again to charm her impressive great-aunt. Yet when she entered the room, she found her smile intended more for the gentleman known to her only as John than for the lady he accompanied.

John merely responded with a polite nod of his dark head.

"Some tea, Aunt Georgina?" Lady Manley offered. "'Twon't be but a moment to have the finest. . . ."

"Tea? Don't be offering tea," Sir Horace scolded as he made his way across the room to the liquor cabinet and began pilfering the shelves. "Ah yes, here's what you'll be wanting."

He removed a bottle of ratafia from the shelf.

"Perhaps some brandy for you, sir," Lady Manley said, recalling just enough of her duties as hostess to accommodate Lady Balford's companion.

Lady Balford indicated her escort with a wave of her hand. "John Tipton, his late lordship's second son's second son."

The Manleys nodded politely.

"Sit down, John," Lady Balford commanded.

Sir Horace leaned over slightly and whispered to Lady Manley from out the corner of his mouth, "No prospects."

Lady Manley shook her head and clucked her tongue, then turned her attention to the truly important person in the room.

"Aunt Georgina, perhaps while you partake of some refreshments you'd like to converse with our daughter Horatia," Lady Manley continued. "Horatia's making her come out this Season."

Horatia quite wisely took this as her signal to come forward, smiling that same charming smile.

Lady Balford squinted and frowned. She cast her eyes up and down Horatia once.

"Adequate," she gave what appeared to be the highest approval she could offer. Then she turned from Horatia and demanded of Lady Manley, "Well, where's the other one?"

"What other one, Aunt Georgina?" Lady Manley asked, eyes wide with innocence.

"What do you mean, what other one? The one you were bringing here to marry off. What's her name? Jane!"

Lady Manley shot her husband a desperate glance.

"Why on earth should you want to see Jane?" Sir Horace asked.

"Well, her father was my brother's son. She's my great-niece too, ain't she? So, where is she?"

"Well. . . ." Lady Manley stuttered. "Jane . . . Jane is not here."

"I can see that!" Lady Balford glared sourly at Lady Manley. "I might be old, but I ain't blind. Do you think I'm stupid as well?"

Both Lady Manley and Sir Horace hastened to reassure her that this was entirely not so!

"Well, where is she, then?" Lady Balford demanded.

Sir Horace made unintelligible grunts while his eyes searched the corners of the room.

"Jane has been kidnapped," Lady Manley blurted out.

"Kidnapped!" Lady Balford exclaimed, gripping the edge of the cushion. "By whom?"

"By . . . kidnappers," Sir Horace ventured.

"Highwaymen," Lady Manley quickly corrected, not neglecting to emphasize her dissatisfaction with her husband's excuse by effectively applying an elbow to his paunchy middle.

"A great band of them," Sir Horace added.

"Waylaid our carriage on the road down to London," Lady Manley continued.

Lady Balford was frowning and staring intently at the two who told the extraordinary tale.

"Tried to fight them off, I did," Sir Horace asserted.

Lady Balford lifted one thin, graying brow and eyed her nephew with no mean degree of skepticism.

"The coachman and valet offered invaluable assistance," Lady Manley tried desperately to cover her husband's blatant falsehood. "All to no avail, alas. They robbed us and carried off Jane."

"Like with the Grimsby maid," Sir Horace finished the tale with a plausible example of just what dangers the highways held.

Lady Balford made some noises that resembled laughter

without containing the least bit of humor. "Where is she—truly?"

"No, truly, Aunt Georgina," Lady Manley hastened to reassure her husband's aunt. "Why, we would never lie to you! Jane was carried off by highwaymen."

Lady Balford pursed her wrinkled lips and nodded her grudging acceptance.

Lady Manley glanced at Sir Horace and heaved a deep sigh of relief.

"Hope you two ninnies had the sense to notify the authorities," Lady Balford remarked sourly.

"Oh, indeed, Aunt Georgina," Sir Horace assured her. "Almost immediately."

Of course, he did neglect to mention that approximately twenty-four hours was as immediate as he had been willing to manage.

"And Bow Street?"

"Oh, indeed, Aunt Georgina," Lady Manley echoed, quite neglecting to clarify that what she meant was that Bow Street would be notified tomorrow, especially now that Lady Balford had insisted upon it.

Lady Balford eyed the two standing before her. "You both know I think you're a pair of addlepated twits."

"Oh, indeed, Aunt Georgina," Sir Horace and Lady Manley replied automatically.

Lady Balford smiled and nodded. "Still and all, I must suppose you've enough sense between the two of you to handle notifying the authorities properly. Let us hope they find the gel soon enough."

The elderly lady extended her hand. John rose immediately, offering his arm to assist his step-grandmother.

"Oh, Aunt Georgina, you can't be thinking of leaving so soon," Lady Manley protested weakly.

"I've seen what I came here for," she stated, glancing briefly once again in Horatia's direction.

Horatia again essayed a charming smile.

"Well, half of it anyway." Lady Balford turned away.

Horatia backed over to the corner of the room near a squared ebony and gold pedestal topped by a small statue of the sphinx. She pressed her full little lips together and scraped at the carpet with the toe of her yellow kid slipper.

'Fie on Great-Aunt Georgina,' she decided petulantly, 'if she wants to pay more attention to Jane than to me.'

That was one of the things which Horatia had always liked about Jane. She was quiet and unobtrusive—and never distracted the center of attention away from herself. And now Jane had managed to do so without even being here!

'Oh, fie on Great-Aunt Georgina! Fie on Jane, too! Fie on this John person as well if he can't be as perceptive as the other gentlemen and see how charming I am,' Horatia thought to herself.

She stole a sidelong glance at the young man who had positioned himself beside Aunt Georgina. Much to her surprise, John was indeed watching her after all.

Chapter 6

"LORD SCYTHE," THE butler announced with his customary sneer.

Lady Manley shot a panic-stricken look to Sir Horace. "Oh, horrors! Not now."

Sir Horace mirrored his wife's expression. "Bloody hell!" he muttered.

"Damn! Knew I should have left sooner," Lady Balford complained quite loudly. "The man's a bloody bore. Why you two ever consented to marry Jane off to him is beyond me."

Lord Scythe paused in the doorway. He leaned against the doorframe and crossed one spindly leg over the other.

"So nice to see you again, too, Georgina," he greeted Lady Balford. He then hiccupped rather loudly.

His lordship blinked, as if using his bushy eyebrows to lift the heavy, red-rimmed lids of his sleepy-looking eyes. He applied his quizzing glass and peered at Lady Balford.

"I believe you've become a bit grayer and just a few stone heavier since last I saw you," he observed.

His lordship took a step to enter the room, swayed and bumped his shoulder into the doorframe.

"Perhaps I have, Derwood," Lady Balford answered blandly. Then her eyes narrowed and she sneered, "How comforting to see that you have not changed in the least."

"Tipton, old boy." Lord Scythe staggered over to John and executed a bow so obsequiously low as to border on the condescending. "What a pity your aging step-grandmama can no longer coax the gentlemen to forego their clubs during the day. How kind of you to accompany her about."

"'Tis my pleasure, my lord, I assure you," John said.

"Indeed," his lordship agreed, nodding carefully so as not to disturb the delicate balance which kept him upright. "I, too, should be exceedingly pleased were someone to offer to pay my way about Town."

John blushed to the tips of his ears. He slowly backed away from his lordship until he was quite safely stationed to the other side of the same pedestal where Horatia had sought shelter.

Lord Scythe's gaze followed John to rest upon Horatia.

"Why hide behind a column, young lady?" his lordship called to Horatia from across the room. "You'll never attract a duke's attention that way."

Horatia's face took on the same coloration as John's.

"Some brandy, Lord Scythe," Lady Manley at last collected her wits sufficiently to interpose.

"No, thank you," his lordship declined. "I find my own stock, of which I keep a generous supply at both my elegant town house in Mayfair *and* my extensive estates in Northumberland, to be far superior to any other I have encountered."

Sir Horace leaned over to Lady Manley and whispered, "What? Don't he keep a supply at his stylish home in Bath?"

Lord Scythe reached for his fob, which hung at the waist of his skintight yellow pantaloons. The fob dangled out in midair from his lordship's protruding paunch.

"Can't stay long, don't you know," his lordship remarked, casually glancing at the elegant timepiece which now rested in his hand. "Have a great deal to do today. So glad my new timepiece is quite accurate regarding the proper hour. Quite expensive, too, if I do say so myself."

He held his newest acquisition directly under Sir Horace's very nose until that gentleman at last conceded, "Yes, yes, damned fine."

"Matter of fact, didn't really come to visit you at all," his lordship continued, dropping the watch fob. "Only stopped by to greet my betrothed."

Lord Scythe readjusted his quizzing glass and glanced about the room once again. "Where is she, by the bye?"

"Jane is . . . ah, not here," Lady Manley broached the subject quite delicately.

"Where is she?"

"She's been kidnapped by highwaymen," Lady Balford stated with exceptional bluntness. "Can't say the gel is any worse off with them than she would have been had she come here and married you."

Horatia thought her great-aunt delivered this information with not only a startling bluntness, but with a great deal of satisfaction as well in being the one to convey to his lordship the horrifying news.

"Kidnapped! How could such a thing happen?" his lordship demanded.

"'Tis not our fault!" Lady Manley told him.

"Certainly not," Sir Horace agreed. "Why, I did my utmost to. . . ."

"Fought the brigands off with his bare hands, he did—almost," Lady Balford corroborated her nephew's tale with a sly grin.

"The coachman and valet rendered invaluable assistance," Sir Horace modestly admitted.

"Not nearly enough," Lord Scythe declared angrily. "You were entrusted with bringing *my* bride to *me.* You allowed a mere highwayman to snatch her from *me?*"

"The authorities are searching for Jane. My gracious, they may find her at any minute," Lady Manley stated with a certainty which she neither felt nor wished for.

"At any rate, the gel is gone, Derwood," Lady Balford said bluntly. "The authorities were notified. Do you think you can do more?"

"We shall see," his lordship said as he pivoted sharply on the heel of one well-polished Hessian. He reeled into the small table beside the sofa, upsetting it.

"No one takes from me what is rightly mine," his lordship finished as he staggered toward the door. "No one!"

Grasping the doorframe, his lordship used its sturdy bulk to shove himself off and propel himself through the entrance hall and out the door.

Horatia scarcely noticed Lord Scythe's departure, since she was occupied in studying the man who stood to the other side of the square black pedestal. John's soft brown eyes had cautiously regarded every clumsy move the inebriated Lord Scythe made. Upon occasion, as his lordship's voice had grown louder, John drew his dark brows into a frown.

"Rather loud, isn't he?" Horatia peeked around the pedestal to whisper to John.

"Rather obnoxious, as well," John replied, glancing in her direction just long enough not to appear rude.

"He is entirely too frank in his remarks," Horatia said, casting her blue eyes up at him. Ah, this gesture never failed to affect all the young gentlemen. "Imagine, censuring you for so kindly escorting your step-grandmama."

John merely shrugged.

Horatia blinked with surprise. How could the man resist telling her that her eyes were like stars? No other gentleman had ever been able to resist.

"Imagine him accusing you of hanging out for a duke," he answered instead.

"Well, Papa *has* ordered me to try for one," she admitted to him with a giggle.

John clasped his hands behind his back and rocked back and forth on his heels. Several times he opened his mouth as if to say something. Then, instead, he drew in a deep breath and said nothing. Horatia was unaccustomed to having *this* kind of effect on men.

Horatia fumed. How could he miss the opportunity to tell her that she was so lovely she would have no trouble at all in securing a duke?

What was the man about? Other young men might even comment upon how delightful she looked in her frock. Why didn't John? Horatia glanced quickly down. Her skirt was hanging properly. Her ribbons were all pressed and tied. She knew the color was becoming. What was wrong with her?

"Delightful weather we're having," John said suddenly, quite startling Horatia.

Should he not be telling her that her hair was the color of sunshine, as the others did?

"Yes," she recovered quickly enough to respond. Slowly, she raised her hand to check upon the arrangement of her curls. Everything was quite in order.

"'Tis not unseasonably warm today."

"No, indeed," she replied, tossing her blonde curls most

provocatively, just in case he had missed her tresses the first time.

"All in all," John continued, "I would say that the entire spring has been neither too cool nor too warm."

"It has been most delightful," she agreed. She smiled and tilted her head in his direction so that he would see the dimple in her soft little cheek.

"Although one could complain that we have seen an inordinate amount of rain."

Horatia was about to scream with exasperation. Was the man so totally immune to all her charms?

Lacking this relief, she found no other recourse but to admit, "Oh, I truly do not mind the rain."

Suddenly, John turned to her and smiled. "How interesting. I, too, often enjoy watching a mild rain and listening to the sound of the raindrops on the leaves."

"Oh, no. I prefer thunderstorms," Horatia declared, her blue eyes widening with renewed interest in this conversation.

"Indeed? Why?"

"Why?" Horatia repeated, blinking her eyes not once but twice. Why? No one had ever bothered to ask her why. Everyone had always been so busy telling her things that they had never bothered to ask her opinion.

My, this John Tipton certainly *is* unusual, Horatia decided.

"I . . . I . . . ." Horatia began, yet could still find no reason for her preference. At last, she managed to seize upon a reason. "Gentle rains are so insipid. Thunderstorms, however, have dark rolling clouds and flashes of lightning and crashes of thunder. They are so full of drama, so full of . . . one could almost say . . . passion," she finished with a breathless little gasp.

"I can see your point, Miss Manley," he agreed. "Yet, you will concede that a thunderstorm must, by the very nature of its ferocity, quickly spend itself. There is passion to be found in the very persistence of that seemingly gentle rain, do you see?"

Horatia stared up at him, undisguised admiration in her gaze. "Indeed, I do believe I see the logic of your argument, Mr. Tipton."

"John, 'tis past time I was leaving," Lady Balford demanded, holding out her hand.

John nodded to Horatia, then made straightway for her ladyship's side.

Horatia pouted as she watched the unique Mr. Tipton following Great-Aunt Georgina from the drawing room. By asking her what she thought, he had surely given her something to think about. Yet, she was greatly disappointed. She was seriously troubled by the fact that, perhaps for the first time in her young life, she had no effect upon a gentleman at all.

"Hadn't I best be taking you home, m'lord?" his coachman offered as Lord Scythe tripped down the last of the three white marble steps of the Manley's town house and fell into the carriage.

"Home? Don't be ridiculous, man. Take me to White's, as usual. I've too much to do today."

"If you don't mind my saying so, m'lord," his coachman made so bold as to imply, "in your condition, I doubt if you'll be accomplishing anything short of casting up your accounts over your Hessians."

"Don't be crude, Attley," Lord Scythe warned.

Lord Scythe settled back into his carriage and pulled the shades up all the way. The sunlight was indeed giving him the most furious ache in his head. Of course, he'd never own that perhaps it was the prodigious quantities of wine he'd consumed last night that made his head hurt him so abominably, although his coachman would undoubtedly have no qualms about pointing out the distinct likelihood of such a thing.

Attley was clearly an idiot, and Lord Scythe would surely have given the man the sack had he not been the handiest coachman in England. His lordship saw no reason to relieve himself of the very best when he had spent his entire life in its pursuit.

Clearly, his station, his fortune, his estates were all he could wish for. The six children his first wife had given him were delightfully exuberant offspring. His mistress was a passionate armful—if the price of his gifts was right.

Lord Scythe frowned darkly. He would have had Jane Manley, too, had it not been for that wretched highwayman!

His lordship's brow grew darker the longer he contemplated his loss.

Jane was everything he desired in a wife. Quiet, complaisant, patient with his six quite lovely, rather lively children.

She might have been rather delightful in his bed, too, he speculated. Betimes the quiet ones were the most passionate—still waters and all, you know, he reminded himself.

And she had been the only lady who had accepted his generous offer of marriage.

Lord Scythe snorted loudly and thumped on the roof of the carriage.

"Attley!" he bellowed. "Turn about immediately!"

"Begging you pardon, m'lord," the coachman answered.

"Bow Street," his lordship ordered. "Take me to the Runners."

How dare any mere highwayman carry off Miss Jane Manley right out from under his very nose. She was his! And if she still lived, he vowed, b'god, he'd get her back!

John Tipton assisted Lady Balford into her elegant carriage.

Blast fate for casting his lot in life as the second son of a second son! he cursed silently. Blast fate again for setting him on this earth with no fortune and no prospects! And blast himself as well for being so deucedly shy!

The loveliest young lady he had ever in his life laid eyes upon and all he could manage to say to her was a trite old remark. A lady as beautiful as Miss Horatia Manley must surely be accustomed to all manner of Spanish coin. Only the wittiest of remarks would make any impression at all upon her. And beetle-headed, cork-brained cake that he was, all he had been able to summon was "Delightful weather we're having"!

She must surely think him the veriest lackwit. Indeed he was, he told himself, and deserved no better than to spend his days following his step-grandmother about on an endless round of shopping and at-homes rather than spending time paying court to the lovely Miss Horatia Manley.

'Ah well,' he tried to console himself, 'it does not signify after all.' Her parents had ordered her to find a duke. With her beauty and charm, she should have no difficulty at all in accomplishing that end.

Especially if she wore that same splendid frock that had shown her pleasantly rounded little figure off to such advantage. Especially if she cast those wide, blue eyes so demurely up at her suitors. Especially if she tossed those sunshine-blonde tresses about so provocatively.

Why hadn't he been able to tell her all these things? he cursed himself for the chuckle-headed lout he was. If he could have thought up enough scathing epithets, John surely would have cursed himself more.

Chapter 7

"I HAVE SO much in store for you today, Horatia," Lady Manley announced as she smeared an enormous heap of strawberry jam over her warm scone.

Horatia eagerly scooped up a forkful of kippers from her plate. Of course, Mama always had exciting plans in store for her.

"The first thing we must do is take you to the modiste," Lady Manley said.

"More money spent," Sir Horace grumbled through his mouthful of kippers and strawberry jam.

"The trouble is, all the best modistes are so terribly busy now, what with everyone preparing for the Season," Lady Manley complained. Then her eyes brightened. "Perhaps we can coax Aunt Georgina to take us to her own."

"Oh, I do hope not, Mama," Horatia pouted. "I should hate to appear in public wearing a turban as horrid as the one she had on yesterday!"

"Nonsense, dear," her mother reassured her. "You will look lovely in anything."

Well, yes, she would. "Still," Horatia protested aloud with a pout.

"I only mean to *ask*," Lady Manley explained. "Only so that Aunt Georgina *believes* we consider her quite stylish."

Horatia, greatly relieved to hear this, took another bite of kippers.

"If Aunt Georgina accommodates us on this one small request," Lady Manley continued, "perhaps she can be presumed upon to invite us to some of her affairs."

"Lord, I hope not!" Sir Horace grumbled through another mouthful. "I heard the damned things are so crowded that one can't take a deep breath without someone else exhaling."

"Not true, Horace," Lady Manley said. "If *you* exhale, there will be room for two."

Her ladyship turned to Horatia. "We *must* be invited to Aunt Georgina's. Her parties are so fashionable that the person inhaling next to you may very well be a quite eligible young duke!"

Sir Horace merely grunted. "She'll have to do more than breathe to catch a duke."

"Never mind your father, Horatia," her mother reassured her. "You've beauty enough to captivate any man."

'Except John Tipton,' Horatia found she was pouting to herself. He may have been polite, but she thought Mr. Tipton to be the least "captivated" man who had ever set eyes upon her.

She also realized she was pushing her kippers around on her plate instead of eating them. She found this even more remarkable, as she was inordinately fond of kippers.

"Perhaps, if we are extremely pleasant to Aunt Georgina," Lady Manley continued, "she might be induced to use some of her influence to obtain for us our vouchers to Almack's." She turned and glared at her husband. "Can you believe the blasted things *still* have not arrived?"

A loud "harumph" from the doorway drew everyone's attention to the butler.

Horatia had learned that his name was Snodderly. She thought the name entirely suited him, as his disdainful expression had not varied since their initial encounter.

"Three, ah, persons wish to see you, m'lady," Snodderly announced these visitors of dubious quality. "I have not admitted them, as I feel certain that they might purloin the silver if the opportunity arose. I have therefore left them awaiting your pleasure upon the front steps. Might I suggest you make haste to dispatch them as they do lend a rather untidy appearance to the premises."

Lady Manley peered disdainfully at the black-garbed gentleman and his plump little wife. "We are not in the habit of making charitable donations from our doorstep," she coldly informed them. "You shall have to contact my husband's solicitor."

"Oh, we're not collecting today, m'lady," Mrs. Willoughby quickly corrected. "We're making a delivery, as it were."

The Reverend Mr. Willoughby stepped aside to reveal a quite bedraggled Jane. She was wearing the same gray dress and brown cloak. Her bonnet was crumpled beyond repair. Her face was grimy from travel.

"Why have you brought this disreputable-looking baggage to our door?" Lady Manley demanded haughtily.

"She had no change of clothing with her," Mrs. Willoughby explained. "I assume her brother neglected to separate her valise from his own. He did depart in great haste."

"I'm sure he did," Lady Manley replied sarcastically.

"We do hope we're not too late for Miss Manley to see her mother's ailing relative," Mrs. Willoughby made another attempt at an apology, "but the Mail can be so dreadfully slow. However, we are quite certain that you're glad to see her again."

"*Again?*" Lady Manley repeated, frowning. She peered directly into Jane's weary, gray-blue eyes and said, "Why, I have absolutely no idea who this person is."

Mrs. Willoughby turned to Jane. "My dear, are you quite certain you gave us the correct direction?"

Jane stood upon the top step of the town house, her mouth hanging open in stunned silence. If she had not exactly expected a warm welcome, neither had she expected them to deny so completely even knowing her.

"Damn the girl for a featherbrained tart!" Sir Horace exclaimed as he came up behind his wife and spotted Jane. "Can't the blasted chit even disappear properly?"

"Oh, Jane!" Horatia cried, pushing through the formidable barrier her parents presented at the doorway. She enveloped Jane in her arms.

"Horatia! What on earth are you doing!" Lady Manley cried, horrified.

"Why, I truly thought I should never see my dear cousin again!"

"Do not be ridiculous. How could this most disgraceful-looking ragamuffin be your cousin Jane?"

"Yes, 'tis I, Aunt Olive," Jane at last managed to reply. "These kind people have brought me home. And I have brought something back to you."

Jane withdrew from beneath her cloak the small leather pouch which contained Sir Horace's money and Lady Manley's jewelry, and extended it to her aunt.

A wide smile suddenly illuminated Lady Manley's face.

"Why, Horace," she cried as she snatched the pouch from Jane's outstretched hand. "'Tis our Jane after all! Our own dear Jane, returned to us."

"So it is," Sir Horace mumbled and turned to resume his interrupted meal. "So it is."

"Why, my dear, you are so terribly grimy, I should never have known you." Lady Manley gingerly patted Jane's shoulder. "How clever of Horatia to have recognized you so easily."

Using only the tips of her fingers, Lady Manley managed to pull Jane into the hallway and propel her toward the stairs. She then turned to the Reverend Mr. and Mrs. Willoughby.

"How can we ever repay you for returning our dear Jane to us safe and sound?" Lady Manley asked.

Then, before the pair could ever tell her precisely how she could repay them, Lady Manley closed the door in their faces.

"No, no, no," Lady Manley scolded as she continued to prod Jane up the stairs and down the hallway.

She pushed her past all the bedchamber doors and on toward the small doorway which accessed the stairs to the servants' quarters on the top floor of the town house.

Jane was directed into a tiny room which faced the front of the house. It contained a narrow bed and a moldy old chest. Thin, tattered curtains hung at the single window.

This high up, 'twould not be too noisy, Jane reasoned. There was a nice window to admit the morning sun. In fact, considering those threadbare curtains, 'twould be extremely difficult *not* to admit the morning sun.

"I shan't have you making a shambles of the best bedrooms in your present condition," her aunt informed her as she and Horatia followed her into the room. "We have no desire to pay for damages to the property. Heaven only knows what sort of vermin you've brought back with you to infest the place."

"The accommodations were rather clean, all things considered," Jane found herself defending the dilapidated little inn she'd been taken to by the highwayman.

"Well, you've had truck with another type of vermin as well," Lady Manley said, her lip curling as she cast her glance disparagingly up and down Jane. "Perhaps an even worse type."

Jane opened her mouth to defend the highwayman, too. How dare Aunt Olive refer to him as "vermin"? He had only ever acted the gentleman, she thought.

Then the image of sea-blue eyes and a crooked smile, and the memory of a firmly muscled back and tapering waist in her arms flashed through her mind. A wicked little voice in the back of her head added, 'Unfortunately.'

Jane gave her head a quick shake to silence that wicked—and persistent—little voice.

Horatia attempted to enter the small room, but Lady Manley quickly interposed her considerable bulk in the doorway.

"I believe you have things to do downstairs, don't you, Horatia, my dear?" Lady Manley informed her daughter, pointing her finger in that direction. "Remember, I told you, we shall be quite busy today. I shall join you just as soon as I clear up this minor inconvenience," she added, glancing disdainfully once again at Jane.

Horatia sighed and disappeared down the stairs.

Her figure was quickly replaced by that of the housemaid lugging up a large copper tub which she set before the small hearth.

A long, hot, soothing, lavender-scented bath would have felt so good, Jane thought, after days and nights of traveling in the same clothing, riding in a stuffy carriage over bone-jarring roads. Yet, Jane quickly dipped into and out of the copper tub. The water was tepid at best by the time the housemaid had carried several buckets all the way up three flights of stairs. The plain lye soap was harsh.

But Aunt Olive had insisted she wash thoroughly. Jane was just thankful that her aunt had not handed her the kind of brush the housemaids usually used to scrub down the front steps.

She supposed she should also be thankful that after such a less than enthusiastic welcome, Aunt Olive had not treated her in the same manner as her gray dress and old brown cloak. At Lady Manley's express orders, the maid had gingerly carted off the entire bundle, right down to Jane's small clothes, to be burned posthaste.

The small fire which had been laid in the grate barely warmed the room. Jane looked about for one of her two morning dresses, but the only clothing the maid had laid out for her was a night rail. Jane quickly donned the clean small clothes and the plain muslin shift.

She was sitting on the floor, drying her long brown hair before the meager fire, when the housemaid tapped upon the door. She entered, carrying a small tray with a plate of food and a glass of water.

The maid looked about and, seeing nowhere else to set the tray, placed it upon the foot of the bed. Some of the water spilled out of the glass onto the food on her plate.

Jane regarded with distaste the now soggy piece of bread, the wilted brussels sprouts, and the three thin slices of overcooked beef, the gravy already cooled to the point of congealing.

"Thank you," Jane told the maid. After all, it was not her fault the meal was so horrid. "However, in the future, I shall take my meals with the family."

"No, no, Jane," Lady Manley said as she bustled in. "Come now, into bed with you."

Jane watched in surprise as Lady Manley herself turned down the thin, patched coverlet on the tiny bed. She also registered a bit of dismay as she noted more water spilling from the glass onto the already cold brussels sprouts.

Quite bewildered, Jane followed her aunt's orders and climbed onto the lumpy horsehair mattress. It was certainly less comfortable than the mattress at the inn—the mattress upon which the muscular highwayman had so easily tossed her, Jane recalled wistfully. She grimaced—and sighed thinking how he'd merely left her there.

"You've been through quite an ordeal," Lady Manley

said, pulling the coverlet up to Jane's waist without actually touching her. "You must rest."

"I'm quite fine, Aunt Olive," Jane insisted. She frowned, suspicious that her aunt should now be so solicitous after her health.

"Come, eat," Lady Manley insisted, indicating the tray.

Jane slid the tray onto her lap, unfolded the serviette, and picked up her fork.

Lady Manley looked as if she were about to sit upon the bed at Jane's side, then suddenly thought better of it and remained standing.

"Now, there is a small but rather important matter we need to discuss, you and I." Lady Manley's manner remained pleasant, but there was a reptilian coldness in her eyes which gave Jane pause.

Jane laid down the fork and held her breath.

"Of course, I am relieved that you are returned to us unharmed—at least to all outward appearances," she added scornfully. "And it was also a great favor that you were able to return with your uncle's money and my jewelry."

Jane merely nodded.

"However, there is the matter of a small garnet brooch which belonged to my mother," Lady Manley continued, her cold stare never leaving Jane's face. "'Tis gone missing and I wondered if perchance you should recall precisely what happened to it."

Jane blinked and frowned. In light of everything else that had happened to her in the past two days, how the deuce was she to remember a small garnet brooch?

Lady Manley's eyes narrowed as she continued to watch Jane.

"You can't think I took it!" Jane declared, shocked and angered by her aunt's unspoken accusation.

"Well, it *is* missing. And you *were* the last person in possession of it—well, you and that highwayman."

"I have never stolen anything!" Jane quickly and firmly pointed out to her aunt. "Not even raspberry tarts from Cook when I was a child!"

"Well, I suppose if you were going to steal my jewelry, it would not have been a mere trinket," her ladyship grudgingly conceded.

"Well, the bag did spill, Aunt Olive," Jane explained. It truly had, in a manner of speaking.

She forced a sigh of dismay. A small gleam of retaliation came into her eyes as she could not resist adding, "It was so difficult to hold on to the jewelry when the highwayman. . . ."

"Never you mind." Lady Manley backed up quickly, shaking her hand before her to forestall Jane's words.

"I truly did try to gather it all up again—after the highwayman. . . ."

"I quite comprehend as much as I should care to."

Jane was sorely tempted to laugh. Lady Manley never failed to beat a hasty retreat whenever anyone came even remotely near the subject of interplay between men and women. In fact, Jane had been counting upon that very fact—and had not been disappointed in her aunt's reaction.

"Well, the brooch was rather old and out of fashion. I don't suppose I shall miss it so very much. Eat, then rest," her aunt ordered, making rapidly for the door. "I do not expect to see you downstairs until I deem you quite recovered."

It seemed hours ago that the housemaid had come to remove the tray. Jane had dozed fitfully in the extraordinarily uncomfortable bed. She had lain and listened to the sounds of horses' hooves and carriage wheels rising from the street below. She had watched the sunlight slowly moving across the whitewashed wall until her little room was now deep in shadows.

All the time, she had been quite, quite alone.

The door moved open a mere hair's breadth. Jane turned quickly to the sound.

Horatia's blonde head peeked through the doorway.

"Jane," she whispered very softly. "Are you awake?"

"You are looking directly at me, Horatia," Jane replied. She never ceased to be amazed at her cousin's capacity for idiocy. "You can see I'm awake."

"Wonderful," she declared, still whispering. She bounced into the room, closing the door tightly behind her, and proceeded to seat herself upon the edge of Jane's bed. "I don't care what Mama says, I think it's everso wonderful to have you home again."

"What does Uncle Horace say regarding my return?" Jane asked.

Horatia paused, then whispered, "I cannot repeat what Papa says."

Jane nodded. She was quite accustomed to Uncle Horace. "Horatia, why are you whispering?"

"Because Mama doesn't know I'm here. She said I was not to disturb you, but I simply *had* to see you!" Horatia declared. "I simply *had* to be the first to have you tell me all about it."

"All about. . . ?"

"About the highwayman, silly," Horatia chided her. "It must have been everso exciting."

Jane nodded in agreement. Indeed, running off with that particular highwayman had been exciting—in more ways than one.

"Were you frightened?"

Jane supposed she might as well agree that she was, although she did not think it a good idea to admit to Horatia that, at the time, she was more frightened of what her aunt and uncle should do if they ever found her again than she was of the highwayman.

"Was he handsome—I mean, after he removed that ridiculous mask?"

Jane merely smiled enigmatically. How she wished she knew!

"Was he gentle?"

Jane's mouth dropped open and she felt her eyes nearly pop from her head. Whatever was her shatterbrained cousin talking about? My gracious, as if Jane needed to ask for clarification! How in heaven's name *could* Horatia ask such a question? Even more bewildering, how was Jane to answer regarding something of which she still had only indirect knowledge. The highwayman had emphatically seen to it that she remained almost as ignorant and certainly as innocent as Horatia.

Jane swallowed hard. "Merciful heavens, aren't we blunt today?" she remarked as a diversion.

"You must tell me, Jane," Horatia coaxed. "After all, we *have* been like sisters, haven't we?"

Jane nodded noncommittally.

"Come now," Horatia wheedled. "Didn't I tell you about the time Roger Paine offered me two farthings to show him my pantaloons?"

Jane was forced to concede.

"Well then?" Horatia insisted, crossing her plump little arms over her breasts.

"But, Horatia," Jane protested. "You were six years old when that happened. I truly do not think that ranks in the same category of shared confidences as. . . ."

"Horatia!" Lady Manley's harsh voice screeched through the tiny room. "Remove yourself from that bed and from this room this instant!"

Horatia quickly leaped from the bed.

"Did I not tell you that Jane has been tainted?" Lady Manley demanded.

"Yes, Mama," Horatia answered, her lower lip jutting out in a pout.

Jane's eyes grew wide with indignation.

"You are my sweet, innocent Horatia, and I intend to keep you that way," Lady Manley said as she escorted her to the door. "I shan't allow you to associate with anyone as depraved as . . . Jane."

Lady Manley pronounced her name with a sneer and a withering glance in Jane's direction.

"After the disgraceful manner in which you have comported yourself, you are not allowed even to speak to Horatia," her ladyship commanded Jane. Then she swept from the room, slamming the door tightly behind her.

Jane could only stare at the fast-closed door.

Well, of course she fully expected that running away with the highwayman would put her beyond the pale socially. Wasn't that why she had done it in the first place?

She had supposed that Aunt Olive intended to see her recovered from her "ordeal," as the lady had put it, and, after causing only just a minor scandal, she then expected to be allowed to retire quietly to a small house in the country.

She thought she should accustom herself to being considered "in disgrace," but she never expected to be so completely ostracized by even her own family.

Jane turned her head to the window to watch the twilight gathering outside.

Horatia pouted as she descended the stairs. Eavesdropping on the servants' gossip had given her only a very sketchy idea of what transpired between a man and a woman. Mama never told her anything. And now she had been forbidden even to speak to Jane, her one truly accurate and accessible source of information. Drat!

Chapter 8

"HOW MANY TIMES must I tell you?" Lady Manley demanded of her abigail as they assisted Horatia to dress for the evening. "The peach shawl is never worn with the primrose-colored gown."

She snatched the offending garment from Horatia's shoulders and replaced it with the proper, white cashmere shawl.

"Oh, how I do miss Jane," Horatia said wistfully. "She always knows precisely what looks well with each gown."

"You do not need *Jane,*" her mother said. "You have *me.*"

Horatia turned pleading blue eyes up to her mother. "Could you not allow Jane to come down just this once? I haven't seen her in two days, and I rather miss her."

"I cannot think why," Lady Manley replied. "Your presentation at Court and your ball were satisfactory, even if Aunt Georgina did decline to attend. And you look quite lovely tonight, too."

Horatia frowned and studied her reflection closely in the cheval glass. Well, perhaps her bosom could be just the slightest bit larger. Perhaps if she stood a bit more erect and kept her feet together, her hips would not protrude so much through the smooth line of the thin skirt. In spite of these minor flaws, every other gentleman of her acquaintance seemed to find her quite attractive. Why didn't John Tipton?

"Where are we going this evening?" Horatia asked.

"'Tis only to the Roscommons' soirée," Lady Manley stated petulantly.

"Who are they?"

"No one," her ladyship lamented. "No one important, at

any rate. That is precisely the problem! Captain Roscommon spent five years in India and still managed to return with only a modest fortune. The entire evening will be quite a waste of time."

"Then why do we bother to attend?"

"Because theirs is the only affair this evening to which we have been invited."

Lady Manley slapped her fan against the palm of her hand as she paced agitatedly back and forth across Horatia's bedroom.

"I vow, if we do not receive invitations to better affairs, we will *never* find you a suitable match and the entire Season will have been a waste! Then there will be absolutely no living with your father. Not to mention, how shall I *ever* show my face in the county again when everyone knows I have a daughter who did not take the first Season? Such an embarrassment!"

"What about Great-Aunt Georgina, Mama?" Horatia asked.

Lady Manley released a great snort of disgust. "Even *she* has not invited us, her own family, to any of her affairs. Imagine! I feel certain that if she would only include us, why, those vouchers to Almack's should appear at our door the very next day. Oh, where *are* those things?"

"Surely we've done nothing wrong, Mama?"

"Who knows the thoughts of these people?" Lady Manley wrung her hands. "Oh, if the news of Jane's kidnapping is the reason for your being rejected, I vow, I'll throttle the chit with my bare hands!"

Horatia drew in a deep breath. It was the fifteenth deep breath she had drawn in tonight, and it was still quite early yet. However, here at the Roscommons, whiling away the hours by keeping a strict account of how many deep breaths one could inhale in any given period of time, was about the most interesting thing she had yet been able to find to do.

Suddenly, Horatia and her mother were approached by a lady whose size Horatia had seen equaled but once, and that was at the county fair by the prized bull. As she drew closer, Horatia decided that the bull had the obvious advantage in that it had smelled better.

"Olive, my dear!" the enormous one exclaimed.

Horatia watched in horror as two immense white arms enveloped Lady Manley. Would she ever see her mother again? Horatia sighed with relief as her mother emerged unscathed from the embrace.

"Lady Constance, your exuberance never fails to lift my spirits," Lady Manley said.

When the huge lady turned her bulk toward her, Horatia could not help but take a quick step backward. She was stopped by an excruciating pain in her side where her mother had just pinched her.

"Come, Horatia. No need to be so shy," Lady Manley said, pushing a reluctant Horatia forward. "Permit me to present my daughter, who is making her come out this Season."

Horatia was forced to endure Lady Constance's embrace, all the while wondering precisely how long she could hold her breath.

"Lady Constance is the sister of the Marquess of Exhampton," Lady Manley explained. She ostensibly searched the room. "I do not believe I have seen Lord Exhampton and his quite charming son here this evening."

"Oh, they've other functions, elsewhere," Lady Constance answered.

"Do call soon, Lady Constance," Lady Manley encouraged, swiftly backing away.

Taking Horatia by the elbow, Lady Manley drew her through the crowd.

"Ah, there is someone whose acquaintance you must make," Lady Manley said, propelling her toward an elderly lady and a thin young man.

The lady's turban was festooned with ropes of large pearls. Long pendants of diamonds dangled from her ears. An immense necklace of rubies and topazes draped her wrinkled throat.

"Lady Gillingham," Lady Manley greeted. "How that red satin gown becomes you!"

'Indeed,' Horatia silently agreed. 'It matches her eyes.'

Lady Gillingham blinked and raised her head with some difficulty. The young man at her side was staring with un-

mitigated adoration at Horatia, his protruding Adam's
apple bobbing up and down with each swallow.

Lady Manley reached out and relieved Lady Gillingham
of her empty wine glass.

"Do be a dear and refill her ladyship's glass," she sent
the young man quickly off to the far side of the room.

"Why, thank you, Olive," Lady Gillingham whispered
hoarsely. "'Twas the very remedy for boredom which I myself was contemplating."

"So glad to have been of assistance," Lady Manley replied
with a smile. "May I present my daughter, Horatia?"

"So pleased to make your acquaintance," Horatia smiled
and repeated one of the pleasantries Mama had taught her.
From the corner of her eye, she could see Lady Gillingham's
companion eagerly approaching, refilled glass in hand.
"And you, too," she added, gracing the young man with one
of her most charming smiles.

Horatia jumped as her mother pinched her again.

"Do call soon," Lady Manley encouraged the lady, who
was already too deeply engrossed in her wine glass to notice
their departure.

"Lady Gillingham must be exceedingly wealthy," Horatia whispered to her mother as she was dragged through the
crowd.

"Not a groat to her name."

"But those jewels. . . ."

"They are all borrowed."

"Then why did you bother. . . ?"

"Horatia, you must come with me," Lady Manley commanded, propelling Horatia up the stairs to the chamber
which the ladies were using to repair their toilette.

"Thank goodness the room is empty!" Lady Manley
closed the door quietly yet firmly behind her and leaned
against it.

"Is something amiss, Mama?" Horatia asked, blinking.

"Amiss? Whyever should you think something amiss?"

"Well. . . ." Horatia began, rubbing the sore spots her
mother had inflicted upon her waist. "I am everso tired of
making the acquaintance of one obnoxious lady after the
other and never, *never* meeting some of the rather nice gentlemen who are also here this evening."

"There are no nice gentlemen here this evening," Lady Manley stated.

"Well, please excuse me, Mama. I mean no disrespect. However, I have seen. . . ."

"The only gentlemen here this evening are those who are without sufficient title or fortune to warrant invitations to better places."

"Then what of the ladies. . . ?"

Lady Manley grimaced as she explained. "While they themselves may be of insufficient means, they could just possibly be related to someone who knows of someone else who might be useful."

Lady Manley drew her daughter down upon the sofa beside her.

"'Tis time I told you a few facts of life, my dear," Lady Manley began.

'Well, at last!' Horatia breathed with relief. 'However, I had thought she might do this in a more private setting.'

"The entire structure of our society depends upon the friendships and animosities of the ladies," Lady Manley explained.

Horatia blinked. These were not quite the facts she had anticipated.

"One simply has no idea of what is possible when a lady is determined to reward or to retaliate."

Horatia wrinkled up her little nose. "That is why you suffered that horrid Lady Constance. . . ?"

Lady Manley leaned nearer her daughter. "Precisely. In our situation, we must be exceptionally careful to be on the reward side of the slate."

Horatia nodded. "I think I see. . . ."

Lady Manley sighed with relief. "I am so glad you are beginning to understand. Now, let us go down again. We have many ladies yet to greet this evening. But do avoid the gentlemen, my dear."

Although she agreed with her mother in theory, Horatia still hesitated when her mother descended the staircase and made straightway for a group of three extraordinarily thin young ladies chaperoned by an equally thin older lady dressed entirely in rusty black crepe. She had been observing the crowd from the vantage of the staircase and determined to go in another direction.

"Do accompany me to the refreshments," Horatia said pleasantly. She seized the eldest by the elbow. "I know we shall have everso much to discuss."

Before the young lady could demur, and before her mother could stop her, Horatia had practically dragged her halfway across the room, making steadily for the punch.

"Pray, excuse me," John Tipton said as he reached for the same glass as the lady coming up behind him.

It was about time he reached for a glass, Horatia decided, as she was becoming deucedly weary of waiting.

"Why, Mr. Tipton," she said, smiling up at him and completely abandoning the lady she had forced to accompany her. "Imagine encountering you here."

"Miss Manley, how nice to see you again." John began to rock back and forth upon his heels.

He was watching her—she knew it! He was taking in every inch of her, and in a manner which, had any other gentleman done so, she should have blushed profusely. Yet, strangely, she found she did not mind Mr. Tipton's perusal in the least.

He glanced from her to his glass of punch, then back and forth once again. Clearly, the man did not want their minimal encounter to end, yet appeared to be at a loss of what to do to continue it.

He drew in a deep breath and at last said, "How do you find the punch, Miss Manley?"

The punch? Why, whoever gave a thought to the punch? "Quite refreshing, actually," she nevertheless managed to reply, as she would never want Mr. Tipton to think her rude.

"I also find lemon juice quite refreshing."

Horatia glanced into her glass of punch. "There is lemon juice in the punch?"

"Can you not taste it?"

Horatia sipped her punch, then considered it a moment. "Indeed. A bit of nutmeg, too."

"Nutmeg? I thought it was cinnamon."

"Cinnamon?" Horatia repeated with a laugh. "Oh, no, Mr. Tipton. Trust me in this matter. Most assuredly, I know nutmeg."

John sipped his punch again. "It *is* nutmeg. How could I have mistaken the two?"

"'Tis easy enough."

"On the contrary. You must have a highly sensitive palate," John said, gazing into her eyes. His gaze traveled slightly downward. "And even more sensitive lips, and tongue. . . ."

His eyes again met hers.

"Do not underestimate your own sensitivities," Horatia said, returning his gaze.

"Mr. Tipton. Good evening and adieu," Lady Manley interrupted, interposing herself between Horatia and John. "Come, Horatia. 'Tis time we took our *congé*."

"But, Mama. . . ."

Lady Manley wasted no time in drawing Horatia to the door.

"Mama, were you not just the slightest bit rude to Mr. Tipton?" Horatia ventured cautiously.

"No more so than he deserved."

When they were farther out of the range of hearing of the rest of the assembly, Lady Manley pinched Horatia once again. "What did I just finish telling you?" she demanded angrily.

"Regarding what, Mama?" Horatia asked, extraordinarily puzzled and rather weary of rubbing her sore side.

"I'll not have you encouraging that Mr. Tipton, or any other gentleman your father and I deem unsuitable for you."

"But he is a relation of Great-Aunt Georgina's, Mama," Horatia felt it necessary to remark in Mr. Tipton's defense. "He's very polite. How can he be unsuitable?"

"The man has no fortune and no prospects," Lady Manley informed her. "If he were a suitable match for you, he most assuredly would not be *here* tonight!"

For several days Jane had watched Uncle Horace depart for his club. She had watched Aunt Olive and Horatia, accompanied by a maid, leave the town house each morning and return, the carriage laden with their myriad purchases, only to go out again on an endless round of at-homes. She had watched them, in their finest attire, leave each evening for some ball or soirée or musicale.

All the while, she had remained alone in her room. As there was precious little else to occupy her, Jane had taken to standing a never-ceasing vigil at the window. The panorama was ever much the same and she drifted into daydreams when the traffic became sporadic.

Suddenly, Jane snapped herself from her inattention and peered more closely out the window. She blinked in surprise as the garish yellow high-perch phaeton drawn by two perfectly match bays pulled to a halt before the Manley's town house and Derwood Marchant, Viscount Scythe, descended and entered.

Jane swallowed hard. Returning to her aunt and uncle had been difficult enough, but Lord Scythe was another matter entirely. She barely knew the man. She had no idea what his reaction would be when she finally confronted him and tried to explain why she had run away with the highwayman.

She was dreading this initial encounter. Certainly, she should not be dreading it any more than she had dreaded becoming affianced to Lord Scythe to begin with.

Actually, she should be anticipating this with a great deal of rejoicing. After all, she would be attaining the goal she had gone to so much trouble to achieve.

She inspected her reflection in the small, cracked mirror which she had persuaded Aunt Olive to have moved down from the attic.

Then she drew in a deep breath and waited quietly at the window until Aunt Olive and Uncle Horace should summon her downstairs to confront her fate.

Chapter 9

"No NEWS OF my Jane!" Lord Scythe repeated. He was apparently attempting to stride forcefully about the drawing room, yet his stagger did manage to detract considerably from the powerfully commanding effect he wished to convey.

"You must be patient," Lady Manley said. "These things take time—weeks, months, years. . . ."

"I have been patient long enough," Lord Scythe informed Sir Horace and Lady Manley.

"We are equally concerned regarding Jane's whereabouts," Lady Manley assured him, wringing her hands in despair.

She glanced upward. Indeed, she was concerned for the girl's whereabouts. If Jane did not remain in her room until Lord Scythe had departed, there would most surely be the devil to pay. Why in heaven's name hadn't she locked that blasted door?

"Then why have you not done more to find my Jane?"

"We've done everything. . . ." Sir Horace began.

"I know what you've done," Lord Scythe interrupted. "Not enough. Not enough by half."

His lordship removed his snuff box from the pocket of his Pomona green waistcoat.

"Allow me to show you my latest acquisition, Manley. Quite an elegant work of art. Deucedly expensive, too," he did not fail to point out. "Saw it in the shop and could not rest until I had made it my own. I feel that way about a great many of the things I eventually acquire. Felt that way the moment I saw my Jane, too. That's why I do not intend to let this matter rest."

Sir Horace and Lady Manley looked at each other with growing trepidation. They had rather imagined that any day now, his lordship would come to tell them that, since the girl hadn't yet been found, they might as well cry off the betrothal. They had never expected *this* to be his lordship's reaction.

"Since I can get no satisfaction from you, or from the deucedly slow authorities, I shall simply have to make use of my rather extensive personal funds to employ certain private parties to make inquiries along these lines."

"Private parties?" Sir Horace repeated.

"Indeed," Lord Scythe informed him. "There are certain segments of the population which can be entrusted—for a nominal fee—to conduct a discreet but thorough inquiry into any number of personal matters."

Lord Scythe attempted to focus his eyes more accurately and peered, frowning, into Sir Horace's face. "You have no objection to that, do you, Manley?"

"No, no."

"Of course not," Lady Manley echoed. "We certainly don't wish to appear unconcerned about Jane." At least not in public, she failed to mention aloud.

"I was certain you wouldn't," Lord Scythe replied with a thin smile. He wobbled as he spun about on his heel and headed for the door.

Jane had waited for what seemed an inordinate amount of time for someone to summon her down at last to confront Lord Scythe.

She stared in bewilderment. Lord Scythe had exited the town house and was climbing up to the seat of his phaeton. His lordship was leaving and Aunt Olive and Uncle Horace had never even called her down!

Sir Horace stared at the doorway long after Lord Scythe had departed. At length, he recovered enough of his senses to turn to his wife.

"Scythe is hiring private parties to search for Jane," Lady Manley repeated in disbelief.

"He *wants* to find her? Does this mean he still wants to marry her?"

"I suppose so," Lady Manley answered, still quite shocked. "I hardly think he'd go to all the trouble—not to mention the expense—of locating a missing girl merely to tell her to go away again."

"Damned unusual," Sir Horace commented. He found it so unusual that he made straightway for the liquor cabinet in order to find some sort of potent elixir which would help him reason it all out.

"This could be very good, Horace."

Sir Horace cast his wife a look which indicated his grave doubts regarding her sanity.

"If he will still marry her, we will get the girl off our hands."

Sir Horace nodded. Perhaps Olive was not so bird-witted after all.

Then Lady Manley decided, "This could also be very bad, Horace."

"Make up your mind, Olive." Sir Horace reverted to his original evaluation of his wife's mental state.

"If he marries Jane, she will still be out in Society. She will ever be a reminder to everyone of her scandal, thus endangering Horatia's prospects of making a brilliant match."

Sir Horace applied the content of the liquor cabinet for assistance in thinking this one out.

"We shall just have to keep Jane secreted away upstairs a little longer," Lady Manley finally decided. "Just until Horatia is married."

Sir Horace grimaced. "That could take a bit of time, considering the way things are currently progressing."

"Indeed," Lady Manley agreed, somewhat disgruntled. "Especially if those blasted vouchers to Almack's do not arrive before all the most eligible bachelors are taken!"

"I believe I saw Lord Scythe call this afternoon," Jane commented to her aunt when the lady came to bid her good evening.

The Manleys were off to yet another soirée—and Jane was once again left upstairs, quite alone.

"Ah well, yes, yes," Lady Manley stuttered as she fidgeted with the gold Brandenburgs which marched down the front of the crimson bodice of her velvet spencer. "Yes, his lordship did come calling."

"He did not come to see me?" she inquired tentatively. "After all, I am his betrothed, am I not?"

Jane hoped against hope that Aunt Olive would give her the dire news that Lord Scythe had seen fit, in view of her immoderate behavior in running off with a highwayman, to cry off from the betrothal immediately.

"Have you nothing better to do with your time than peer out windows all day?" Lady Manley countered.

"Indeed not, Aunt Olive," Jane replied. "I have no books, no companionship. There is precious little else to do here but stare out the window. Since I have only one of them available to me, I am growing rather weary of the view from it as well. I am completely recovered from my ordeal, as if I had suffered any ill effects from it in the first place. I do so want to rejoin the family," Jane pleaded.

Lady Manley slowly shook her head. "Impossible!"

"Why must I remain here when there are other bedchambers for me on the floor below?" Jane asked.

Still her ladyship adamantly refused.

"I realize I am not invited, nor am I prepared to accept invitations to any of the affairs which you attend," Jane reasoned, although she knew that reasonableness was not one of her aunt's major attributes. "But I should be content to take my meals with the family. I would spend the rest of my time in the library or garden, where I shan't be a bother to anyone," she hastened to reassure her aunt.

Lady Manley's cold eyes stared at Jane.

"You will remain in this room until I tell you otherwise," she informed her quite bluntly. "Your appearance in public after your disgraceful action will only harm Horatia's prospects of making an excellent match."

Jane silently considered her shatterbrained cousin. Indeed, the future held little if anything for Horatia were it not for marriage. While Jane could be content living alone in a modest country cottage on what little income her parents had left her, or even make a living as a governess, lady's maid, or companion, should circumstances warrant, certainly Horatia was without such resourcefulness.

In all good conscience, Jane could hardly condemn her cousin to a life for which she was so ill-suited.

"I understand," Jane replied at length. "I would not wish to do anything to harm Horatia. . . ."

"You should have thought of *that* before you ran off," Lady Manley chastened her.

"Be that as it may, Aunt Olive," Jane continued, "would it not be better for Horatia if I were not in Town at all?"

"Indeed," the lady replied with an indignant snort.

"Then could I not simply retire to the country—to a small cottage—quietly, with no further scandal?"

Jane held her breath. Would fate be so kind as to grant her this simple wish?

Lady Manley shook her head. "We cannot have you taking trips about the countryside at this time."

"It isn't trips about the countryside," Jane corrected. "Just one short journey. Once in my own little cottage, I assure you, I shall stay put."

"You should have stayed in your uncle's carriage," Lady Manley grunted irritably. "At any rate, neither your uncle nor I can leave London just now. Nor would we want to. There is simply too much to do for Horatia."

"You needn't accompany me. . . ."

"Do you actually believe that we would allow you to travel on your own?" Lady Manley demanded, regarding Jane with a mixture of shock and ridicule. "Why, just look at the problems you caused when accompanied by two excellent chaperones."

"Who?" Jane asked, frowning with incomprehension.

"Why, your uncle and I, of course!"

"Oh."

"I shudder to think what kind of scrapes you could get yourself into when left to your own devices." Lady Manley deliberately shook her plump shoulders to emphasize her horror. "Then what tales there would be for the scandal-mongers to bruit about! Horatia's prospects would be ruined for certain!"

Jane nodded.

"At any rate, we haven't the funds available just now."

"I would not use your money, Aunt Olive," Jane ventured. "My father did leave me a small income of my own."

"Ah, yes. Well, that's not available just now, either."

"Aunt Olive, you haven't spent my money. . . ." Jane suddenly felt her knees turning to the consistency of Devonshire cream as she saw her hopes of independence, no matter how modest, rapidly disappearing.

"Of course not! What kind of aunt and uncle do you think us?"

Jane was so relieved to hear she still retained her modest income that she wisely decided to refrain from answering her aunt's question. She breathed deeply as she felt sensation restored to her lower limbs.

"It's just . . . well, it's all so heavily invested—for your future—that we cannot make use of it just now," Lady Manley explained rather clumsily. "You do understand, don't you?"

Jane understood perfectly well. She also understood that there was little she could do about it. She looked at her aunt and nodded.

"You will remain in this room, where I can be *absolutely certain* that you will do nothing further to interfere with Horatia's come out," Lady Manley said with great finality as she headed for the door.

Just before her aunt closed the door behind her, Jane ventured to ask, "Could I at least have access to the library?"

The only reply she received was the cold metallic click of the key in the lock.

Jane crossed her arms over her chest and walked to the fireplace. The size of the fire in the hearth had remained inadequately the same all the while she had been here.

She rubbed her hands up and down her arms the better to warm herself, yet still found no relief. With a dread that caused her to shake even more, she realized that the chill came not from the insufficient heating of the room but from her dawning realization that she was a virtual prisoner here.

Jane swallowed hard and moved to the window, now truly her only contact with the world.

Far below, in the gathering twilight, Aunt Olive and Uncle Horace were leaving the town house. Jane leaned closer to the windowpane, following her old habit of monitoring Horatia's attire.

Jane nodded in approval. She had watched her cousin

every evening, and each evening she had looked even more lovely than the previous one, if that were possible.

Jane was comforted with the small hope that her beautiful, if somewhat shatterbrained, cousin would succeed in making a brilliant match soon, very soon—and Jane could at last escape to the country.

The very thought of escape recalled to mind her short-lived adventure. Had it been a mere fortnight ago that she had been traveling in her uncle's carriage toward her own inescapable fate?

Then she had been watching the stationary world as she traveled by. Now it was she who was standing still at the window, watching the entire world as it quite completely passed her by.

Once, not so long ago, the highwayman had been there to stop the moving carriage. He had been there for her to seize hold of and to escape with.

She squeezed her arms more tightly across her breasts, remembering the feel of the warm highwayman's body in her arms on that chilly night.

If she closed her eyes, she could still recall the unusual blue of his eyes and the soft creases in his eyelids, the hollow between his cheek and his strong jaw, and the smooth line of his fine lips. She smiled as she imagined hearing his voice accusing her of having such fine tendencies toward becoming a highwayman herself. She thought she might even be able to endure him scolding her if she could only be a fugitive with him again—instead of a lonely prisoner here.

She opened her eyes and, from the great height of her window, she watched the tops of the elegant carriages rolling by. She sighed. She truly doubted that any highwayman would be passing by up here to help her.

Oh, where was that blasted highwayman when she *really* needed him?

Chapter 10

"I DON'T BELIEVE I am acquainted with Mr. and Mrs. Baxter, Mama," Horatia said as their carriage pulled up before the tall, brick-fronted town house.

"That doesn't signify," Lady Manley said. "What matters is that we are out."

"Mama, we have been out every evening this week," Horatia complained.

"And we shall be out every evening that we are invited," Lady Manley replied. "The important thing is that we are among people whose acquaintance we may cultivate to make the acquaintance of other, more important—and more useful—people."

Lady Manley heaved a heavy sigh. "Oh, if only someone could obtain for us those vouchers to Almack's—especially since Aunt Georgina hasn't bothered to. Oh, I just know you will find a simply splendid match there!"

"But, Mama, I am becoming just a bit bored by all these. . . ."

"*That* does not signify, either," Lady Manley informed her quite bluntly. "We are not attending these things to be entertained."

"Your mother is correct, girl," Sir Horace growled from his corner of the carriage. "I haven't been entertained at a one of these things yet—no, not a bloody one."

"Have you made the acquaintance of my brother?" Lady Constance inquired as she approached them from across the Baxter's drawing room and embraced Lady Manley.

"Why, I believe I have not," Lady Manley answered quite

92

coolly, but Horatia could detect the gleam in her mother's eye.

"Then I shall secure you an introduction forthwith," the large lady announced, seizing Lady Manley by the hand and dragging her along.

Horatia found her own wrist grasped by her mother. The three made a rather unusual procession as they snaked through the crowd.

Horatia found herself drawn to a halt before the enormous Lady Constance's equally enormous brother, the Marquess of Exhampton. His lordship merely nodded, then returned to his passionate affair with the contents of the refreshment table.

Horatia watched her mother. Surely she would be incensed at Lord Exhampton's cavalier treatment of them. However, Lady Manley was still smiling most pleasantly— and directing that smile at the beefy, red-faced young man who had remained standing beside Lady Constance.

"My nephew, Percival, Viscount Brinshire," her ladyship beamed. "My brother's only son and heir. And as his doting aunt, may I modestly add, the most eligible bachelor this Season."

Ah, Horatia inhaled a deep breath of comprehension. Of course. Mama would have been exceedingly polite to these people even if Lord Exhampton had seen fit to eat her reticule.

Still, Horatia suppressed a small shudder when she saw Lord Brinshire's squinty little eyes regarding her with much the same voracity that his father eyed the refreshments.

"I should have known you in a trice," Lady Manley said to him in her most musical of voices.

Indeed, Horatia agreed silently, as in a few more years, not to mention quite a few more meals, he would attain every bit of the dimensions his father had already achieved.

His doting aunt might declare him the most eligible bachelor of the Season, but Horatia decided he was only eligible for an attack of the gout.

"It is not every evening one encounters a young lady whose hair equals the sun for radiance," Lord Brinshire commented to Horatia, "yet whose eyes rival the very stars for brilliance."

Horatia forced herself to smile. She was quite weary of hearing this remark. Strangely, she now found herself longing to hear a certain other gentleman say something very different to her.

"Are you fond of boxing?" Lord Brinshire inquired.

Horatia grimaced. This was not quite the something different which she had in mind.

"Capital! So am I."

Horatia blinked. Indeed, his lordship must be possessed of extraordinarily acute hearing, as she most certainly had not heard herself make any reply.

"Why, just this morning, I attended the most rousing mill," he continued, quite oblivious to Horatia's disinterest in the subject.

Horatia glanced in despair toward her mother. She could hope for no relief from that quarter, as Lady Manley was listening quite contentedly to the enormous Lady Constance—and all the while she smiled and nodded her encouragement to Horatia.

"Of course, they have taken to wearing gloves," he complained. "I detest when they do that. Takes all the bottom out of the sport. Man likes to see a bit of blood with his mill, if you take my meaning."

Horatia grimaced. Indeed, she did not take his meaning. Her stomach was of such a disposition that she felt it begin to tumble if there was too much red in her slice of roast beef.

"Now, last October, there was the most smashing mill at Crawley," he continued, unmindful of the increasingly green coloration to Horatia's normally fair complexion.

As no rescue was to be forthcoming from her mother, Horatia began to scan the room for some other—any other—acquaintance.

"No gloves on these coves, I can tell you!" Lord Brinshire crowed with bloodthirsty delight. "One plants a facer direct to the other. Not only knocks the fellow's two front teeth out, but slices his own knuckles wide open in the process. Fellows in the first row got spotted rather red."

"Pray, excuse me," Horatia interrupted. "There is such a clamor about the refreshments, I can barely hear your intensely interesting account. Why do we not take a stroll to where I can hear you better? Say over there."

She pointed to the other side of the room, to a corner filled with large potted palms. She had spied her means of escape and definitely intended to make use of it.

When they arrived at the palms, Horatia waved her hand before her face.

"Oh, Lord Brinshire, 'tis everso warm. Could you get me a glass of punch, please?"

"But we just left the . . . why did you not ask then. . . ?" he protested.

"I wasn't thirsty then. Surely you would not want me to bother you when I *wasn't* thirsty."

When Lord Brinshire strolled away, John Tipton emerged from behind the potted palm where Horatia·had first spotted him.

She found herself grinning with affectionate familiarity as he began again to rock back and forth upon his heels. Oh, if only he could find something about her which appealed to him as much as the things he did appealed to her!

"How good to see you, Miss Manley," he said.

"Indeed, I scarcely could see you behind this. . . ," Horatia reached her arm up to bat at the intruding palm fronds, " . . . this vegetation. Are you in hiding, perhaps?"

"Only sometimes," John answered. "Certainly not now."

Horatia grinned. "I wish I had the advantage of carrying a potted palm about with me. They appear to be quite useful for concealment," she said, running her fingers along the slender leaves of one frond.

"I believe they are only useful when they stand erect," John said, reaching out to straighten the same frond which Horatia held. Briefly their fingers touched. "Drooping branches are abysmal."

"Indeed, quite useless," Horatia concurred.

John shyly glanced at Horatia, who was still stroking the palm fronds. Then she raised her wide blue eyes to his. One engaging smile from her soft pink lips gave him the final incentive he needed.

"Miss Manley, might I . . . might I be so bold as to call upon you tomorrow?"

"Mr. Tipton, I should be delighted."

The look which Horatia bestowed upon him made John feel like a man who has been at the bottom of a pit for too long and has suddenly just returned to the welcomed, warming light of day.

"The, ah, person has arrived, m'lord," Raleigh informed Lord Scythe from the doorway of his study.

'Twas not without good cause that Lord Scythe was a trifle apprehensive. One did not bring this sort of character into one's home every evening, and certainly not at this late hour.

Still, he did suppose it was better than going to the sort of places such people usually frequented.

"Show him in, Raleigh," Lord Scythe said. "Just keep an eye upon him—and the silver."

Lord Scythe quickly polished off his brandy and was about to pour himself another when Raleigh again appeared at the door. "A Mr.—ah. . . ."

"Just Davey," the swarthy little man completed as he poked his head into the room. After a quick glance to the left, then right, he slipped into the room. "Red Davey, to me business associates."

'Whyever should they call him "Red"?' Lord Scythe silently wondered, inspecting the man's curly dark locks and black eyes. 'The man is swarthy as an Egyptian.'

Unless, of course, his name derived not from his personal appearance but rather from his reputation in his chosen profession, Lord Scythe pondered with a small, nervous gulp.

"Won't you come in," his lordship said most cordially, prudently deciding to be exceedingly polite to his new business associate.

"Thankee, m'lord," the dark little man replied, carefully watching as Raleigh left, closing the door behind him.

Red Davey glanced from side to side as he slowly moved from the doorway. Instead of directly crossing the wide-open expanse of room, the little man edged his way to the bookcase at the side, then moved to the window. All the while, the wiry little man never actually ceased watching the doorway.

Red Davey slowly ran his grimy finger over the leading between the small panes of colored glass in the long, narrow window. Lord Scythe watched with growing apprehension as Red Davey's finger continued to pass back and forth over the latch.

Lord Scythe debated whether Red Davey was looking for a quick route of escape this evening—or an even quicker means of entrance some other night.

Red Davey cast one more furtive glance toward the doorway before coming to stand before his lordship's desk. He picked up the crystal decanter and twirled it against the candlelight, examining each facet.

"Please be so good as not to handle that," Lord Scythe requested. "'Twas deucedly costly. . . ."

Lord Scythe quickly silenced himself. Perhaps it was not such a good idea to remind this fellow of the cost of the contents of his town house.

"May I offer you some brandy?" Lord Scythe asked as a diversion.

Red Davey quickly replaced the decanter upon the desk. "No thankee, m'lord. I'd rather keep me wits about me just now."

"Won't you have a seat, then?" Lord Scythe invited.

"No, thankee, m'lord. I'll remain standin', if it's all the same to you."

"As you wish," Lord Scythe replied. He himself thought that he would feel much more comfortable seated, yet with this fellow constantly on the prowl about his study, he decided to remain standing as well.

From the desk, he took the miniature of Jane which the Manleys had given him upon his betrothal.

"This is the young lady. . . ." he began, attempting to extend the miniature to the little man, who had been standing in front of the chair the last time he saw him. But when he looked up, Red Davey had skirted the chair and was now circling the desk.

Lord Scythe turned slowly around until he was facing the wall, and the strange little man. He glanced down at the miniature.

"This is the young lady. . . ." his lordship began again.

But when he looked up, Red Davey had moved over to the window.

"Blast it, man! I'm trying to show you her likeness so you can find her. Be so good as to stand still long enough. . . ."

"The man who stands still 'long enough' is still forever," Red Davey remarked enigmatically as he returned to the desk. He stood before his lordship just long enough to take the miniature in hand.

"Aye. I can see *why* you want her returned to you," Red Davey observed, tucking the miniature into his righthand jacket pocket. He began patting his left side. "Now, what have you for this pocket so that *I* will want to see her returned to you?"

Chapter 11

"GOOD EVENING," DALTON called to the occupants of the elaborately outfitted berlin which he and his two companions had just stopped. "My friends have detained your coachman momentarily."

"Didn't think they'd be able to stop," Clive whispered to Tony as he trained his pistol on the quaking coachman.

"Traveling hell for leather, they were," Tony agreed. "Never seen such speed, and this Jehu appears to be sober."

"While your coachman is thus preoccupied, I am afraid you will have no alternative but to pass the time in my company," Dalton was telling the unseen occupants of the carriage. "I trust you will not find me too tedious a companion."

There was no reply from inside the berlin.

"Kind sirs, ladies." Dalton raised his voice to carry into the dark corners of the interior. "You will be so good as to unburden yourselves of your valuables. . . ."

"We have no valuables," the softly feminine voice replied.

"Come, come. Traveling in a carriage such as this and possessed of no valuables? How gullible do you think me? Please be so good as to open the door," he demanded with his customary politeness.

The quivering hand of a young girl slowly pushed open the door.

Blast! There was a child traveling with them. How he hated frightening children.

Dalton glanced quickly up to the coachman. Both of his upraised arms were shaking with such violence that Dalton began to suspect that the sight of a band of mere highwaymen could not be the cause.

Cautiously, he inched Paladin farther from the door of the berlin and cocked his pistol.

Blast the authorities, he cursed. If they wanted to lay a trap for him, then so be it. He was prepared. But damn them for involving women and children in their plot.

The feminine voice gasped in what sounded like a single, suppressed sob. Suddenly, from the interior of the berlin, a horrendous duet of wailing arose to accompany her deep lamentations.

Paladin backstepped in fright. Dalton, still suspicious, thumbed the hammer of his pistol for assurance and edged his horse closer.

"We have already been robbed once this evening," the lady informed him above the resounding sobs of the other occupants of the carriage. "Please let us pass—and quickly, sir. Quickly! We must reach the nearest physician before my husband. . . ."

The lady's explanation was interrupted by more racking sobs.

Dalton frowned and lowered his pistol. He was not usually so incautious, yet some feeling deep within urged him to leniency.

"Coachman," he called. "Bring the lantern."

Tony waved his pistol to ensure the quaking coachman's obedience. Once shaken from his inertia, the man quickly clambered down from his seat to swing the lantern into the berlin.

"My God!" Dalton exclaimed at the sight.

Two young girls, barely twelve and thirteen he supposed, clung to each other, wailing in fright. The fragile-looking woman seated opposite the girls held the man's head in what remained of her lap, as she was obviously increasing. The front of the man's jacket was flung open to reveal the spreading red stain which covered his once-white waistcoat.

"You two," Dalton summoned his companions, his eyes never leaving the injured man. "Come quickly! I need you!"

Dalton uncocked his pistol and shoved it into the top of his black breeches. Quickly slipping from Paladin's back, he entered the berlin and knelt at the injured man's side.

"What happened?"

He did not stop to listen to her reply, but immediately unfastened the man's waistcoat and tore open his shirt.

"The highwaymen. . . ." she gasped between sobs.

Dalton could barely hear her quivering voice over the crying of the children.

"They took our money, my jewels . . . they can have them," she said, shaking her head as if none of that mattered. "But then the leader went for my Julie. . . ."

She swept her eyes from her husband to the elder of the two girls.

"She's just a child!" Dalton exclaimed. Damn this other highwayman, whoever he might be! Dalton minded only a little that the hard-hearted scoundrel and his band were making life difficult for him, but did the soulless bastard have to cause others to suffer so?

The lady reached down to stroke the perspiration from the man's blanched forehead.

"That's when Randolph caught him off guard and struck him, knocking him from the carriage. But before he rode off, he shot. . . ." Her sobs prevented her from continuing.

"Oh, I say! This is horrendous!" Tony declared as he arrived at the doorway of the berlin.

"Give me your shirt," Dalton ordered.

Tony slipped out of the lady's sight and stripped off jacket, waistcoat, and shirt. He began to tear the fine lawn fabric into long strips of bandage and hand them inside to Dalton.

A short time later, Dalton leaned back on his heels and heaved a deep sigh of relief. Turning to the woman, he said gently, "That stops the blood—for now. It appeared much worse than it really was."

The lady breathed a deep sigh of relief. She leaned over and patted the girls on the arm.

"'Tis all right," she told them. "Papa will recover."

Greatly relieved, the two little banshees ceased their wailing—much to Dalton's even greater relief.

"He'll recover if he's not moved just now," Dalton corrected. Then he turned to Clive. "Ride for the apothecary."

Clive nodded, departing immediately on his errand of mercy.

"Remain here," Dalton ordered the lady. "We must go. The apothecary will come."

Dalton dug into the pocket of his black jacket and withdrew a few shillings. He pressed them into the lady's trembling hand.

"Seeing as how the other highwayman left you with nothing, I doubt you've the wherewithal to pay the apothecary—and those fellows do demand to be paid," he added with a weak grin.

The lady, obviously completely bewildered, could only glance from the coins to Dalton and back again.

Dalton grinned at her, shrugged his shoulders, and left the berlin.

What else could he have done? he asked himself as he mounted Paladin and he and Tony galloped away.

Dalton raised a silent prayer that the man would recover from his wounds. He'd done all he could to help the man. He made another silent plea that the prayers of a wretched highwayman such as himself would be heard.

Damn that other highwayman for his violence and stupidity! Dalton cursed under his breath as he and Tony traveled the well-worn path through the woods to the tiny, dilapidated inn to await Clive's return. That slimy wretch was giving a bad name to honest, conscientious thieves like himself.

Yes, he might still be a thief, Dalton had the courage to admit to himself, but blast it all! Somebody had to take care of these people, especially with such black-hearted scum preying on the innocent.

He pushed out of his mind his speculations regarding how many unfortunate people had been set upon by that other highwayman in the same tragic manner when Dalton had not been there to aid them.

He had heard that, several weeks ago, some wealthy travelers had had their maid carried off. What would have happened to the little girl he had just seen had her father not bravely intervened?

Dalton suddenly found himself pondering the fate of the young lady who had tried to run away with him.

As he galloped along on Paladin, he realized he would have enjoyed the feel of her slender arms about his waist right now, and her thigh pressing against the base of his spine.

In the company of the clergyman and his wife, had she reached London safely? He certainly hoped so.

Was she married by now to the man she had been so desperate to avoid? Odd how he found himself hoping that she was not.

"Thompson, you look as if someone had just stolen your Shakespeare," Dalton said upon seeing the long face with which his valet greeted him when he arrived the next morning at Milbury Hall.

"So sorry, sir," Thompson replied. He then raised his voice to pronounce, " 'The nature of bad news infects the teller.' "

"Bad news?" Dalton repeated frowning. "What bad news?"

"Aren't you even going to guess, sir?" Thompson asked.

"Must I guess what the bad news is?"

"No, sir. My quotation of the Bard."

"Oh, heavens," Dalton threw up his hands with exasperation. He hadn't been correct in all this time. Why try now? "You know I'll suppose 'tis from *Hamlet.*"

Thompson smiled smugly. *"Anthony and Cleopatra,* sir." Then he shrugged. "And, sir, 'tis not exactly bad news."

Dalton sighed with relief.

Then Thompson coughed and added, "'Tis not exactly good news, either."

He scuffed his shoe against the red brick floor of the kitchen. "On the other hand, 'tis most likely bad news."

"Oh, for heaven's sake, Thompson," Dalton cried. "Decide one way or the other!"

Thompson shrugged again.

"Or tell me the news outright and I shall decide for myself whether 'tis good or bad."

"Very well, sir," Thompson agreed and handed Dalton the morning post. "Please forgive the lack of a tray, but Lord Milburton's agent from London arrived while you were out yesterday and took some more of the plate back with him to be sold, I assume to cover his lordship's gaming debts."

Dalton grimaced. "Undoubtedly."

He took the proffered envelope. 'Twas his uncle's stationery, Dalton confirmed as he turned the embossed, cream-colored paper over in his hand.

With some apprehension, Dalton slit the seal and unfolded the missive. His brow darkened as he read the short message.

"Oh, 'tis bad, sir," Thompson decided, disappointed.

"My uncle summons me to London," Dalton explained, his outright astonishment rendering his voice strangely flat.

"Oh, 'tis very bad, indeed."

"Whyever should he be summoning me?"

"I cannot imagine, sir. His lordship hasn't contacted you since you plagued him to have a new well dug on the home farm as the old one had run dry four months previous and the tenants had been having to carry water from the neighbor's well two miles away."

"'Twas a legitimate complaint," Dalton defended his actions. "My uncle had no cause to berate me so."

"I seem to recall his words were something to the effect of you being 'more annoying than the pox and to remove your posterior from his presence forthwith and never return.' "

"You have an astonishing memory, Thompson."

"If it is any consolation, sir, you have been very cooperative regarding compliance with his lordship's wishes."

Dalton nodded. Since that day two and a half years ago, he and his uncle had succeeded admirably in their efforts to avoid each other.

Dalton had never wanted to hate his uncle. However, his father's elder brother had never liked him and had taken every opportunity to demonstrate that fact to Dalton.

Dalton could recall no specific incident from which his uncle should have conceived such animosity toward him. He could only suppose it was because Lord Milburton had no surviving offspring and it galled him to know that his younger brother's son would one day succeed him. It seemed to Dalton that Lord Milburton was doing his level best to ensure that there was precious little to inherit.

As grim as the recollection of his uncle was to him, Dalton thought with affection of his aunt. After her only child had died in infancy, Aunt Sophie had transferred all her affection to him. She had been as a second mother to him after his own parents had passed away years ago.

Lord Milburton had made every effort to alienate his nephew. Dalton held out no false assumptions as to making peace with his uncle. Aunt Sophie alone still maintained hope for a reconciliation between her husband and his heir-presumptive.

"Shall I begin packing, sir?" Thompson inquired, rousing Dalton from his contemplation.

Dalton crumpled the letter in his hands.

"You're upset, sir," Thompson observed.

"Just like my uncle to be so selfish as to choose this particular time of year to make his unreasonable demands upon my time," Dalton complained. "The cows are calving, the spring crops are ready for planting. I must be here now."

Dalton tossed the crumpled paper into the cold hearth.

"Still, I suppose no harm would come from a quick trip to London, just to see what wild scheme the man has concocted for the sole purpose of annoying me," Dalton decided.

"A wise move, sir," the valet offered his approval.

"Pack very little, Thompson. I shall be returning quickly."

Chapter 12

SNODDERLY ENTERED THE drawing room. One eyebrow was raised to its customarily censorious angle. His lip was curled back in its usual sneer of distaste.

He held before him at arms' length—as if fearful of being contaminated by the offensive article—a small bouquet of purple violets.

"For Miss Manley."

"How charming!" Horatia exclaimed, jumping to her feet.

As excited as she was, Horatia was not as quick as her mother. Lady Manley interposed herself between her daughter and Snodderly.

"How utterly ordinary," Lady Manley pronounced the floral offering. "I certainly would have thought that, with his means, Lord Brinshire could have sent a bit larger bouquet."

"Perhaps Lord Brinshire did not send it," Horatia ventured cautiously, peeking over her mother's shoulder at the small bouquet. Indeed, she hoped it was not his lordship! She should hate to think that gentleman would even consider paying her court. With what fear and loathing she should anticipate family gatherings!

"Nonsense," Lady Manley declared forcefully. "Who else. . . ?"

"If I may be so bold," Snodderly interposed through tightly clenched lips. "Perhaps her ladyship could solve this perplexing conundrum by reading the accompanying card. Then I should not have to remain standing here. I feel, personally, that I make a rather wretched flowerstand."

106

"Indeed you do, Snodderly," Horatia readily agreed. "Flowerstands are pleasantly silent." Horatia blinked with astonishment. Wherever had she come by the audacity to say that—and to the intimidating Snodderly, of all people!

With a disdain that rivaled Snodderly's, Lady Manley withdrew the small card and peered at it for what seemed to Horatia an interminable amount of time.

"Mama!" Horatia exclaimed. "I can bear it no longer. Who has sent me this lovely bouquet?"

Lady Manley crumpled the card. She seized the bouquet from Snodderly, who seemed greatly pleased to be relieved of his burden. She marched to the window, pulled the curtain aside, and flung the bouquet into the path of the carriage passing along the street below.

"Mama! What have you done?" Horatia cried in horror as she sped to the window. She leaned out, attempting to catch sight of her vanished flowers. Then she ducked back inside the window to stare at her mother in disbelief at what had been done to a bunch of small, relatively harmless flowers. "Who could have angered you so by sending them to me?"

"You know perfectly well. They were from that horrid John Tipton."

Horatia could not prevent the wide smile of satisfaction that spread across her face.

"Horatia, I specifically forbid you to encourage that man!"

"But he's terribly nice, Mama."

"He sends you violets . . . common, ordinary violets."

"What is wrong with violets?" Horatia demanded. "That horrid Lord Brinshire would have sent me boxing gloves! Would *that* have made you happier?"

Before her mother could reply, Horatia spun about on her heel and strode angrily from the room. Once in the hall, she broke into a most unladylike run and did not stop until she reached her own bedchamber. She slammed the door and threw herself down across the bed.

When she tired of lying across the bed, punching her pillow, she rose and paced about her bedchamber, slapping at pieces of furniture with her pillow. When she wearied of that pastime, she once again flung herself across her bed, the better to gather strength for another round of furniture slapping.

She was in the middle of making the fourth circuit of her room, and just about to hit the chair of her escritoire, wondering if this time she could actually succeed in knocking it over, when she heard the distant sound of the front door knocker.

Flinging the pillow onto her bed, Horatia raced to her window and peered out. She could neither see nor hear what transpired below. She opened the window to remedy the situation.

"Miss Manley is indisposed and is not receiving callers," she heard Snodderly's voice informing the unseen person.

"Why, that's ridiculous," Horatia exclaimed aloud. "I feel perfectly well."

She leaned farther out the window, the better to see who was being turned away. She almost tumbled out when she saw John Tipton replacing his hat and walking away from her door.

Quickly recovering, she cried out the window, hoping to attract his attention before he was gone.

Horrors! He continued to walk away. He had not heard her. Wait! What was he doing? He stopped. He was coming back. He had heard her after all!

No, he had only stopped to bend down. Whatever was he after? It was her poor mistreated violets, crushed and bedraggled from a day spent in the street. Oh no! How could she tell him that it was not *she* who had so callously discarded them there?

Drat! If she had only maintained her hold on that pillow, she would have it to hand now to fling out the window. Surely that would attract his attention!

Lacking the pillow, she tried to call out again, but a plump hand clamped over her mouth.

"I was afraid you might try something so . . . so disgraceful!" Lady Manley lamented. "I suppose this is what comes from allowing you to associate with that shameless cousin of yours. Imagine, my own daughter hanging out the window, calling to a man in the street like some common. . . ." Lady Manley quickly pressed her lips together to prevent herself from saying the next logical word.

"Why did you turn John away?" **Horatia** demanded.

"Oh, I do hope none of the neighbors heard you cater-wauling like some milkmaid!"

"I don't care if they did," Horatia boldly asserted. "In fact, I wish they had. Then John would have heard me, too."

"How dare you embarrass me so?"

"How dare you embarrass *me* so!" Horatia countered angrily. "You bring me to Town to make a match, yet you turn away the one gentleman who calls upon me."

"Well, I would certainly admit any *acceptable* caller," Lady Manley explained. "But this John Tipton? Why, he has no title, no fortune—and no prospects whatsoever. If we expect to recoup our expenses for your Season, you will certainly have to make a much more brilliant match than Mr. Tipton."

"But I haven't met anyone I like half so well as John," Horatia declared. She began to pout, a tactic which had always seemed to work before to get her what she wanted. Perhaps it still would.

"Not to worry, my dear," Lady Manley said just a bit more kindly, patting her daughter's hand in her customary gesture of consolation. "As soon as we receive those blasted vouchers to Almack's, you will meet many gentlemen possessed of both title and fortune, and choose one as your husband."

She cast her mother a darkly skeptical look.

"Trust me, my dear," Lady Manley assured her. "After all, a successful marriage is merely a matter of deciding which of a man's faults to change and which to overlook. Lack of fortune is one which you cannot readily change and it most certainly is one which cannot be overlooked!"

Horatia would have preferred to remain at home, this evening and every other evening. She saw no point in attending scores of boring parties and being introduced to hordes of boring gentlemen. There was only one man she truly wanted to talk to, and her mother adamantly refused to allow her to see him.

Only a few more weeks of this tedium. Oh, grant me patience, Horatia prayed as she endured the countless greetings, the interminable introductions, and one tiresome conversation after the other.

Then she spied him across the room. At the same moment, he lifted his head and saw her as well. Horatia moved to leave her mother's side.

"Oh, no, you don't." Lady Manley seized Horatia's wrist. "I see him, too. You are staying right here with me," she whispered.

Horatia drew in a short sniff of exasperation and tapped her foot impatiently. From across the room, she sent John a pleading glance.

With a surge of hope, she saw John return her smile and begin to advance, like some knight errant of old, to where her wretched mother held her prisoner.

"Good evening, Lady Manley, Miss Manley," John said, bowing to each in turn.

Lady Manley eyed him coldly and said nothing. When Horatia opened her mouth to respond, her mother remarked effusively over a quite ordinary watercolor painting and turned her sharply to the wall to face it. Each time Horatia tried to turn to John, she felt a sharp pain pinch her side.

Fighting back the tears, Horatia stared at the intensely boring painting for what seemed ages!

"Is he gone?" Lady Manley asked.

"I do not know, as every time I try to turn around, you pinch me," Horatia fumed, rubbing her side with her free hand.

Lady Manley ventured a peek. She breathed a sigh of relief and released her grasp. Horatia rubbed both her sore side and her injured wrist.

"Begging your pardon, Lady Manley. We met at Mrs. Edgeley's musicale two days ago," a plump gentleman reminded her.

Lady Manley merely smiled politely. "Indeed, Mr. Peters."

"Permit me to make your acquaintance to my friend Edward Pratt, Viscount Nuxton," Mr. Peters said, gesturing to the gentleman at his side.

"How *very* delightful to meet *you!*" Lady Manley suddenly beamed.

Indeed, if her mother could manage to beam just a bit

more, Horatia believed the Philbys might extinguish a few dozen candles.

"You appear to be greatly interested in paintings, Miss Manley. Might I escort you about the room to view some of them?" Lord Nuxton invited.

Horatia imagined her mother was about to burst into a wild, multicolored pyrotechnic display.

"You are most kind," Horatia accepted. Indeed, if she had refused his lordship, she believed with great certainty that her mother would have strangled her with the strings of her reticule right there in the Philbys' drawing room. Horatia stifled a laugh. *That* surely would have enlivened this tedious evening!

Yet, Lord Nuxton was not interested in paintings nor in her, Horatia discovered, as he merely promenaded her into the next room, to an anxiously waiting John Tipton.

"I am eternally in your debt, Ned," John said to Lord Nuxton as he strolled away.

"For my part, think nothing of it, John, old boy," Lord Nuxton replied. "However, I do believe Peters will recall this vividly to your recollection the next time you try collecting his vowels."

"My, you are the clever one," Horatia said, smiling up at John with admiration.

John took up her smooth white hand in his. "I was greatly distressed to hear you were indisposed this morning."

"But I was *not* indisposed," Horatia quickly corrected his erroneous impression. "'Twas my mother's doing, as was the sad fate of my lovely flowers."

"Miss Manley—Horatia, if I may."

"Oh, indeed, you may . . . John."

"Would you care to accompany me on a stroll about the park tomorrow afternoon?"

Horatia sighed. "How shall I manage that? I fear I'm not as clever as you in arranging to escape my mother's ever-watchful eye."

"You underestimate your own intelligence, Horatia."

She blinked at him. He thought her *intelligent*? My gracious, no one had *ever* accused her of being intelligent!

"I shall meet you, John," she announced with determination. "Somehow, I shall."

Chapter 13

"I AM *INORDINATELY* displeased!" Lady Balford announced as she swept through the hall and into the drawing room. Sir Horace and Lady Manley trailed helplessly along behind as if they had been snared in an invisible net.

"Well, where is she?" Lady Balford demanded, planting herself firmly on the sofa.

Lady Manley's mouth hung open for a few seconds until she finally replied, "Horatia is in the garden. . . ."

"Wasn't asking about Horatia," Lady Balford interrupted. "You *always* know where that one is."

Lady Balford alternated her cold, steely glare between Sir Horace and Lady Manley. "Why was I not informed?"

"Informed?" Lady Manley and Sir Horace chorused.

"Don't play stupid with me, although Lord knows you two do it so well." Lady Balford looked Sir Horace and Lady Manley up and down with undisguised disdain. "Where is Jane?"

"Our Jane?" Lady Manley repeated, nervously fingering the lace at the neck of her gown.

"Damned peculiar world it is," Lady Balford complained with a disgruntled snort, "when a gel's own great-aunt has to find out secondhand that she has returned. Mind you, I've never been one to listen to the idle chatter of servants. Denotes damned bad breeding, it does. Why, I detest the very notion of it!"

She nodded her head emphatically, then reached up and readjusted her large turquoise turban.

"However, I understand from my abigail, who apparently heard it from my cook, who heard it from the brother of

112

one of your footmen, who apparently has been having rather extensive conversations with one of the housemaids when the two are not involved in other pastimes, that Jane returned." With a dark frown, Lady Balford added, "Some time ago."

"Well, yes, she did, Aunt Georgina," Lady Manley admitted. Just as well to confront the old dragon with the truth, she reasoned.

"Safe and sound?"

How could Aunt Georgina think the girl was safe and sound when she'd been at the mercy of a highwayman? "As well as can be expected, I suppose," Lady Manley replied.

"Then why wasn't I informed?" Lady Balford demanded.

Lady Manley swallowed hard. "Jane has been . . . still is . . . indisposed," she ventured.

"Indisposed?" her ladyship repeated. "You just said she was safe and sound."

Before Lady Manley could protest that she had said no such thing, Lady Balford commanded, "Summon her down."

Lady Manley felt her stomach twist. Why in heaven's name would Aunt Georgina be wanting to see the disgraceful chit? How in heaven's name could she prevent it? "Jane really has been *dreadfully* indisposed. . . ."

"Nonsense!" Lady Balford declared. "At my age, if I can travel all the way from Mayfair just to see her, the least she can do is come down a flight of stairs for me. Summon her."

"Yes, Aunt Georgina," Lady Manley replied with resignation. Very slowly, she moved toward the door.

"Oh, we're in the soup this time," Lady Manley muttered to herself once she was in the hallway and safely out of hearing of her husband's formidable aunt. She released a painful moan as she mounted the stairs. "Heaven only knows what the girl will tell Aunt Georgina about running off with a highwayman or how we've kept her locked in the attic for the past week!"

Lady Manley plodded slowly down the corridor. She straightened a crookedly hung painting, she rubbed her finger over the edge of the wainscotting to remove a thin layer of dust—anything she could think of to postpone the inevitable confrontation.

"If that girl says anything to make us look even worse to Aunt Georgina than we already do, I vow, I'll throttle her with my bare hands!"

Lady Manley paused when she reached Jane's door and drew a deep breath.

"Blast! I cannot even do *that,*" she lamented. "Just think how *that* would ruin Horatia's prospects!"

Lady Manley unlocked the door.

"I have such wonderful news for you, my dear," Lady Manley greeted Jane in her falsetto voice.

Jane was quite taken aback. She never in her life imagined that she would hear her aunt addressing her in such dulcet tones.

"Lord Scythe has cried off the betrothal?" Jane offered hopefully, although she could not recall having seen his lordship's garish little phaeton today—and, indeed, she had been keeping a vigilant watch over the street all morning. There was precious little else to do up here.

All she had observed was a strange carriage arrive and the top of a rather unattractive turquoise turban enter the town house.

"Why, no, my dear," Lady Manley answered, quite surprised. "Why should you think that good news?"

Jane grimaced with disappointment. Then her face brightened again. "Horatia has made an exceptionally brilliant match, and now I may at last come downstairs."

This time it was Lady Manley who grimaced. "Unfortunately, no." Then her ladyship announced with great formality, as if trying to impress Jane with the importance of the caller, "Lady Balford—your Great-Aunt Georgina— has arrived, and she is most anxious to see *you.*"

Jane was not impressed. The last time she had seen Great-Aunt Georgina had been at her parents' funeral. She recalled her ladyship as a rather loud, rather blunt individual who apparently had little use for Uncle Horace or Aunt Olive. Jane had been but a young girl at the time, and Aunt Georgina had expressed even less use for children. Why on earth would her ladyship be asking specifically to see her now?

"You informed her that I am indisposed," Jane reasoned,

as her aunt had allowed her to see no one but the housemaid since her return.

Lady Manley smiled benevolently and said, "No, I deem you quite recovered. Come now. Tidy yourself up to greet your great-aunt."

Puzzled by Aunt Olive's sudden change, Jane moved slowly across the room to peer at her image in the cracked mirror.

"However," Lady Manley began, moving closer to Jane. "There is a small matter regarding the highwayman which needs . . . how shall I say this? Clarification? Rectification?" Lady Manley searched for the appropriate word.

"Falsification?" Jane offered.

"Yes," Lady Manley answered slowly. "In a manner of speaking, yes."

Jane waited for her aunt to elucidate.

"When you, ah, *left* with the highwayman, your uncle and I made it known that, well, that you had been kidnapped instead."

Jane blinked with surprise that they had invented such a plausible excuse.

"Actually, it was Horatia's idea," Lady Manley acknowledged.

Now Jane was truly astonished. Had she underestimated Horatia all these years?

"It did rather diminish the stigma," Lady Manley said. "After all, we wouldn't want a scandal to cause Horatia to remain unmarried and unhappy, would we?"

Jane might have marveled at her aunt's insistence, except for the fact that it was more like pleading. Jane had never before seen Aunt Olive plead.

Jane pursed her lips, considering her answer. She understood completely. It was so difficult for Jane not to grin. For so long, she had been dependent upon the whims of her aunt and uncle. Now they were dependent upon her. Indeed, this was an opportunity not to be missed. And while she truly did not wish to make Horatia—or anyone else for that matter—unhappy, she could not resist making her aunt suffer the pangs of anxiety for a change—at least just a little.

Blackmail was such a sordid term, Jane thought with distaste. However, reason had not induced her aunt and uncle to allow her to retire in peace to the country. Pleading had been equally ineffective. Perhaps, under the circumstances, a mutually agreeable bargain might be struck—her cooperation in exchange for a small cottage in the country.

At length, Jane conceded magnanimously, "I suppose it would do no harm to maintain the illusion."

With great relief, Jane proceeded toward the open door.

"Turned out rather plain, didn't you?" mused the tiny lady wearing the enormous turquoise turban. "What a pity. Your mother was such an exceptional-looking woman."

Jane fought down the urge to turn about and march directly back to her attic room, especially if she had been summoned down here only to be criticized. She got sufficient of that from Aunt Olive!

"Come and sit with me," Lady Balford invited, patting the place beside her.

Cautiously, Jane inched closer. Her ladyship seized Jane's hand and drew her down beside her.

"Quite a brave little gel, ain't you?" Lady Balford exclaimed. "Damned clever, too, to have managed to escape from the highwayman."

Jane realized with surprise that everyone believed Aunt Olive's tale that she had been kidnapped. Great-Aunt Georgina even assumed that she had managed to escape instead of having been ransomed. She wondered what people would think if they knew the highwayman had actually sent her away just to be rid of her?

"Get us some tea, Olive," Lady Balford ordered. "Jane and I intend to have a nice little coze." Then her ladyship turned to Jane. "I insist you tell me everything."

After her great-aunt's less than cordial greeting, Jane fully expected to be ostracized by that august lady as well. She was quite unprepared to become her immediate confidante.

Lady Balford patted Jane's hand. "Were you frightened?"

Before Jane could reply, Lady Balford continued, "Of course you were. A gel would have to be a damned ninnyhammer not to be. I remember I was frightened my first time, too, and I'd known the man for, oh, months."

Her ladyship leaned closer to Jane and grinned, "But it

was exciting, too, wasn't it?" Barely taking time for another breath, she continued, "Of course it was. A gel would have to be a damned fool not to be just a little excited, too."

Jane felt the color rushing up her cheeks. Her ladyship winked slyly at Jane. "Oh, he must have been a prime one!"

Lady Balford plunged forward. "When I was a gel, my father's carriage was stopped by a silly bandit who insisted upon kissing all the ladies. Oh, he didn't kiss *me,*" she denied in a voice that sounded just the slightest bit disappointed. "I say if a man's got to hold a gel at gunpoint to get a buss, he don't deserve one! But I thought it was damned exciting at the time."

For the first time in many weeks, Jane genuinely smiled.

Suddenly, her ladyship's gray-blue eyes narrowed. She peered intently at Jane and asked in a gentle whisper, "He didn't hurt you, did he? I mean beyond the usual."

Jane could not prevent her mouth from dropping wide open. Merciful heavens! Great-Aunt Georgina asked questions which were even worse than Horatia's!

"Dreadfully sorry about that, my dear. 'Tis inappropriate for a lady to discuss." She patted Jane's hand. "Well, anyone can see you're in fine fettle."

Suddenly, her ladyship rose from the sofa. In spite of all those quite personal questions, Jane found she was rather disappointed to see her great-aunt prepare to depart.

"I've planned a soirée for two days hence," Lady Balford announced to Jane. "I'll see you there."

Before Jane could politely decline the unexpected invitation, Lady Balford turned to leave.

"I know everyone will be just as curious as I to hear the exciting tale of how you were kidnapped by a highwayman and how you so cleverly managed to escape. I can't wait to introduce you to my friends—Emily, Sally, and Sophie will be simply green with envy. Just think—*I* invited you first!"

"But, Aunt Georgina," Lady Manley stuttered her protest as she suddenly recovered her senses. "Jane cannot possibly . . . she's been . . . I mean, she still is indisposed. . . ."

Lady Balford glowered at her nephew's wife. "The gel looks recovered to me. She has a certain prettiness which makes for an acceptable appearance. She talks like she's got good sense, which is more than I can say for a great many of the people who will be attending."

Lady Balford asked Jane, "Got a gown for the evening, gel?"

Quite overwhelmed, Jane nodded dumbly.

"Then I expect you there," her ladyship pronounced. "Damn me, if this isn't as thrilling as some of those novels. Better! *This* actually happened."

"But, Aunt Georgina!" Lady Manley made one last appeal.

"*Now,* what is it?" Lady Balford stopped in her tracks again. "Oh, I see. Yes, you and Horace may attend—and you may as well bring Horatia, too," her ladyship grudgingly conceded. "But I warn you, if you do not bring Jane, you may as well not come at all."

Jane stood staring after her formidable great-aunt. She was invited—no, practically commanded—to attend the soirée.

Jane heard in Aunt Olive's voice the very unfamiliar tone of defeat as she told her, "You may as well move down to the other front bedroom. Not much sense in trying to hide you now that Aunt Georgina knows."

With light steps, Jane mounted the stairs. How wonderful to move from that wretched room into a proper bedchamber. How gratifying to be personally invited to a soirée, not just trailing along because she was a member of the Manleys' party.

Jane stopped abruptly in the middle of the stairs. Great-Aunt Georgina expected her to recount to the guests the tale of her kidnapping and escape from the highwayman.

She had hoped her rash actions would cause her to be social anathema. How in the world could she have become the object of social curiosity? What in the world was she going to say about her adventure with the highwayman? And what in the world was she going to wear?

"Damned miserable old witch," Sir Horace muttered. "From the first, she's excluded us, her very own family, from her parties!"

He tipped the wine bottle up to drain the last of it.

"But *now,* when she thinks she may make some use of

Jane as entertainment," he continued to fume, "*now* she invites us. Where was she at the beginning of the Season, when Horatia needed invitations to her affairs? Just like Aunt Georgina to think that drawing everyone's attention to Jane's scandalous behavior would be prime entertainment— and at our expense!" He thumped the empty wine bottle on the arm of the bergere.

Lady Manley swiftly came to his side and removed the bottle from his hand. "Have a care not to do a damage to the furniture, Horace. 'Tis only let."

"I think I have a bloody good right to be angry, Olive," Sir Horace insisted. "Damn me if I went to all this trouble and expense just to return home with Horatia unmarried!"

Lady Manley stood silently stroking her chin, as if that would assist her in thinking.

"We must look at the practical side of this, Horace," Lady Manley said at last. "Aunt Georgina has ever been up to the mark when it came to the latest rage of the *ton.*"

"Except for that bloody awful blue turban."

"The color is called turquoise, Horace," Lady Manley corrected.

Sir Horace shrugged. "Looked blue to me."

"The way you drink, I'm surprised everything doesn't look blue to you," Lady Manley grumbled. "Be that as it may, if Aunt Georgina thinks Jane will be quite a sensation, then I say let the girl go to the soirée—and we'll be very certain that Horatia is with her every minute."

Sir Horace began to grumble unintelligibly.

"Just think, Horace." Lady Manley grasped her husband's arm and explained, "No more tedious soirées at the Philbys or the Roscommons. This is, at last, our opportunity to see Horatia launched in the best of circles, and to find her an excellent match."

Sir Horace was nodding his grudging acceptance.

"After all," Lady Manley said, nodding her head sagely, "if one has a relation who is invited to all the best places, one really should take advantage of the situation."

Chapter 14

"COME OUT TO the garden and read to me, Jane," Horatia whined.

"I really should like to move to a proper bedchamber first."

"Oh, let the maid do that," Horatia told her.

When Jane still hesitated, Horatia said, "I should think that after being in that dreary little attic for so long, you would absolutely *crave* some fresh air and bright sunshine and spring flowers."

Jane had to own, Horatia's proposal did sound delightful. Still she hesitated.

Horatia pulled her lips into a pout. "You know how I do so love it when you read to me," she wheedled.

Jane abandoned the pair of slippers she was preparing to transfer and took the book which Horatia held out to her.

The sunlight dappling through the fully opened green leaves felt good on Jane's face after her enforced confinement. Horatia led her to a bench under an arbor at the far end of the garden.

Jane began to read aloud. However, after only a page or two, Horatia began to pull at her skirt and fiddle with the leaves and twist and untwist one blonde curl.

Jane paused in her reading. "Is something amiss, Horatia?"

"Amiss?" she answered quickly. "Why should anything be amiss?"

"Oh, no particular reason," Jane replied. She resumed reading.

Horatia left off toying with her surroundings and appeared to be intensely interested in what Jane was reading. Then, gradually, she resumed her fidgeting.

Jane closed the book with a thump and looked directly at her cousin. "Something *is* amiss, Horatia."

"'Tis just . . . 'tis just that . . . this book is so . . . so dreadfully boring!" she complained.

Jane glanced down to check the title. "But, you always said that *Cecilia* was one of your favorites."

"Well, yes . . . that's precisely it. I've heard it so often it's become boring."

Horatia rose quickly from the bench and snatched the book from Jane's hand. "I shall get another that I like even better," she declared, and bounced off toward the library.

"Shall I help you find. . . ."

"Oh no, indeed," Horatia called over her shoulder. "I think myself quite capable of finding what I'm looking for all on my own."

Fie on this boring book! Horatia decided as she tossed it into the lilac bushes. From under the same bushes she retrieved the bonnet and pelisse she had bullied the maid into placing there earlier this morning.

Glancing cautiously all about her one more time, Horatia slipped through the servants' gate and made her way quickly to the park, where John was waiting for her, just as they'd planned.

"Where on earth have you been!" Jane exclaimed when she finally spied Horatia tiptoeing down the hall past her bedchamber.

Horatia startled. She quickly glanced to her left, then to her right, then darted into Jane's bedchamber and closed the door tightly behind her.

"I waited and waited for you," Jane scolded. "I know how slow you are when deciding upon a book. Then I thought, 'Not even Horatia could be that slow.' So I went inside to help you."

Jane grasped her cousin's arm to emphasize her concern. "I searched for you all through the house. Can you imagine how frightened I was when I did not find you?"

"You didn't tell Mama that I was missing, did you?" Horatia cried as she threw off her bonnet and pelisse.

"And have her scold *me* because *I* had lost you?" Jane cast her cousin a look of reproach.

"Did she notice at all that I was missing?"

Jane shook her head. "She must have assumed we were in the garden together all afternoon."

Horatia released a deep sigh of relief.

"But she *will* know if you don't tell me where you disappeared to," Jane threatened.

"You wouldn't!" Horatia asserted. "You would be in as much trouble as I. And you cannot afford to be in any more trouble just now."

Jane placed both hands upon her hips and glared at her cousin. "Horatia, after everything that I have been through, do you think any of your problems could possibly harm me?"

"I don't suppose so," Horatia mumbled into her bodice.

"Now, where have you been?"

Horatia scuffed at the carpet with the toe of her brown morocco-leather walking shoe. "If I confide in you, will you promise . . . I mean most sincerely promise. . . ?"

"Oh dear, Horatia? What have you done?"

Very softly, Horatia admitted, "I was with John Tipton."

Before she scolded her shatterbrained cousin, Jane supposed she ought to know the details of Horatia's offense. "Who is John Tipton?"

Horatia blinked and stared wide-eyed at her. "Oh, Jane, Mama did keep you locked in the attic too long!"

Horatia flung herself face-up across Jane's bed. Her blue eyes were dreamy and she kept releasing wistful little sighs. "John Tipton is merely the most wonderful man on the face of the earth. He has the most marvelous, soft brown eyes. . . ."

"So does a cow, Horatia. However shall I tell the two apart?"

Horatia looked up, frowning. Then she saw the playful grin on Jane's face. "Oh, you are teasing me again," she said, returning her smile. "Well, I shall tell you. I am not inordinately fond of cows, but I do like John Tipton."

"You also like Yorkshire pudding and kippers. . . ."

"Be serious! John is . . . well, he's different from any other gentleman I've ever met."

"How so?"

"He . . . well, he talks to me."

Jane nodded. "Indeed, I should say that quite eliminates any resemblance he might have to a cow."

Horatia frowned and pointed a warning finger at Jane's nose. "I am becoming exceedingly irritated with your sarcasm."

Jane regarded her cousin with surprise. My, Horatia was inordinately sensitive regarding this Mr. Tipton.

"The other gentlemen I meet, all they do is waste time with empty flatteries or endless drivel about themselves," Horatia attempted to explain. "It doesn't matter what John and I talk about—and we talk about so many things. The point is, he doesn't just talk *at* me. He talks *with* me."

Jane nodded her comprehension. Indeed, it was extremely easy to find a man who would talk to you. The difficulty lay in finding a man who would also listen.

"How did you encounter this unique individual?"

"John is the second son of the second son of the late Archibald Tipton, Earl of Balford. . . ."

"Great-Aunt Georgina's husband?"

Horatia nodded. "We met when John accompanied Great-Aunt Georgina here on a visit. I've encountered him at various parties I've attended." She heaved a heart-wrenching sigh. "Unfortunately, he has no money, no title, no prospects of ever attaining either. . . ." Horatia made a dreadful-looking grimace. "And Mama and Papa are *ever* reminding me of such."

"You know they are hoping for you to make a better match than the penniless, untitled second son of a second son," Jane reminded her cousin as gently as she could.

"But I like—no, Jane—I love John!" Horatia declared. "I know he loves me, too. I don't care what Mama and Papa say. I want to be with him. I *shall* be with him!"

Jane's eyes widened. This was quite unusual behavior for her complacent, compliant little cousin. What effect was this Mr. Tipton having on Horatia? Jane wondered.

"Is that where you were today?" Jane asked, a chill of foreboding creeping up her arms.

Horatia nodded.

"Unchaperoned!" Jane exclaimed. "How could you be so shatterbrained?"

"Do not scold *me*, Jane Manley," Horatia countered. "That is like the pot calling the kettle black. I merely went for a pleasant stroll about the park in plain sight with a very honorable gentleman. *You* are the one who went riding off into the night with a highwayman. My John is certainly more trustworthy than that!"

Jane made no reply. How could she refute Horatia's accusations? How could she defend the highwayman?

"Oh, you must help me," Horatia cried, throwing herself at Jane's feet.

Jane drew in a deep, apprehensive breath.

"I *must* see John. Oh, please help me to escape from Mama so that I can continue to meet John each afternoon in the park."

Jane looked down at her cousin. She was just about to scold her again when she noticed the tears welling up in Horatia's blue eyes.

Jane paused. For eleven years, she had watched Horatia whine and wheedle and cajole Aunt Olive and Uncle Horace into giving her whatever she desired—as if they had ever denied her what she wanted! But never could Jane remember having seen Horatia actually cry—real tears—for anything!

Did her cousin truly care so much for this John Tipton? Apparently so, since Horatia had never before disobeyed her parents. Moreover, she intended to continue her clandestine meetings with Mr. Tipton.

Jane *had* told Aunt Olive that she would do nothing to interfere with Horatia's happiness. Would she be willing as well to do *something* to allow Horatia to be happy?

'Certainly, I once had the opportunity to escape Aunt Olive and Uncle Horace and *I* took it,' Jane recalled.

'Yes, and look what it resulted in for me,' she then reminded herself. 'Horatia is so innocent, so naive. She has a much better life ahead of her than the one facing me when I ran off. She should do nothing to jeopardize her future.'

Jane shook her head. All her mental faculties told her to refuse Horatia's request.

'But what sort of life will it be for Horatia,' Jane coun-

tered her own argument, 'if she is married to some other
man and still in love with John Tipton?'

Jane looked down again at her cousin and her heart told
her to agree.

"Horatia, you must be very, very cautious."

Suddenly, Jane and Horatia startled.

"Horrors!" Horatia exclaimed. "What is that awful
noise?"

Jane could hear him raving all the way upstairs. She
shook her head in dismay. "I have the most dreadful feeling
it is Lord Scythe."

"I must own, I had thought one husband might be very
much like any other, until I met a man I truly loved. Now
I understand why you ran away, Jane," she said sympathetically. "I suppose even a highwayman would be an improvement over that drunken, pompous ass."

Jane regarded her cousin with a startled stare. *Never* before had she heard Horatia use that term, even if it *were* the
most accurate description.

The tiny tap on Jane's bedchamber door and the housemaid's message of Jane's summons downstairs was barely
heard above the noise rising from the drawing room.

Jane turned to Horatia. "Best go to your room now. If
Aunt Olive has noticed your absence, we shall tell her that
you developed a headache and retired to your room to nap
while I retired to mine to continue reading."

Horatia squeezed Jane's hand. "See, you *are* everso
clever!"

As she descended the staircase, Jane wondered if she
would be everso clever enough to think her way out of this
meeting with Lord Scythe. Even though he would now
surely cry off the betrothal, just as she had hoped, Jane still
dreaded this last confrontation.

Lord Scythe was thumping his silver-handled cane
sharply against the floor. "Why was *I* not informed?"

The blue veins at his temples were standing out in livid
lines against the purple of his face. His bulging white eyeballs were lined with a network of red veins. All in all, Jane
decided that his lordship was quite a colorful fellow.

Jane noticed that Sir Horace was finding either courage
or consolation in his bottle.

"Jane is *my* betrothed, is she not?" his lordship demanded.

"Indeed," Lady Manley assured him. "But we have been taking care to ensure that she recovers completely from her ordeal before. . . ."

"But why was I informed by Lady Balford, that witch, instead of by *you?*"

"Because Aunt Georgina's broomstick flies faster than Olive's," Sir Horace muttered at his bottle.

In her anxiety, Jane was unable to stifle her laughter at her uncle's remark. A grave error on her part, she decided quickly, as it caused Lord Scythe to take notice of her presence.

Turning quickly, he advanced upon her.

She rapidly backed away. She had expected he would be angry, but she had never anticipated that he would consider a physical attack upon her. She was so shocked that she was unable to move another step.

"Jane! My dearest, my own. Mine! How good to have you returned to me," Lord Scythe exclaimed, extending both arms wide to embrace her. Each spiritous word drew sharp tears to her eyes.

She endured not only his embrace, but the wine-soaked kiss he planted on her cheek. She tried very hard, but could not stop her shudder.

'My greatest fear has come true,' she lamented. 'In spite of everything, Lord Scythe still wants to marry me!'

"However. . . ."

That one word gave Jane hope. She rapidly began to blink away her tears.

"However, I shall not marry my Jane until I have caught the dastardly highwayman who caused such concern to me . . . and my betrothed—and, yes, you people as well. . . ." he added, waving at Sir Horace and Lady Manley. "I intend to see the blackguard hanged."

"Hanged?" Jane repeated.

"I have heard news of increasing numbers of people passing through that particular area being waylaid by highwaymen," his lordship recounted. "At first they were merely robbed. Now they are being assaulted, abducted, even murdered!"

"Murdered? No, no. That cannot be," Jane protested.

"But it is," Lord Scythe affirmed. "And *I* intend to stop this man!"

"These atrocities cannot possibly be the work of the highwayman I ran . . . who kidnapped me."

"How many highwaymen do you think there are?" Lord Scythe demanded, frowning.

"But highwaymen are, by the very nature of their profession, rather transient," Jane offered, desperate for any excuse. "Surely the highwayman who kidnapped me has moved on by now. Some other bandit is committing these crimes."

"You mustn't contradict his lordship, Jane," Lady Manley scolded. "He's a man of the world. He knows much more about this than you do."

"I seriously doubt that," Jane asserted. "My highwayman was kind and gentle. . . ."

"*Your* highwayman?" Lord Scythe demanded. His bloodshot eyes narrowed suspiciously.

"Kind and gentle?" Lady Manley repeated incredulously. "Jane, do you truly think you should be discussing this particular aspect of your kidnapping in front of his lordship—or me?"

"It does not signify, Lady Manley," Lord Scythe said, waving away any offense with a clumsy swipe of his hand. Then he turned to Jane. "My dearest, this precisely proves my point. You are *my* intended. *Mine.* But you will not be truly mine until I see this man dead!"

Jane suddenly felt her stomach turn cold. She wished she had not eaten luncheon as then she would not have felt such a churning inside, threatening still worse to come.

Her highwayman surely did not deserve the fate Lord Scythe had in mind for him. Perhaps she should be angry with him for rejecting her, for consigning her over to the Willoughbys' care, and especially for returning her to Lord Scythe, but none of that was sufficient reason to wish the man dead.

Lord Scythe continued, "Why, already, nay, even as we speak, plans have been set into motion which I am certain will ensure the capture of this dastardly bandit."

Jane had managed to fight back the tears which had

threatened her when she faced the inescapable fact that, for the rest of her natural life, she would be the wife of the pompous Lord Scythe—not to mention the stepmother of his six obnoxious children.

But the very thought of her highwayman swinging at the Tyburn brought tears that would not subside. The image of that crooked smile forever stilled, those sea-blue eyes forever closed, hurt Jane as nothing had ever hurt before.

Chapter 15

DALTON REINED PALADIN to a halt before the large town house. A liveried footman immediately took the horse's head as Dalton dismounted.

The London residence of the Marquess of Milburton was a bright, clean, rather pleasant-looking abode, Dalton thought, as he looked up at the sheer, whitewashed facade—not at all like one of those darkly forbidding castles one encountered in the numerous Gothic novels circulating the libraries. Yet, before he entered, Dalton felt the need to draw in a deep breath of courage to chase away the sense of unease which enveloped him.

Ever since he left the cheap lodgings he had let in Blackfriars to conserve his scanty resources, Dalton had been dreading this confrontation. What could the man want now?

Whatever it was, Dalton decided, it was certain that his uncle would couch his demands in the most unpleasant manner possible.

These misgivings were somewhat allayed when Dalton was greeted in the hall by his beloved Aunt Sophie. He smiled broadly.

"My dearest boy," she whispered in his ear as she reached up to embrace him. She placed a light kiss on his cheek. "I have missed you dreadfully."

"I have missed you, too, Aunt Sophie."

"We must speak. . . ." Lady Milburton began. She was interrupted by the furious bellows emanating from the next room. She sighed and wrung her hands together in agitation.

"Calm yourself, Aunt Sophie," Dalton said, placing a

consoling hand on her shoulder. "You know how he rages when he's forced to wait for the slightest thing."

"Is that my brother's boy, Sophie?" Lord Milburton screamed. "About time he arrived. Send him in!"

"I should like to speak with you first, Dalton," she said, laying a quivering hand upon his arm.

"As would I," he responded, gently disengaging her quaking grasp. "But you know very well that when he gets himself into one of his tempers, you are the one who eventually suffers."

Dalton pressed his jaws together in exasperation. How he wished there were something he could say or do to deliver his aunt from her miserable life with this impossible tyrant. But if she felt it her duty to remain, what could he do?

"Damn it, woman! Send him in!" Lord Milburton shouted.

"Then I must speak to you afterward," Lady Milburton conceded. "But, Dalton, make him no. . . ."

As he approached his uncle, his lordship's shouts grew even louder so that Dalton could not hear the last of his aunt's warning.

Dalton was not surprised by the bloated appearance of Lord Milburton. For years the man had eaten everything within his grasp. He had drunk enough to float Nelson's *Victory*—and pickle Nelson in the bargain. Sooner or later, Dalton reasoned, the ravages of his uncle's dissipated life were bound to show.

Yet as he drew nearer, Dalton noted that there was an unwholesome gray pallor under the bloat. Perhaps there was more to his uncle's unhealthy appearance than was at first apparent.

If the hatred in Lord Milburton's eyes could have been physically projected, Dalton would have been unable to advance across the room. Even when he stood directly before the man, Dalton could almost feel the black looks his uncle was casting in his direction.

"Good day to you, m'lord," Dalton remarked, bowing respectfully. In order to do so, he continually needed to remind himself that he was honoring his family's ancestral title rather that the current embodiment of that venerable name.

"I want you married," was all his uncle replied.

"Married?" Dalton repeated, unsure that he had heard aright. "Begging your pardon, Uncle, but since when are you so concerned for my connubial bliss?"

"I want you married," his lordship repeated. "You are thirty years of age. Time to stop playing farmer out there in the country and settle down and provide a continuation to the line."

"That seems rather pointless to me," Dalton remarked. "For the past three years, you have been intent upon ensuring that there will be nothing to pass on to the next generation."

Lord Milburton still glowered darkly at Dalton. "Are you a gaming man?"

Dalton frowned, puzzled at his uncle's question. What had that to do with the Milburton inheritance? Dalton drew in a breath of dismay. Unless the old fool has wagered the entire estate on whether or not I marry soon, he speculated.

"You know I haven't the funds to be frittering them way as you do," Dalton replied cautiously.

"You have other things of value worth staking," his uncle told him.

Dalton debated whether the things he truly valued in this life were worth losing.

"You will marry and produce an heir within the year," his lordship stated.

"Is that your proposed wager?"

Lord Milburton nodded.

"If I succeed?"

"I will allow you sufficient funds to repair and maintain the Milburton estates," his lordship offered, "until my death, when you will inherit it all."

"And if I fail?"

"You will never again set foot on Milburton property, and I will disinherit you."

Dalton stared at his uncle, aghast. Within the year? he repeated to himself. Within the year he must find, wed, and bed a wife, as well as produce an heir! Oh, not that Dalton doubted that he could find any number of young ladies who would leap at the opportunity to wed the heir-presumptive of the Marquess of Milburton. It was simply that he had hoped to take his time in the matter of a wife, choose one who truly suited him.

Dalton frowned. He did not have time right now to be prowling about Almack's.

On the other hand, if he did not comply with his uncle's demands, perhaps there would be no Milburton estates to inherit.

His personal happiness for the sake of his posterity? Quite a decision.

'Damn!' Dalton thought to himself as he knew there really was very little to debate. 'Why do I have to be so deucedly noble?'

He regarded his uncle cautiously for several moments before replying. "Eighteen months?" Dalton bargained.

"One year," his lordship insisted.

Dalton pressed his fine lips tightly together. "Very well, Uncle," he replied with a nod. His blue eyes narrowed with the challenge. "I shall take you on."

Lord Milburton nodded. "Now get out of my sight," he growled. "I don't want to lay eyes on you until you return with that heir one year from today."

Lady Milburton met him in the hallway.

"Oh, Dalton," she sighed, taking him by the arm. "What have you done? What has he made you do?" She led him into the library, closing the door quietly behind her.

"I merely made a small wager with uncle. . . ."

"To marry within the year," Lady Milburton said sadly, nodding her head. Her gray eyes peered into Dalton's blue ones. "I did try to warn you."

"And produce an heir," Dalton added.

"An heir, too?" Lady Milburton repeated, her eyes growing wide. Then she shrugged her small shoulders. "Well, Roger always does demand high odds when he wagers."

Dalton attempted a grin. "Perhaps 'twas time I began looking for a bride, Aunt Sophie."

"Do not choose hastily," she cautioned as she seated herself upon the sofa. Dalton sat beside her. "Do not rush into marriage with someone you do not love."

"I promise I shall do everything in my humble power to find within the year someone I could love," he replied with a wry grin.

Lady Milburton did not return his smile. "There is no need to rush. The physicians have informed me that your uncle will not live out the winter."

Although they never really got on well together, Dalton was shocked and dismayed to hear the predictions of his uncle's imminent demise.

"Does Uncle Roger know?" he asked.

Lady Milburton nodded. "But he refuses to believe them. You know your uncle. He thinks *no one* knows more than he does."

"He tricked me!" Dalton exclaimed, his sadness suddenly turned to anger. "He tricked me, the damned old charlatan! And fool that I am, I fell directly into his trap!"

"Then you need not feel you must be obligated. . . ."

"Oh, indeed, I must, Aunt Sophie," Dalton replied, rising to his feet. "My uncle may be a conniving cheat, but I hope I may still call myself an honorable man. I have given my word, and I will keep it."

"Well then," Lady Milburton said, rising after him. "I suppose you had best begin. The least I can do is help you find a suitable bride. There is a soirée at my friend Georgina's tomorrow—the perfect opportunity for you to begin your search."

"Well, adequate," Lady Balford assessed Jane as she entered the large Mayfair town house. Yet, dressed in her pale peach sarcenet gown—the best she owned—Jane felt very inadequate.

"Not to worry," Lady Balford assured her. "You'll suffice."

But Jane *did* worry. Not about her appearance, of course. She was quite accustomed to being plain. In fact, she rather hoped she might be completely invisible tonight.

Suddenly, Lady Balford clapped her hands and exclaimed, "Come, everyone! Gather round and listen to the tale."

Jane realized with dismay that Great-Aunt Georgina had no intention of allowing her to remain invisible. Great-Aunt Georgina expected her to entertain them with the tale of her menacing highwayman.

What in heaven's name was she going to say?

With her fan, Lady Balford waved a wide path through the crowd for Jane and herself. She seated Jane in a single chair, placed in front of the fireplace precisely for this purpose.

As many ladies as could fit had crowded onto the chairs which Lady Balford had ordered arranged in a tight semicircle facing Jane. They came right up to the edge of her chair, leaving Jane precious little room. Behind the rows of chairs, several more rows of ladies were standing. There were only a few gentlemen gathered at the very outside edges of the crowd.

"Come now, gel," Lady Balford encouraged her. "All the guests are waiting."

Jane felt the hot color rising to her cheeks. She had always been made inconspicuous by Aunt Olive and Uncle Horace. Being the center of attention was quite a new and not altogether pleasant experience for her.

She swallowed hard and, in a tiny, little voice, began, "The highwayman stopped our carriage. . . ."

"Oh, do speak louder," a lady called. "We cannot hear you back here."

"So sorry," Jane apologized in the same small voice. She tried for more volume. "They held pistols on the coachman. . . ."

"Come to the exciting part," another lady cried.

Indeed, Jane realized, they were probably all conversant with the initial procedure of stopping a carriage.

"He reined his sleek, black horse to a halt close beside the carriage. He pointed a pistol directly at my head. He shouted 'Give me your money and your jewels.' Then he pointed to me. 'This young lady will assist me.' "

"You helped him?" a man's incredulous voice demanded.

"He held a pistol directly to my head," Jane explained nervously.

"Why, *I*'d have given the blackguard a set-down. . . ."

"Oh, do be quiet, Mortimer!" a lady's voice declared. "You had an attack of the vapors the night the mouse jumped out of your boot. *I* think she was dreadfully brave." Then the lady demanded of Jane, "Tell us of when he kidnapped you."

Every lady turned her gaze intently to Jane, waiting with baited breath for her answer.

They did not want to hear about the robbery at all, Jane realized. They wanted to hear about the highwayman—*her* highwayman.

"As I was about to hand him the bag of money. . . ." Jane swallowed hard. Well, I can hardly tell them I jumped, can I? she rationalized the huge lie she was about to tell.

"Suddenly, he seized me about the waist and threw me over the back of his horse."

Embarrassed, Jane quickly glossed over how the highwayman had taken her to his room at the small, dilapidated inn. Yet she fabricated a fantastic series of events worthy of Mrs. Burney herself regarding how she had managed to escape him, eventually.

"But what did he *look* like?" the lady sitting directly before her asked.

Oh dear, Jane worried. This *was* going to take some imagination!

Planning how to describe the highwayman to her audience recalled him even more vividly to her mind. "He wore a scarf of black, yet from under the scarf, I could see his hair, burnished golden brown in the light of the setting sun, curling about his small ears."

The ladies whispered 'ooh' and 'aah' in response.

Jane's heart began to beat faster. Being the center of everyone's attention was not as horrid as she had at first thought it. In fact, she was rather beginning to enjoy herself.

"He also wore a mask, but I could see his lips, finely made and well shaped. His chin was cleft. The corners of his mouth turned up into dimples when he smiled."

Jane felt herself drifting into vivid memories as she spoke of her highwayman. "His eyes were not blue, nor green, but . . . but the color of the sea which is left in the little hollows of the sand after the rest of the tide has gone out. . . ."

Suddenly, she ceased speaking. She had been so involved in recalling the image of the highwayman that she had hallucinated! That could be the only logical explanation, she told herself, because, for the life of her, she could swear she had seen the highwayman's sea-blue eyes, twinkling with devilment, peering back at her from the crowd.

"How thrilling!" a lady's shrill voice exclaimed, snapping Jane's attention back to the group. When she again searched the crowd for the highwayman's eyes, he was gone.

Indeed, she had been hallucinating! What in heaven's name would the highwayman be doing here at Great-Aunt Georgina's soirée?

Jane felt herself slowly returning to reality as Lady Balford, accompanied by several imposing-looking ladies, approached her.

"I should be most pleased to have you call when I am at-home and tell that stirring tale!" one lady smiled and said.

"Indeed," Lady Balford accepted for a bewildered Jane. "You'll call upon Lady Sefton, won't you, dear?"

Jane nodded.

"I insist upon your attending my next soirée. You must recount your extraordinary adventure," another impressive-looking lady requested.

"Jane will be most pleased to attend," Lady Balford responded. "How kind of Lady Castlereagh to invite you, dear."

Jane nodded again.

A horde of other would-be hostesses began to besiege her.

"Come, come, now," Lady Balford interposed herself between the clamoring horde and her great-niece. She waved her fan to clear a path through the throng. "Give the gel some room to breathe."

Lady Balford and one of the ladies who accompanied her each took one of Jane's arms and led her away.

"Let us get you some punch, my dear," said the other lady.

"Thank you. . . ." Jane began. She paused. She had no idea to whom she was speaking.

"Lady Milburton. My niece, Miss Manley," Lady Balford threw out, as if she were just as glad to dispense with the bother of formal presentations.

"You do look positively parched," Lady Milburton commented sympathetically.

"After telling such a tale, she must be as dry as an old bone, Sophie," Lady Balford said with a laugh.

"Do be a dear and get us a punch, Dalton," Lady Milburton called to the gentleman walking a bit ahead of them.

"Certainly, Aunt Sophie," he replied as he turned around.

Jane's knees gave way beneath her. She had found her highwayman again!

Chapter 16

HOW RELIEVED JANE was to have Great-Aunt Georgina and Lady Milburton at her side. She needed their support to remain standing.

She had never imagined that she would ever meet her highwayman again! She certainly never expected to find him eavesdropping on what she was saying about him—especially when she was telling such blatant falsehoods! Well, at least he should be glad that she told everyone he was handsome.

She had recognized him immediately, of course. She knew the manner in which the man's cheek curved in, then smoothed out to the firm line of his jaw. She knew the way his mouth twisted up to create a dimple at each side when he smiled. She could never in a thousand years mistake the rare color of those eyes!

She grinned with satisfaction as she studied the man's face. So this is what he looked like without that blasted mask. Why on earth, she wondered, would a man that handsome *ever* take to a profession which necessitated wearing a mask?

"Miss, you appear quite unwell," the gentleman said. His familiar voice flowed like honey to her ears.

Jane stared at him, too bewildered to respond immediately. Finally, in a weak voice, she managed to explain, "'Tis the heat."

"Allow me to bring you that glass of punch, then." He bowed and turned to go.

"What a prize he is, Sophie," Lady Balford told her friend. "Pity he doesn't come to Town more often."

Lady Milburton nodded. "I do miss him."

"If he came to Town more often, he'd be married already."

Lady Milburton shrugged her shoulders. "I suppose he has other matters which are more pressing upon his time just now."

"Pity I'm not thirty . . . well, forty years younger," Lady Balford added with a laugh. "He's quite a capital-looking fellow, that nephew of yours."

"Your nephew?" Jane managed to repeat.

"Dalton St. Clair," Lady Milburton replied with obvious pride. She and Lady Balford guided Jane to the comfort of a large, soft chair in a secluded alcove. "The son of my husband's younger brother."

"Lord Milburton's heir," Lady Balford made a point to whisper to Jane.

Jane accepted the glass of punch which the returning Mr. St. Clair extended to her. She did manage to retain her grasp upon the slippery sides, even though her hand was shaking quite badly. She did manage to murmur, "Thank you."

She took several sips of the cool liquid to restore her composure. How she wished she had something which would restore her senses!

In the shadows of the alcove, she examined the gentleman's features. By the glimmer of candlelight, she could see that his hair was much darker and simply brown, without any trace of the bronze she had detected in her highwayman's hair. Mr. St. Clair's eyes appeared to be pale blue, not the halfway blue-green of her highwayman.

'No, Jane, you've been gravely mistaken,' she told herself, and found she was exceedingly disappointed. 'He's an exceptionally handsome man, no doubt, but he's not your highwayman.'

"Does something about my appearance disturb you, Miss Manley?" Dalton asked.

"Oh!" Jane roused herself. "I beg your pardon."

"You were staring at me. . . ."

She quickly attempted to explain, "I . . . I thought you resembled . . . someone I once met . . . but I was mistaken. Please excuse me. I was most rude."

"Not at all," he replied. "What a pleasant way for a gentleman to spend an evening—having such a lovely lady stare at him."

Jane blushed and feigned an intense interest in the contents of her glass of punch.

How sap-skulled can you be? she berated herself. What in heaven's name would the heir of the Marquess of Milburton be doing riding about the countryside disguised as a highwayman, anyway?

How could she be so shatterbrained to have taken on so? She had seen very little of the highwayman's face. This man's features merely bore a slight resemblance to the highwayman. Her much too fertile imagination had done the rest. And she had embarrassed herself in the bargain—quite deservedly, too.

Mr. St. Clair's jawline was not quite as squared as the highwayman's, she decided as she observed him further—from out of the corner of her eye, of course, so as not to draw his attention again. And where is the cleft in his chin? she asked herself.

'Don't you remember?' she answered herself. 'The cleft only appeared when your highwayman smiled.'

Suddenly, the corners of Mr. St. Clair's lips curved upward in a smile. A slight cleft appeared in his squared chin. Jane startled. She did indeed most vividly remember! Her hand began to tremble uncontrollably. Thank heavens there was very little punch remaining in the glass.

Now she was truly confused.

Dalton smiled down upon the young lady. He watched her slim, tapering fingers as they wrapped around the glass which, from time to time, she raised to her soft, full lips. From where he stood above her, it was deucedly difficult for him to resist staring at the glimpse of smooth, white breasts which the rather low-cut gown so kindly provided for his appreciation.

He hoped his smile would be taken by those who might observe him as simple benevolence to the great-niece of his aunt's friend, who was feeling rather poorly after recounting her ordeal. Thank heavens no one would know the true reason for his expression. He was so relieved to see her alive. He was glad to know that his silly little runaway had been brought safely to London. He felt a strange satisfaction in learning at last that her name was Jane Manley.

"Dalton arrived late and missed the beginning," Lady Balford said to Jane. "I'm sure he would be interested in hearing your exciting tale. Why, he resides near that area. Perhaps he may even know something of your highwayman."

"Oh, I doubt that very much," Jane responded immediately.

Dalton felt the tension in his shoulders dissolve. Miss Manley had been staring at him so intently that, for a moment, he feared she recognized him as the highwayman in her tale. He silently thanked his lucky stars that he had continued to wear his mask the entire time he spent with her, no matter how deucedly hot the thing was. Yet she answered her great-aunt's question in the negative so quickly that he felt quite reassured.

So reassured, as a matter of fact, that he deemed it safe to indulge himself in thoughts to which, in moments of leisure, he had allowed his mind to drift. How pleasant it might be merely to converse, quite at ease, with the lady.

"*Your* highwayman, Miss Manley?" he repeated, grinning at her. "I fear I have been in the country too long. I was not aware that having one's personal bandit had become all the crack."

"I had little choice in the matter, Mr. St. Clair," Jane answered quietly. "He rather thrust himself upon us uninvited."

"I understand completely," Dalton replied. "I, too, have had the occasional uninvited guest."

Miss Manley looked so pretty, sitting on the edge of the chair, wearing the softly colored gown, gazing up at him with her gray-blue eyes. Even prettier, if that were possible, he thought, than she had looked that night in the inn with her cheeks all flushed from the exertion of the horseback ride and the excitement of the robbery, with her slender body enveloped in that impossibly plain and unflattering gray traveling dress.

Seeing her like this, Dalton decided, what harm could come from saying it?—so he did. "Of course, had circumstances warranted, my uninvited guest might not have been quite so unwelcomed."

Dalton extended his hand to relieve Jane of her empty glass. "Would you care to take a stroll with me to the dining room for more punch?"

She rose and took his arm. Yes, she was every bit as fragile as he had remembered her. Still, he wished he might feel her slender arms not in the crook of his elbow, but about his waist once again.

"On the way, perhaps you would tell me your exciting tale in its entirety," he suggested.

If she were spreading tales of the highwayman, the least he could do was to be certain they were accurate—or at any rate flattering.

As they walked, Miss Manley began to recount her adventure. The girl had as much talent for getting out of a scrape as she had for getting into one, Dalton decided as he listened. Not only did she run away with a highwayman, but when she returned home, she made up the most astonishing lies about it. Not only had she managed to avoid being socially ostracized, she had actually become quite a sensation! She even appeared to be enjoying her infamy.

Yet she spoke slowly, as if she were actually reluctant to be reliving her adventure. What a strange little piece of baggage she was!

"Imagine, being kidnapped by a highwayman," Dalton commented as Jane and he made their way through the throng to the refreshments. If that was the excuse she chose to have bruited about, then he would not gainsay her. After all, he had secrets of his own to keep. "Were you frightened?"

Jane swallowed hard. Merciful heavens, she thought with a start. How she hoped Mr. St. Clair's line of questioning did not run along the same vein as that of Horatia and Great-Aunt Georgina!

"The highwayman was very. . . ." Jane paused to consider her words. It was difficult to discuss her highwayman with a gentleman who bore a likeness to him. Even if the likeness were not exceptionally striking, it was just a bit disconcerting.

"He was very . . . polite," Jane finished, feeling that this was a safe description.

"Merely polite?"

Jane thought she detected just the slightest bit of disappointment in the sound of Mr. St. Clair's voice at her assessment of the highwayman. She nodded. "Polite" would have to suffice for this situation.

"Indeed, he must have been extraordinarily polite."

Mr. St. Clair was glancing up and down her figure in a most audacious manner, making it decidedly difficult for her to concentrate on a reply.

"I should say that the man must have been extraordinarily *stupid* as well, to have allowed *you* to escape him."

"Mr. St. Clair!" Jane protested, blushing profusely.

Dalton's lips turned up in a teasing grin.

"Are you saying that your highwayman was *not* stupid? Are you saying that this black-hearted devil was extremely intelligent, perhaps?"

Jane stuttered and stammered and at last managed to reply, "Perhaps."

"From the manner in which I heard you describe him, I would wager that you thought this dastardly villain extremely handsome as well."

Jane no longer stammered. As a matter of fact, she was becoming rather disgruntled by Mr. St. Clair's verbal abuse of her highwayman.

"Indeed, he was," she asserted.

"You sound as if you had grown rather fond of him in the time you spent together."

"He treated me well enough, I suppose," she answered noncommittally. She felt the flush of crimson again rise up her cheeks.

"If the man treated you so well, I marvel that you ever wanted to escape from him."

Jane made no reply. How on earth could she admit that the highwayman had actually sent her away?

"Miss Manley, dare I suppose that this highwayman has stolen your heart as well as your purse?"

The corners of Mr. St. Clair's lips turned up to reveal two crescent-shaped dimples. The barest trace of a cleft appeared in his squared chin. In the brightly lit dining room,

Jane could almost swear that this man's hair looked burnished and that his eyes took on a blue-green hue.

Surely she was losing her mind! How could this man bear such a striking resemblance to a man whom she'd never actually, completely seen? Why was he pursuing this strange line of questioning regarding her highwayman?

"I do believe I need another glass of punch," Jane decided, hoping that Mr. St. Clair would fetch her one and leave off these rather delicate, and dangerous, questions.

Lady Manley seized Jane's elbow from behind and announced, "'Tis time for us to depart."

Behind her aunt stood Uncle Horace, his pudgy fingers wrapped securely about the wrist of Horatia, who was valiantly struggling to hold back her tears.

"And stay away from that Mr. Tipton," Uncle Horace was telling Horatia.

Jane never thought that she would actually be glad to see Aunt Olive. Still, it was with reluctance that she bade Mr. St. Clair good evening. She most certainly was glad to be away from his probing questions and impertinent looks. She was not so certain that she was glad to leave the man behind.

Dalton watched her depart. Miss Manley was in the company only of her aunt, uncle, and cousin. What of the man she had been on her way to London to marry? Had he simply not attended tonight? Or, in light of her notoriety, had he cried off the betrothal?

He smiled, recalling her impetuous efforts to that end, efforts which had resulted in their initial meeting. Had she actually achieved her desired goal?

Dalton found himself hoping that she had.

"I knew it! I knew it!" Lady Manley shouted with glee. She waved the small papers she held in her hand high over her head as she did an awkward jig about the hall.

Horatia merely stared at her mother.

Jane watched, mouth agape. Never in her life had she seen such a sight. Indeed, she hoped never in her life to see its likes again!

"Our vouchers! Our vouchers!" Lady Manley sang, dreadfully off-key. "I just knew as soon as Aunt Georgina invited us to one of her soirées that everyone would see how delightful Horatia is and that we should then receive our vouchers to Almack's!"

Lady Manley danced up to Horatia, seized one of her daughter's hands, and began to lead the girl about the hall.

"At last, you shall be with the sort of people you deserve to be," Lady Manley declared. "You shall meet the most exceptional gentlemen there."

Lady Manley spun Horatia about to face her. "And you will entirely forget about that worthless John Tipton!"

Horatia disengaged herself from her mother's grasp.

"I am so happy for you, Mama," Horatia remarked flatly. She patted her hand over her mouth, making the barest concession to politeness to hide her feigned yawn. "I do believe the excitement is more than I can bear. Pray, excuse me while I attempt to control my emotions—in the library."

"Look, Jane," Lady Manley continued in a surprised tone of voice. "How kind of them. Even *you* may come."

Jane nodded. "Indeed, how wonderful. I hope I may control my excitement better than Horatia did."

"Well, I shall never understand you two," Lady Manley told Jane with an indignant snort. "Whatever do young people consider important these days?"

Jane had no wish to attend Almack's. She was quite fearful of having people flock about her, waiting for her to recount her adventure once again. They were all ready and willing to believe her fraudulent tale. How would they ever accept it if they knew the truth?

Horatia emerged from the library, carrying a familiar volume. She made a very different appearance from when she had left them. She now smiled sweetly.

"Are you coming to read to me in the garden again, Jane," she asked enthusiastically. "Oh, do say you will. 'Tis my absolute favorite book. . . ."

"What are you reading?" Lady Manley stopped dancing long enough to ask.

"Oh, ah. . . ." Horatia glanced down at her book, then turned it over quickly so that she could see the front of the cover. "Oh, 'tis *Cecilia*. Yes, indeed. My absolute favorite."

Horatia turned to Jane, the stilted smile still pasted across her face. "You *are* coming to read to me, aren't you, Jane dear?"

"I suppose I am."

As soon as Jane and Horatia reached the arbor, Horatia carelessly threw the book onto the bench and withdrew her pelisse from under one of the cushions and her bonnet from behind another.

"Did you have to pick *Cecilia* again?" Jane complained, retrieving the book.

Horatia shrugged as she fastened the buttons of her pelisse. "It was the closest to hand."

"But you have chosen it three days in a row," Jane protested. "Now I shall be stuck out here all afternoon with a book I have already read. If you expect me to continue this sham so that you may meet Mr. Tipton, the least you could do is provide me with more varied reading material."

"Oh, fie! Next time, *you* choose." Horatia departed through the servants' gate.

Jane sighed with apprehension. This truly was not the right thing to do. Or was it? She wished she could be certain.

Lord Scythe poured himself a snifter of brandy from the intricately cut crystal decanter. A man needs to keep his wits about him, Red Davey had said. Suddenly, his lordship frowned and replaced the snifter upon his desk. Surely this was one of those times.

Escorted by Raleigh, an elderly man stood in the doorway, clutching his battered felt hat in his hands, until Lord Scythe motioned him to enter and be seated.

"I understand you have seen this lady," Lord Scythe said, holding up for the man's perusal the miniature of Jane which had miraculously reappeared on top of his desk one morning.

The elderly man said nothing, but merely shuffled the brim of his hat round and round in his hand.

"Damn it, man!" Lord Scythe shouted, pounding the top of the desk with frustration. "Don't make me drag every word out of you!"

The man glared back at Lord Scythe. "See here, guv, I'm a working man, here to do you a favor, but I needn't stand for any abuse."

Lord Scythe grimaced. If he wanted to get the needed information from this man, perhaps he should try a different tactic.

"Come now," Lord Scythe began in a much softer tone of voice. "Have a brandy, won't you, old fellow?"

The man warily eyed Lord Scythe, but accepted the drink. He downed it in one gulp.

'To think what I paid to have that blasted stuff imported!' Lord Scythe silently lamented. Then, slowly and softly, as if the act of speaking civilly were foreign to him, he asked, "You've seen this lady?"

"She was in a coach I drove," the man answered.

"In a coach?" Lord Scythe repeated incredulously. "Alone?"

"Nay, there be two with her. A preacher from York, I think. And his wife, or sister, I suppose."

"I need to know exactly where your coach stopped. . . ."

The coachman began to cough loudly.

". . . where your coach stopped. . . ." Lord Scythe repeated, to no avail. The coachman continued to cough loudly.

"Have another drink, won't you?" Lord Scythe offered.

"'Deed I will. Thankee, m'lord," the man replied, quite clearly. He downed the second snifter as quickly as he had the first.

"I need to know where you acquired the young lady on your journey."

"Couldn't rightly tell ye. I was . . . ah, in me cups at the time, m'lord, and a bit lost."

Lord Scythe grimaced in frustration.

"However, 'twas an old inn and very run down." The old coachman stroked his bristly chin. "No one ever goes there now, 'cept the locals. Many years ago when I was just a lad and first taken to coaching, I seem to recall hearing about what used to be quite a fine inn somewhere abouts in that vicinity."

The coachman raised his eyes to the ceiling in contemplation. He began tapping on the snifter.

Lord Scythe reached over and served the coachman again. He shot back the brandy.

"A horse. Blue? Yellow? Wretched color for a beast. Yes!

The Green Horse Inn. Find what used to be that place and ye've as good as got yerself a highwayman."

Lord Scythe smiled broadly. "Do have another brandy, my good man."

Jane looked up and rubbed her weary eyes. Horatia was silently creeping in through the servants' gate. There was a happiness in her cousin's eyes which she had seen every day since Horatia had first confided to Jane her and John Tipton's love for each other.

Yet, there was another aspect to her expression, one that Jane had not seen heretofore—a strange, wistful look. What could have caused such a change? Jane did not even want to contemplate the possibilities.

Chapter 17

"'TIS A PACKAGE," Snodderly announced after the footman who brought it departed.

"How huge!" Horatia exclaimed.

"'Tis for Miss Manley," Snodderly announced.

"Who could have sent it? What could it be?" Horatia cried excitedly as she reached for the box.

Snodderly refused to relinquish his burden. "'Tis for Miss *Jane* Manley," he corrected.

"Oh," was all that a very crestfallen Horatia said.

"For me?" Jane asked incredulously.

No one had sent her a gift for so long—not since her parents had died. She hardly knew what to do.

"What could it be?"

Snodderly raised one bushy eyebrow. "Might I suggest you open it to find out, miss?"

"Yes, do open it, Jane," Horatia said, recovering her spirits somewhat.

Jane's fingers trembled with childlike excitement as she undid the twine.

Under the layers of thin, white paper lay a new silk gown of a soft, creamy shade which would enhance the golden highlights in Jane's usually nondescript brown hair. Gasping with delight, Jane held it up to her and swirled the gently floating skirt about.

"I forbid you to keep it! I can tell you, no proper lady receives such expensive gifts from a gentleman," Lady Manley scolded. "No proper gentleman would send a *true* lady. . . ."

Jane poked through the myriad layers of tissue until she

found the card. "Great-Aunt Georgina sent it!" she exclaimed breathlessly.

"Where is Horatia's?" her ladyship demanded.

"Only one box was delivered, m'lady," Snodderly responded.

"'Tis not right," Lady Manley insisted.

"Oh, Mama," Horatia said, "after all we have bought, I don't need another new gown. Jane most assuredly does."

Lady Manley looked Jane up and down. "Well, I suppose so, especially if she is going to be seen with us at Almack's."

Until only a few days ago, she had always been Plain Jane. Although she had been dreading this first evening at Almack's, Jane found it quite an intoxicating experience to be greeted so effusively by the Patronesses. It was pleasantly bewildering to be besieged by so many important people, all clamoring to hear of her exciting adventure or to invite her to one of their soirées so that she could recount it once again for their guests.

However, it was not a pleasant experience at all to be escorted the entire evening by the bothersome Lord Scythe!

Two giggling, freckled young ladies approached them.

"Do tell us, Miss Manley, was the highwayman truly as handsome as we've heard others say?" one girl said. Her blush obliterated her freckles.

"Oh, even more so," Jane answered with a smile.

The two girls disintegrated into a chorus of giggles.

At the mention of the highwayman, a small crowd of ladies and gentlemen began to encircle Jane.

"Makes no difference how handsome he was," Lord Scythe declared, interrupting Jane's response to their questions. "The man will be dead within the fortnight!"

"How so, Scythe?" asked a rotund gentleman.

Indeed, how so? Jane agonized silently.

"Even as we speak, my men are making inquiries," Lord Scythe boasted. "Each day draws closer to the bandit's doom."

Lord Scythe appeared to draw energy from the attention of the crowd. "Mark my words, I will see him hunted down and trapped like the beast he is, then brought to execution, even if I must do it myself—and I am just the man for the task!"

"Pray, excuse me, Lord Scythe," Jane interposed. The small glass of weak lemonade which she had drunk when she first arrived was gnawing at her otherwise empty stomach. "I am feeling rather ill."

"Nonsense, my dear. You look quite fit to me."

Lord Scythe then returned to the crowd. "I will be most delighted to see him swing! Only wish I could place the noose about his neck myself, and pull the lever that opens the trapdoor which will send the perfidious wretch to perdition! Oh, the man will rue the day he crossed Derwood Marchant!"

"A bit overdone, wouldn't you say, Scythe?" another gentleman commented.

A bit overdone, indeed, Jane would say.

A horde of restless young bucks gathered about Jane and Lord Scythe. The two freckled young ladies, along with the rest of the feminine sector of the group, silently slipped away.

Jane felt exceedingly out of place among these rather bloodthirsty young men, yet could not release her hand from Lord Scythe's grasp. Nor would he respond to her pleas to be excused.

"Shan't rest until I see the duplicitous devil's eyes bulge from their sockets and his tongue turn black in his head!" Lord Scythe nodded emphatically.

The image of her highwayman's sea-blue eyes rolling back in his head and his swollen tongue hanging from his slack lips made Jane begin to swoon.

"I feel I am . . . exceedingly ill," she began, but Lord Scythe was too engrossed in regaling the group of men with his intended feats of courage.

A thousand tiny stars twinkled in the blackness that encroached upon the edges of her vision. Her knees began to collapse.

Suddenly, Jane felt a supporting hand beneath her elbow. She turned to the kind person who offered his assistance.

Her knees collapsed completely. It was Dalton's firm grasp alone which upheld her.

Jane looked up at Dalton with gratitude, yet also with

a strange feeling of relief. She leaned back against his chest for additional support. He felt strong and safe and secure.

She suddenly wished she could turn to him and bury her face in the warmth of his jacket and the strength of his chest and never have to face this bewildering world again. She wished that he would dare to envelope her in his arms and that she could remain there, safe, forever.

'How can he make you feel so safe?' she wondered. As safe as she had felt with her highwayman when confronted by the men in the courtyard of that old inn.

'Why, you just met Mr. St. Clair briefly a few evenings ago,' she scolded, rousing herself from her wanton speculations. 'How can you feel this way about a man you barely know?' Yet, she found that indeed she did.

"Scythe, your betrothed is ill," Dalton forcefully interrupted his lordship's tedious monologue. "Seeing that you are exceedingly preoccupied, I shall be happy to escort her into her aunt's care."

Lord Scythe tightened his grasp upon Jane's hand and glared at Dalton. "I shall take care of my own, sir."

A strange feeling of loss overcame Jane as she felt Mr. St. Clair drop his comforting hand from her elbow.

"Do you not think an execution an inappropriate subject to discuss in the presence of a lady?" Dalton inquired.

Lord Scythe shot him a scathing look. "*I* will decide, sir, what is or is not appropriate for *my* betrothed to hear."

"Do you not think," Dalton continued, apparently undaunted by Lord Scythe's set-down, "that the lady might have preferences of her own?"

Lord Scythe's bushy eyebrows shot up with surprise. "The late Lady Scythe never had any preferences of her own. Why should Miss Manley?"

"Indeed, why should Miss Manley?" Dalton asked. 'If you only knew her preferences,' he thought, with a silent laugh of ridicule at the pompous Lord Scythe.

Clearly her preference had not been to be attached to this man, Dalton thought. Seeing his lordship now, he could hardly blame her for attempting to run away.

An intense abhorrence arose in Dalton as he watched Lord Scythe proprietarily enfolding Jane's smooth, tiny hand in his wrinkled, spotted grasp. He found it increasingly unbearable to remain in their presence.

A strangely disquieting feeling arose in him as Dalton realized that *he* was to blame. He was to blame for the tiny droop to the corners of her soft, pink lips. He was to blame for the lackluster glaze to her gray-blue eyes. All because he had sent her back, had returned her, all unwilling. Seeing the life to which he had consigned her, Dalton now rather wished he had kept her.

Twice he had relinquished his helpless runaway into the hands of persons unknown, allowing the Willoughbys to transport her back to her aunt and uncle. Now, having made the acquaintance of her family, as well as her betrothed, Dalton knew that he could not abandon her again.

"Why, my dearest Jane, you *do* look just a shade piqued," Lord Scythe at last observed with some surprise.

Jane sighed with relief. "If I could but sit for a moment, I know I should feel much recovered," she suggested.

"Gentlemen," Lord Scythe excused himself from the encircling crowd. He elbowed past Dalton on their way to the place where Lady Manley was seated.

"Pray, do not let my indisposition interfere with your pleasure, my lord," Jane told him as she seated herself on the small chair beside her aunt. She gestured toward the waiting group. "They appear to be most interested in hearing a continuation of your plans to bring security to England's highways."

She really didn't give tuppence whether the men were interested in Lord Scythe's diabolical plans for the unfortunate highwayman. She didn't give tuppence for Lord Scythe, either. But she thought it was a most ingenious way to rid herself of his lordship's tedious company, if only for a few moments.

She need not have worried. Lord Scythe was already eagerly returning to his avid listeners, where he would probably be occupied the remainder of the evening.

Sitting quietly beside her aunt, listening to the music, Jane's queasiness began to subside. She breathed more easily. She smiled and tapped her foot in time with the lilting music.

"See here, gel! What are you sitting for when 'tis plain

as the nose on your face that you want to be dancing?" Lady Balford demanded as she approached Jane. "Just because you're betrothed to a wretched antiquity, no need for you to act like one yourself!"

Jane was surprised not only by Great-Aunt Georgina's unexpected appearance, but by the presence of Mr. St. Clair at her side. How glad she was to see him again.

Dalton bowed respectfully. "Miss Manley, with your aunt's kind permission, might I have the pleasure of this dance?"

He extended his hand to her. Jane smiled and rose from her chair.

Lady Manley coughed loudly. She was frowning darkly from Jane to Lady Balford and back.

"Oh, do relax just a bit, Olive," Lady Balford scolded, quickly taking the seat which Jane had just vacated. "Dalton is my friend Sophie's nephew—and Lord Milburton's heir."

"Oh," Lady Manley said with a startle. The expression on her face brightened considerably. Then she frowned at Lady Balford and whispered, "Jane is already betrothed. Why didn't you bring him over for Horatia?"

Lady Balford grinned and shrugged.

Dalton led Jane to the floor. A waltz was called. He smiled that fate could, for once, be so kind. He would be allowed to hold her in his arms at last—and all quite honorably, too.

He stood facing her, his body the proper distance from hers. He extended his left arm, but not too far lest Jane, with her smaller, shorter arms, should be made uncomfortable in any way. Slowly, he placed his right hand upon the center of her back.

He cursed the conventions of society which forbade him from doing as he truly wished. He wanted to draw her slender body close and press her tightly to him. He was sorely tempted to slip his hand down the small of her back and over her softly rounded derriere—just as he had wanted to do in the dark courtyard of the inn, not so very long ago.

They began the three small steps which propelled them about the floor.

"Forgive me for broaching an unpleasant subject, Miss Manley. . . ."

Jane grinned up at him. "Are you referring to Lord Scythe's plans for the poor highwayman or to his lordship himself?"

Dalton laughed and spun her slowly about the floor. "How unusual to speak so of one's betrothed."

"Sometimes one's betrothed is, like certain guests, thrust upon one uninvited."

"Do his lordship's plans for your highwayman bother you so much?"

Jane nodded most emphatically. "The highwayman was no black-hearted villain who would deserve such a horrendous fate as his bloodthirsty lordship has in mind."

"I have heard your assessment of both Lord Scythe and the highwayman," Dalton said cautiously. "Permit me to observe that you seem to prefer the company of the highwayman to that of his lordship."

"Mr. St. Clair, 'tis no secret mine is an arranged marriage," Jane said. "I'll tell you quite frankly, if the highwayman were to walk through that door this minute, I would run. . . ." She caught her breath and coughed.

"Pray, continue, Miss Manley," Dalton prompted. "What would you do?"

"I would be quite willing," she began slowly, then, apparently gathering courage, stated quite bluntly, "to allow him to kidnap me yet again."

"What a loss for poor Lord Scythe," Dalton commented. "And how fortunate for your highwayman."

Dalton smiled as he watched the tinge of pink suffusing her smooth skin. She was so close to him now that he need only incline his head slightly to place a kiss upon her soft cheek.

"Indeed, the prospect could almost induce one to take up the noble profession of the road."

Jane lowered her gaze. Her eyelids concealed from him the expression in her eyes. Dalton watched affectionately as the pink of her cheeks deepened to scarlet.

"Mr. St. Clair, I do not think Lord Milburton would be very happy to discover that his heir has taken to trade."

When she looked up to him again, Dalton could see the

merriment twinkling in her soft, gray-blue eyes. Dalton drew her closer to him, so slightly that he was barely conscious of the movement. Yet, as they gazed into each other's eyes, both knew that they now stood closer than when the dance had begun.

Much too soon, the waltz ended. Dalton reluctantly returned Jane to her aunt.

"Miss Manley, I cannot recall when I have enjoyed a dance more," Dalton said. "Perhaps you will favor me with another in the near future."

Very slowly and very softly, Jane responded, "Indeed, I shall."

With great reluctance, Jane watched him move away until his broad shoulders were swallowed up by the throng of laughing, dancing people.

Jane shook from her head any doubts she may have had regarding the identity of Mr. Dalton St. Clair. The highwayman may have been handsome and exciting, but he harshly scolded her, coldly rejected her, and quite callously abandoned her.

Dalton was not only every bit as handsome, he was also courteous, witty, even solicitous for her health. He could not possibly be her highwayman—and she found she was rather glad of it.

"Vetiver!" Jane whispered loudly.

Lady Manley turned to her. "Did you say something, Jane?"

Jane's eyes grew wide. She certainly had not meant to say it aloud, but the snap of recognition had compelled her.

It was vetiver, she recalled. Vetiver. She had finally identified the scent which she had first noticed on Dalton when he had upheld her in the crowd of men and then again as they had danced. Vetiver—the same fragrance worn by her highwayman.

Not to mention dozens of other gentlemen, she reminded herself.

Now, was he or was he not the highwayman? Oh, how she wished she could make up her mind!

*　　　*　　　*

Horatia was quite miserable. It seemed as if she had been sitting beside her mother, looking about the ballroom all night.

Well, not *all* night. She *had* danced a few dances. Quite a few, really. Rather a lot, as a matter of fact, her pride finally forced her to admit. Yet none of them signified, as not a one of those dances had been with John.

Great-Aunt Georgina was always dragging the poor man about from one affair to another. Why wasn't he here with her tonight? She thought she had glimpsed him once or twice in the crowd, only to have him vanish before her very eyes.

Suddenly, her pulse quickened as she saw him advancing toward her. She smiled broadly as his soft brown eyes met hers.

John stopped abruptly, glancing to his right, then to his left, almost as if he were looking for some means of escape, some way to avoid her! Then, very slowly—she could almost have said reluctantly—John resumed his advance.

John bowed to Lady Manley, who blatantly ignored him. He bowed to Horatia as well.

'He has come to ask for a dance,' Horatia thought with joy. 'Fie on anything Mama might say. I *shall* accept.'

Instead, John then turned to Lady Balford. "If you wish, I am prepared to escort you home now, Grandmama."

Lady Balford extended her hand and John assisted her to rise.

Through tears which verged dangerously close to the surface, Horatia stared after John, watching him depart.

'What is wrong?' she agonized, suddenly exceedingly anxious to go home. 'We were so close, so . . . intimate,' she admitted. 'Beyond a doubt, he no longer respects me. Perhaps he never did love me. Oh, God, what a fool I've been!'

Chapter 18

"QUITE STYLISH, I think," Lord Scythe declared.

"Oh, indeed," Lady Manley agreed. "An extraordinarily stylish new carriage."

Jane regarded the bright-orange lacquer carriage with its purple velvet upholstery and bright green tassels. If this was what his lordship considered stylish, she sincerely hoped he would never take it into his head to choose her wardrobe!

"Do you not think my new carriage *le dernier cri,* my Jane?" Lord Scythe asked.

"I must admit, I've never seen its like, nor do I think I ever shall," was the safest comment Jane could think to make.

"Devilishly dear, too, if I do say so myself," his lordship continued to praise his latest acquisition.

"I should not imagine less from you," Jane said.

"Ah, you are beginning to know me better, my Jane." Lord Scythe took her hand into his with great propriety.

Jane suppressed a groan of despair and removed her hand from Lord Scythe's hold. She opened her fan and began to beat it furiously back and forth before her.

The sun was not that intense this early in the year and this late in the day. If the truth be told, Jane felt rather a chill from the breeze which had sprung up as the sun lowered in the sky. However, even more so she felt the need to do something with her hands to free herself from Lord Scythe's grasp.

She turned her face from the occupants of the carriage to regard the sunlight shimmering upon the smooth expanse of the Serpentine.

The lovely spring afternoon had drawn out all manner of carriages and riders. Yet, amid the crowd, one figure attracted her attention immediately—the tall, broad-shouldered man on the coal-black horse.

Beneath his hat, his hair shone burnished in the light of the late afternoon sun. As Dalton drew nearer, Jane could quite plainly see his eyes, like two blue-green pools of the sea.

She expected to see him draw a loaded pistol upon them and demand their valuables. Indeed, she was quite certain that if he did, she would not be able to prevent herself from leaping from this atrocious carriage and trying once again to escape with him.

No doubt remained now in her mind. Dalton St. Clair, nephew and heir of the Marquess of Milburton, was also her highwayman. Why in heaven's name he did such a thing, she could only conjecture. To any casual observer, the man appeared quite sane. Perhaps it had something to do with the full of the moon.

Merciful heavens! she realized. Here is the man who, with one word, could refute her exciting tale. He could tell them all how she ran away with a strange man. Jane would be quite in disgrace. Poor Horatia would remain forever unwed. Heaven only knew what Aunt Olive and Uncle Horace would do.

No more new gowns, no more invitations, no more soirées. With one word, this man could spoil all the lovely fun she had been having.

Ashamedly, she realized that in exposing her as a liar, Dalton would most assuredly be condemning himself to the gallows—a much greater risk than her paltry concerns.

On the other hand, the man had given no indication that he had recognized her as one of his erstwhile victims. Why had he not? *She* had made it easy for him. *She* had not been the one wearing a mask.

But then, why *should* he recognize her? He had never even wanted her in the first place. He had probably forgotten all about her as soon as he left the inn.

Why, the man probably did not even realize how badly his rejection had hurt her.

Jane frowned. Why had he left her then, when he was so

exceedingly attentive to her now? Clearly, he found her attractive or he would not have sought her company at Almack's nor have said the things he did.

Of course, there was always the possibility that he *did* recognize her, yet refrained from saying anything to her for fear that she would identify him.

Jane imperceptibly shook her head as she continued to watch his approach. Shouldn't he know by now, from the manner in which she had always defended her highwayman, that she would never wish to expose or endanger him?

She could only hope that Horatia and Lady Manley would not recognize Dalton as the highwayman! Those two would have no qualms whatsoever about turning him in to the authorities.

As he drew his horse into step with their carriage, Dalton's eyes sought out her and her alone. It was upon her alone that he bestowed that lovely, crooked smile. Gladly, she returned his smile.

"Capital piece of horseflesh there, St. Clair," Lord Scythe commented. "Must have been deucedly expensive."

"Not at all, Scythe," Dalton replied. "Sired and foaled at Milbury Hall. I trained Paladin myself."

Jane smiled as she watched Dalton's pride in his horse as well as in his own accomplishments shining in his sea-blue eyes.

"Is that his name? Paladin." Jane extended her hand to stroke the horse's velvety muzzle.

Dalton nodded and patted his mount's gleaming neck.

"I suppose you named him yourself, too," Lord Scythe remarked sarcastically.

Dalton raised one eyebrow. "Why not? He's my horse. You, of all people, Scythe, should appreciate the satisfaction of taking care of one's own."

Lord Scythe snorted and nodded his agreement.

"Paladin. Doesn't that mean knight?" Jane asked.

Dalton smiled his crooked smile into her eyes. "A knight of Charlemagne, champion of a noble cause."

"How clever. How . . . noble," Lord Scythe continued his sarcasm.

"How beautiful," Jane said, smiling back into his sea-blue

eyes. "A name . . . for such a magnificent-looking animal," she quickly added, turning her attention to the horse.

"Marvelously outstanding color, St. Clair," Lord Scythe conceded. "Must have him. Name your price. Money is no object."

Jane rolled her eyes up in exasperation. 'If that man makes one more mention of money, cost, or expense,' she vowed to herself, 'I shall throw him in the Serpentine and pile all his filthy lucre on top of him so he might never surface again!'

When she glanced back to Dalton, he appeared to be struggling mightily to withhold his laughter. My gracious, had he seen her expression? And what if he had? Apparently, they were of the same opinion regarding his lordship and his money.

"So sorry, Scythe," Dalton responded. "Paladin is not for sale—at any price."

"Come, come, St. Clair," Lord Scythe coaxed. "'Tis no secret your uncle keeps you a mere two steps ahead of the duns. For the price I'd be willing to pay, the horse will carry you farther sold than kept."

Still Dalton refused.

"See here, now, St. Clair," Lord Scythe persisted. "The price I'd name would enable you to buy any number of horses just like him."

"There are no others just like him," Dalton said, shaking his head. "Paladin is one of a kind."

"One of a kind?" Horatia repeated. "But, Mama, I have seen a particularly beautiful black horse. . . ."

"As have we all, Horatia," Jane quickly interrupted.

"I wish I could recall. . . ."

"Lord Flaxon had an exceptional pair of black horses to pull his black-and-silver carriage," Lady Manley recalled. "Of course, that was before you were born, I think, so how could you know?"

Lady Manley waved her hand in the air. "It doesn't signify, at any rate, as he's dead now and his half-wit son gambled the entire estate away at loo and was forced by the duns to go away and live in Philadelphia, or Baltimore, or some other wretched, uncivilized place like that. I can't think where, at the moment."

How fortunate, Jane decided, that no one ever actually expected Horatia to recall any fact with anything remotely resembling accuracy. Even when she did, they still ignored her.

Lord Scythe had been silently pulling at his chin during this entire debate. At last he nodded and said, "There are rumors that the highwayman infesting a particular area of Yorkshire sometimes rides a coal-black horse."

"Sometimes?" Jane repeated. An icy feeling began to sink from her heart, directly through her stomach, and down to her very toes.

"Some say black, some say roan," Lord Scythe told them.

"Quite a difference in the two colors, if you ask me," Dalton said. "A pity your witnesses cannot get their facts correct."

Lord Scythe nodded sagely. "Myself, I am inclined to believe the reports of the black horse, as these have been given by what appear to be more accurate and trustworthy persons."

"How so?" Dalton asked.

He was studying his fingernails intently, as if not caring in the least about the varying reports of the highwayman's horse. Yet Jane could see his brow draw into a worried frown.

"I should tend to disregard the testimony of the passengers of the Mail," Lord Scythe replied with a sneer. "The more reputable travelers in private carriages most frequently report a man on a black horse. Even you, Jane, have reported it to be black."

Jane swallowed hard. If anyone were to equate Dalton's black steed with the description of her highwayman. . . ! If anyone were to use even half his wits. . . ! If anyone had only one eye in his head and actually *looked* at Dalton. . . ! Jane had told such gargantuan falsehoods regarding every other aspect of her adventure with the highwayman. Why had she been so deucedly accurate regarding his appearance?

"All horses are black at night," Dalton observed with a laugh.

"And all horses are roan by the light of the setting sun," Lord Scythe countered.

"If everyone riding a black or roan horse were to be hanged as a highwayman, there'd be deucedly few equestrians," Dalton said.

"How will you find your highwayman on that small shred of evidence?" Lady Manley asked.

Lord Scythe set his mouth into a smug little grin. "Oh, I am not concerned. I *shall* find him. I have more to trail the blackguard by than merely the color of his horse."

Lord Scythe suddenly released what Jane considered a most unpleasant laugh.

"Why don't you let us all in on your witty jest, Scythe?" Dalton asked sarcastically.

"Indeed," his lordship corrected himself after he had managed to cease laughing. "I should say that the color of the horse is by far the most important piece of evidence I have."

"To find a man by the color of his horse," Horatia remarked, "it had best be a horse of a most unusual hue."

Lord Scythe said nothing, but merely chuckled again with that extremely unpleasant sound.

The entire journey home, Jane was plagued with worry for Dalton. Lord Scythe and Aunt Olive's continued conversation regarding the highwayman did nothing to lift her spirits. And if Aunt Olive made one more mention of the supposed theft of that tawdry little garnet brooch which Jane had lost, Jane thought she should most certainly scream.

What was Scythe up to? Dalton worried as he rode away.

Any half-wit, even Lord Scythe, could see that Dalton was rather taken with Miss Manley, his lordship's betrothed—and, Dalton believed, she was rather taken with him, too. That alone was enough to create quite a bit of enmity between Lord Scythe and Dalton.

His lordship had shown quite an interest in Dalton's horse as well. Dalton hailed from the highwayman's county. Should his lordship succeed in putting together all the pieces of the puzzle, Dalton could be in a vast amount of trouble.

Chapter 19

"LORD SCYTHE!" JANE exclaimed, hastily leaving her bonnet and pelisse on the small bench by the stairs. She had not expected him to call. "I am so sorry. I have made arrangements to visit the shops with Horatia, Aunt Olive, and Great-Aunt Georgina today."

Oblivious to her excuses, he seized her hand with his cold, clammy grasp.

Jane jumped back, but not quickly enough to avoid him. She held her arm rigid, to keep his lordship at a distance.

"Ah, my Jane! This could not wait. I have news. . . ."

His lordship's beady, brown eyes stared intently into hers. Jane was rather surprised to see that his eyes were lacking their customary network of little red veins. Noting this, she also recalled that he had managed to enter the room without bumping into anything. He even managed to stand upright without leaning against the wall. Had Lord Scythe left off his excessive drinking?

" . . . such dreadful news to impart!"

That was hardly dreadful news.

Short of Bonaparte escaping from St. Helena and sailing up the Thames with his army, or the drawstring of her pantaloons suddenly breaking during a dance with Lord Scythe in the middle of the ballroom floor at Almack's, Jane could think of only one thing more dreadful.

"We are to be married tomorrow," she stated blankly.

"No, no." Lord Scythe laughed. "I said 'dreadful,' my Jane. No, the fact is, I must leave you, my dear."

"Oh, that is not so dreadful," she said, attempting to hide her smile of relief.

"I am glad you are taking this so well, my Jane." His lordship hastened to explain, "'Tis only for a little while."

"Ah well," Jane consoled herself aloud, "nothing lasts forever, does it?"

"Indeed not," he assured her. "After I return, we shall be wed."

Jane startled so that she was at last able to free herself from Lord Scythe's grasp.

"But . . . but you said. . . ." she stammered as she began to pace the room.

"I know, my dear. I said we should not be married until I had trapped or killed the black-hearted devil who caused me . . . us such suffering."

"I know you are a man of your word," Jane reminded him. She hoped to keep him to his promise.

"I know it has been the height of wretchedness to wait. . . ."

"Oh, it has not been so bad," Jane demurred.

"But my . . . our wait is almost over!" his lordship declared. "I have found the highwayman's hideout—a place called the Green Horse Inn."

The Green Horse? Merciful heavens! It had been headless and weather-beaten, but that *had* been a horse painted on the discarded old sign in the courtyard of the inn where she and the highwayman had stopped—and the horse had been green.

"When I return from that inn, I will have avenged the great wrong he did to me—and to you, too, my Jane," he added. "Then we can be married."

Jane breathed a bit more easily. It did not matter if Lord Scythe went searching for her highwayman at the Green Horse Inn. It did not matter if his lordship's search sent him to the very ends of the earth. Jane knew now that Dalton, her highwayman, was in London, safe.

If his lordship never found the highwayman—did that mean their wedding could be postponed forever? Jane heaved a great sigh of relief, which she hoped his lordship might mistake for one of resignation at his imminent departure.

"I wish you a pleasant journey, my lord," she said, moving toward the door to see him out.

His lordship followed close upon her heels. He suddenly seized her shoulders with both hands. He turned her to face him and, drawing her closer, placed an enormous, wet kiss directly upon her lips.

When he released her, Jane reeled backward. She certainly never wished any harm to Lord Scythe, she thought as she watched him leave. At times, he was rude, boring, and overpossessive, and she, personally, found him physically repulsive—but he was not a truly bad sort of fellow.

He had gone to a great deal of trouble and—what probably meant more to the man—a great deal of expense to right the wrong he believed had been done. He had probably been a very good husband to the first Lady Scythe, Jane decided. His lordship simply was not the man for *her*.

"So now you will not have Lord Scythe to escort you to Lady Milburton's ball," Horatia commented from where she stood at the top of the stairs. "Poor Jane. I know how that distresses you."

"How long have you been eavesdropping?" Jane asked as she closed the door.

Horatia trailed her plump little finger listlessly down the banister as she descended the stairs. "Poor Jane. You and I both sitting out the dance with the dowagers. Just as well for me, as I do not care to dance." She heaved a great sigh and sauntered off toward the library.

"Horatia, you love to dance!" Jane called, following after her.

Jane had more than a slight suspicion that Horatia's reluctance owed to the fact that she would rather dance with John Tipton, with whom she was forbidden to associate, than with anyone else her mother might approve.

"*I* certainly intend to dance with anyone who may ask me," Jane said.

Yet, she knew perfectly well that the only person she truly cared to dance with was Dalton St. Clair. Of a certainty, he would be there—it was his aunt's ball.

Her heart beat just a little faster with the anticipation of dancing with him once again. How wonderful to feel his arms about her, to smell the earthy scent of the vetiver he wore, to gaze into those sea-blue eyes.

"Then you certainly may," Horatia said. "*I* shall have no partner."

"As pretty as you are, you will never lack. . . ." At that point, Jane actually looked at her cousin. She frowned with surprise and examined her more closely.

"When was the last time you arranged your hair?" Jane demanded.

Horatia shrugged. "This morning, I suppose."

"You look positively wretched!" Jane exclaimed. "Did you not sleep well last night?"

Horatia shrugged again. "I slept like a baby, for an hour or two, I suppose."

"Then it was you I heard roaming about last night. For a while, I had begun to believe this house haunted." Jane smiled, trying to cheer her extraordinarily blue-deviled cousin.

Horatia gave Jane a perfunctory smile which quickly faded from her lips.

"I wish you had awakened me, especially if you were sneaking down to the pantry for what was left of that *gateau génoise,*" Jane tried again.

Horatia shook her head and turned her lips back in distaste.

Horatia reject *gateau génoise?* Jane marveled. Or any other food, for that matter! On the eve of Lady Milburton's ball, one of the most eagerly anticipated events of the Season, Jane sincerely hoped her cousin was not becoming ill.

"I have but one new gown, so my choice is limited," Jane made one last attempt. "What are you wearing to Lady Milburton's ball?"

Horatia sighed. "Oh, a gown."

"I certainly hope so! I know Aunt Olive wishes you to create a stir among the *ton,* but I do not think that appearing in your night rail is quite what she had in mind."

Horatia ran her index finger listlessly across the bookshelf and sniffed.

"Come, let's go up to your room and decide which gown you will wear," Jane suggested.

"I shall find something—later," Horatia replied, waving her hand carelessly in the air.

Jane stared in surprise. After food, fashion was the one

thing which never failed to attract Horatia's interest. She had always been pleased to have Jane spend hours assisting her in choosing the perfect accessories for each gown.

"To own the truth," Horatia continued, "I have no desire whatsoever to attend any more of these tedious affairs."

Well, this come out *has* been quite a burden on Horatia, Jane reasoned. Perhaps she does need a bit of a rest.

"Why don't we just sit and I shall read to you until Great-Aunt Georgina arrives? Come, let's find a book—a *new* book," Jane insisted. "We shall go out to the arbor. . . ."

"I think not, Jane," Horatia said with a little sniff. "Our little times of . . . of reading aloud just. . . ." She sniffed again several times and heaved a deep sigh. ". . . just do not hold the same interest for me which they once did."

Horatia released a loud wail and ran out of the library, across the hall, and up the stairs. Jane heard the bedchamber door slam shut.

"Whatever could be Horatia's problem?" Lady Manley asked as she descended the staircase. She glanced back in the direction in which Horatia had just disappeared.

"I'm not sure," Jane answered, deeming it a wise move not to confide in her aunt. "I hope she is not ill."

Lady Manley stopped to adjust the angle of her bonnet in the hall mirror. "She needs to arrange her hair. She had best hurry, too, or we shall be late for our shopping expedition with Aunt Georgina."

"I doubt that Horatia wishes to accompany us," Jane offered. *Especially* if John Tipton were escorting his stepgrandmama about today.

"Nonsense!" Lady Manley insisted. "Why, to go shopping with Lady Balford is a social *coup!* Anyone may be invited to her soirées, but to be seen buying a pair of drawers with Lady Balford is the epitome of social acceptance. Horatia *will* go!"

"Perhaps if you talked to her," Jane suggested. "Horatia has *always* listened to *you.*" At least, she had, until a few weeks ago.

Lady Manley mounted the stairs to seek out her daughter.

Only moments later, Snodderly admitted Lady Balford. "Aren't you ready yet, gel?" she demanded.

"Aunt Olive will be with us directly," Jane explained,

fetching her bonnet and pelisse from the bench. "I am not sure Horatia is coming with us."

"Don't tell me," Lady Balford said, holding her hand up before Jane. "The gel's not feeling well."

"Why, yes, she . . . she does appear rather unwell," Jane answered.

"No regard for personal hygiene?"

Jane hesitated, then replied, "Actually, she appears *very* unwell."

"Can't sleep."

"Not a wink."

"Won't eat."

"Not a bite."

"Won't go out."

"Precisely," Jane replied, surprised that Great-Aunt Georgina should so accurately sum up Horatia's malady without even having seen her.

Lady Balford grimaced and nodded. "Know it well. That blasted John fairly drove me mad the way he moped about the place that same way. He even refused to accompany me about. At last, I ejected the ninnyhammer from the premises, made him live at his club—especially as he hardly bothered to bathe or shave!"

"Horatia is behaving in exactly the same strange manner. . . ." Jane confided in her Great-Aunt Georgina, " . . . aside from the shaving."

"If I knew it was going to take this long just to get to the house, I'd have saved myself some time and dressed in the carriage," Sir Horace grumbled as they waited in the long line leading toward the Milburton town house. "Might as well just get out and walk up to the door."

"*You* certainly may, if you wish to appear no better than a mere tradesman," Lady Manley haughtily informed him. She then informed Jane and Horatia, "*We* shall be arriving by carriage."

"I should prefer just to continue driving until we reach Dover," Horatia mumbled.

"What on earth is in Dover?" Lady Manley demanded.

"Lovely cliffs from which one might leap into the sea," Horatia replied with a wistful sigh.

Lady Manley glared at Horatia. "Not in that expensive gown you don't!"

When Horatia opened her mouth to reply, Lady Manley pointed her finger directly at her daughter and cut her off with, "And I don't want to hear of you washing up on the beach in France naked, either!"

The wait had been worthwhile, Jane decided, when at last they alighted and entered the magnificent hall. Just a bit bewildered, she searched the crowd. She smiled with relief when she saw Dalton, leaning against the wall across from the door.

He had been watching each guest as they entered, yet only when he saw her did he push his long-legged frame away from the wall and move toward her—as if he had been waiting just for her!

His sea-blue eyes locked with hers. When he smiled, the soft creases about his eyelids deepened. She rather wished that every other person in the crowded hall could suddenly disappear and that only Dalton and she were there together—alone.

In spite of the crowd and the distance, Dalton needed only a few long strides before he stood directly in front of her.

"I am glad you could attend my aunt's ball," he said politely, for the benefit of all those around him who might take great delight in eavesdropping on the heir of the Marquess of Milburton and his conversation with the future Viscountess Scythe.

The scandalmongers would make quite a feast of it if Lord Scythe's betrothed appeared overly friendly with Mr. St. Clair.

"I would not have offended your aunt by declining her gracious invitation," she replied, attempting to emphasize with her eyes what she could not express in words.

"I do not see Lord Scythe here with you this evening. I hope nothing unfortunate has occurred."

"His lordship left for pressing business in Lincolnshire," Jane explained. "Hardly an unfortunate occurrence."

Dalton chuckled and extended his arm to Jane. "I would consider myself fortunate if you allowed me to escort you this evening."

Jane tucked her hand into the warm crook of his elbow.

"How exceedingly kind of you, sir. I'm certain if his lordship were here, he would express to you his own opinions on the matter."

"Then I am doubly glad for his lordship's absence, as the ballroom is already greatly overheated."

Dalton escorted her from the crowded hall into the equally crowded ballroom. Jane paused when she saw the sea of elegantly attired ladies and gentlemen swaying to the strains of the excellent music.

"Doubtless you will be besieged tonight with innumerable invitations to the dance," Dalton observed. "May I claim the first dance as my own?"

"You may."

"At the risk of appearing extraordinarily greedy, may I now claim the last as well?"

"I should be extremely disappointed if you did not."

Dalton had barely led her to the edge of the dance floor and gently placed one arm about her when she was besieged, not by a horde of would-be partners for the dance, but by a group of giggling ladies, bright-eyed with curiosity.

"Oh, Miss Manley, *do* tell us about the highwayman!" the apparent leader gushed.

"Oh, yes, do," the chorus behind her echoed.

With great dismay, Jane felt Dalton's strong fingers slip from her grasp. She turned one quick, pleading glance to him.

"The crowd clamors for you, madame. I shall wait quite impatiently for our dance," Dalton said, his eyes smiling reassuringly.

Jane was not reassured. If there was one thing she did *not* want to do, it was to discuss her supposed adventure with the highwayman in the presence of Dalton St. Clair!

"We've all heard how handsome he was," the leader said. Her ladies chorused enthusiastically, "The waving brown hair! The broad shoulders! Those devastating blue eyes!"

"I scarce need tell the tale," Jane acknowledged with a feeling of relief, "as you appear to have already memorized it."

Much to Jane's consternation, one thin, elderly lady at the edge of the crowd continued in a breathless whisper that nevertheless carried quite far, "How he held you in his arms! How he carried you up the stairs of the inn and into his room! How he kissed you! How he embraced you and . . . . Oh, were you frightened?"

Why did everyone ask that question!

A bright flush raced up Jane's cheeks. She could hardly credit how her original story of adventure had, at the hands of others, turned into quite a lusty tale.

She turned to the sound of Dalton's chuckles.

Oh, the wretched man! His face was almost as red as hers, she was sure. But hers was due to the embarrassment these ladies were causing her in his presence—or was it from the embarrassment which his presence was causing her in front of these ladies?

Dalton's face was red not from embarrassment, but from his efforts to control the laughter which threatened to explode from him at any second.

Suddenly, the tension was more than she could bear. Jane began to laugh.

Dalton's lips were quivering with merriment as he offered his hand to her and said, "I believe we were about to dance, Miss Manley."

Still laughing, Jane nodded her farewell to the puzzled group of ladies.

"For shame, Mr. St. Clair," Jane scolded. "You are an incorrigible tease."

His sea-blue eyes were wide with feigned surprise.

"I was merely amazed by the fact that you appear to have a more diverting adventure with the highwayman each time I hear the tale retold."

"Are you amazed that I am capable of enjoying myself or that I found the highwayman . . . likable?"

"It is not the former," Dalton replied. "I should believe *you* capable of anything."

The light pressure of his strong hand upon her back guided her about the floor. With each step he was drawing her closer to him. Merciful heavens! If this process continued, by the end of the dance she should be pressed directly against his tall, strong body.

A few steps on her part in the opposite direction would have put an easy halt to his advance, yet Jane felt herself not merely reluctant, but absolutely averse to the very thought of moving away from him. As a matter of fact, had she but a scintilla more courage, she believed she might have taken a step toward him on her own.

Jane's heart pumped faster. She would have held her breath with anticipation but for the need to speak. She felt that if she did not say something soon, she would be hopelessly enchanted by those eyes.

"Then apparently you find it amazing that I should have found the highwayman likable," she said very softly.

Dalton's gaze shifted away from hers momentarily. After a small cough, he replied, "A highwayman, by the very nature of his chosen profession, does not generally leave his victims with a favorable impression."

"Generally, I should say that was true," she replied. "Generally."

"Then, specifically, there was something about this highwayman which made a favorable impression upon you. . . ?" Dalton asked, his sea-blue gaze pinioning hers. "Something which another man might do to gain your favor as well?"

Before Jane could reply, the waltz ended. They stood directly before Lady Milburton.

"Come now, Dalton," her ladyship chided him. "It was kind of you to entertain Jane upon her arrival. Now, I should like some of my other guests to meet her."

"As you wish, Aunt Sophie." Dalton turned to Jane, still grinning. "Miss Manley has several diverting tales to relate."

Just as well that she had not had the opportunity to answer Mr. St. Clair's question, Jane supposed. How could she explain the ache in her breast which merely looking at him caused her? How could she explain the longing in the pit of her stomach just to have him hold her once more? How could she tell him that he already did all these things—and more?

The entire evening, Jane did not sit out a single dance. Her legs ached. She had worn a hole in the sole of one of her slippers. She longed for a large, cool glass of punch and a large, comfortable chair!

She felt she had quite enough of dancing, and, as the evening wore on and the wine flowed more freely, she felt she had quite enough of her dance partners as well.

They began with mere compliments of a rather personal nature regarding her appearance. Then their remarks had degenerated to comments regarding the graceful way in which she moved about the dance floor and their conjectures regarding how these movements might be transferred to other, more intimate locations. Jane had done her best to ignore them all.

But this gentleman—Jane decided she was being extremely charitable in styling him thus—was the outside of enough!

"You appear quite flushed, my dear," he slurred his words. When the dance ended, he did not release his hold upon her hand. "Why, I'll wager that pink goes from your cheeks all the way down to your. . . ."

"Please excuse me, now," Jane said, pulling away from him.

For a man who had not been able to dance without tripping over her toes, he maintained a surprisingly—and distressingly—strong grip.

"A little stroll in the garden should cool some of that hot blood," he said, leering at the generous amount of cleavage which her gown exposed. "As if I should ever want to cool you down when. . . ."

"I should truly prefer just a glass of punch," Jane pleaded as he pulled her across the shadowed porch and into the darkened garden.

He stumbled several times on the twisting pathway. He sprawled into a secluded alcove and pulled her down on top of him. Jane scrambled to rise.

"How delightful you feel," he said, running his hands up and down her sides.

"Let me go!" Jane cried, striking at his face.

"That Scythe is a damned lucky man," he continued, pinning her arms to his side so that she could not rise. "But he's too old for a ladybird like you. A bit o' muslin as lovely as yourself should share her favors."

"I beg your pardon!" Jane exclaimed as she still struggled to rise.

"I'm not as rich as Scythe," he said, "but I can be very generous if you would become my mistress."

"I am betrothed to Lord Scythe," Jane informed him—as if the loutish cad had forgotten! "When he hears of your insulting behavior . . . and believe me, he surely shall. . . ."

"Come, come, no counterfeit virtue with me, my little doxy," he continued, oblivious to her threats. "You've made no secret of your adventure with that highwayman. Everyone knows one man is not enough for a woman like you."

He quickly rolled over, pinning her beneath him. His hand began to move from her cheek, down her neck, to the curve of her breast.

Chapter 20

THE MAN WAS lifted from her chest with such force that Jane was caught up with him. In his surprise, the man released her at last and she fell back upon the bench.

"Get out of here! Now!" Dalton barely choked back his rage. Holding the man by the collar of his jacket, he flung him away as he would have discarded so much trash.

The man stumbled backward. Catching his balance, he raised his fists.

"I'll not fight you, you drunken sot," Dalton sneered as he scornfully regarded the man. "Now, begone from these premises before I change my mind."

The man stood there, clearly bewildered by Dalton's refusal to answer his challenge.

"You've no right to order me about, St. Clair," he mumbled defensively as he lowered his fists. "'Tis not your house yet."

"I'll not have you disrupting my aunt's ball nor insulting her guests with your boorish behavior," Dalton countered. "Now, begone!"

Dalton advanced a single step. The man spun on his heels, toppled over a bush, and ran up the walk.

Using the arbor for support, Jane pulled herself up to stand on her trembling legs.

Dalton wrapped one arm about her waist. He placed his other arm across her shoulder and drew her close to his chest.

The night was warm, but she was shivering with fright. With great relief, she leaned against him. She pressed her face into his warm, comforting chest. She could hear his heart thumping and could feel his chest heaving with rage.

She drew in a deep breath of vetiver. Indeed, holding him close while he faced her was even nicer than embracing him from behind. She released a sigh that was half shuddering fear and half relief.

Suddenly, he seized both of her arms and held her back from him. "Did he hurt you?" he demanded, sweeping his gaze up and down her body in a most piercing manner. "I swear, if he hurt you. . . ."

Jane shook her head. "He frightened me," she replied. "That was all."

The anger eased from his tightly compressed lips. As she watched his eyes, the rage ebbed and another emotion appeared. Very slowly, the little creases about his eyelids softened, yet his sea-blue eyes took on the fiery passion she had once only imagined could be there. He gently pulled her closer and, with excruciating slowness, lowered his lips to hers.

His lips were warm and soft and tasted sweet. She gave very little thought that anyone passing by might discover them—and even less thought to Lord Scythe. This was all she had ever wanted!

Yet one kiss was not enough. His lips caressed her cheek and slipped down her slender throat. She pressed her face into the warm hollow between his ear and his neck and breathed deeply of his masculine scent.

Oh, how could she ever endure Lord Scythe's cold embrace? How could she cry off her misbegotten betrothal? How could she let Dalton know that she had loved him, that she had wanted him to hold her like this from the very first moment she had laid eyes upon him?

"Once again, you came to my rescue," she dared to whisper in his ear.

Dalton ceased his caresses and eased his firm embrace.

Oh, now you have done it! she lamented. Why could she not leave well enough alone?

He held her just the slightest bit back from him, yet he still held her. "Once again?" he repeated, regarding her cautiously.

Jane took a deep breath before beginning. "Dalton, I . . . I know you are my highwayman. . . ."

"Jane, you most surely are mistaken," he said, shaking his head emphatically. "When caught, the highwayman will be hanged. 'Tis not I."

Jane cast him an admonishing frown. "'Twas *you*. No need to deny the truth to me, Dalton."

"And what if you *have* trapped the dastardly highwayman?" he asked cautiously still. "Do you intend to turn him over to the proper authorities—or to Lord Scythe's summary justice?"

She took a step forward, so that she was once again pressing against his strong, lithe body. She reached up to cradle his cheek soothingly in the palm of her hand. "I shall do neither. How could I ever betray you?"

Dalton allowed a small smile to appear upon his fine lips. Raising one dark brow, he asked, "How can you be so certain 'tis I? Your highwayman was masked. . . ."

"Mask or no, I would recognize you . . . your lips . . . your eyes." She ran her finger lovingly over his cheekbone and into the little hollow above his jaw.

In countless dreams, both sleeping and awake, she had made this very gesture. The reality was infinitely better than any fantasy.

He reached up to move her hand to his lips and placed a warm kiss in the center of her palm.

"Did you not remember me?" she asked.

Dalton chuckled. "How could I have forgotten you, my little runaway?"

He slipped his hand up her back and across her shoulder to rest gently at the base of her throat. She reached up, quite willingly entwining her arms about his neck.

"Do you have any idea how happy I was to see you at Lady Balford's, safe and sound—even if you were telling such preposterous tales about me?"

Jane buried her face into the warmth of his chest to hide her embarrassment.

"I worried every day after you left that you would return home safely. I had no way of knowing . . . no one to ask. . . ."

Jane looked up. Slowly, she disengaged her arms from about his neck.

"Then why. . . ." She wanted to stop herself, yet some perverse necessity of pride prodded her to continue. "Then why *did* you send me away? Why did you not want me?"

"Not want you?" he repeated incredulously, attempting to pull her closer once again. "How can you think I don't want you?"

"Oh, yes, you want me *now.*"

She pulled out of his arms completely. She did not want to argue with him. She wanted to return to his arms, to find comfort in his strong embrace, to feel the warm insistence of his kiss again. Yet the anger she felt at being rejected and abandoned by him at the inn, the anger and hurt she had held within her for so long, surged to the surface, compelling her to speak.

"Did you prefer that Nell person?" she asked petulantly.

"Nell?" He laughed. "You must be joking." He stepped forward to take her into his arms again, yet she continued to back away.

"You think that because I ran away with you, that because I have invented a few amusing incidents. . . ."

"Amusing?" Dalton interrupted. His lips curved up into that teasing smile. "Scandalous might be a better term. As a matter of fact, some of the versions I have heard circulating the *ton* have bordered upon the lascivious!"

Jane had a great deal of difficulty finding her sense of humor at this point.

"Just because I invent a few tales is no cause for you to think that I am now a . . . a lightskirt. You are as bad as that other fellow who only wanted me for his mistress!" Jane accused.

Dalton at last managed to break through her angry tirade. "I want you, Jane—and not for a mere dalliance. I want you now. I wanted you then, but I could not . . . I would not. . . ."

Dalton extended his arms, attempting once again to embrace her. "If you cannot understand how I feel about you without words, I don't know how I *can* explain."

But Jane wanted an explanation. She needed an explanation. Even an egregious lie might provide some clue to his exasperating behavior. But the blasted man expected her to be able to know what was in his head! If only he would tell her why he acted the way he did.

But he merely stood there, watching her with those beautiful, sad, sea-blue eyes. Saying nothing was the worst response he could have made.

Oh, men! she fumed. How could she ever hope to understand a one of them!

She cast Dalton one last sad, pleading look. She hoped he would take this chance to explain. When he still said nothing, Jane quickly turned and fled back to the ballroom.

Jane carefully draped her gown over the back of her chair. After donning her nightrail, she began to brush out her hair. What a pity she had not enjoyed the rest of Lady Milburton's ball as much as she had the beginning.

It was all that wretched Dalton St. Clair's fault, Jane decided. Oh, why couldn't the man just say what was in his thoughts? Why couldn't he make up his mind?

The light tapping at her bedchamber door roused Jane from her dismal contemplation.

"Oh, Jane, I just *have* to talk to you," Horatia said as she peeked her head around the door. She slipped quietly inside, then closed the door tightly behind her.

"Horatia, you've been crying," Jane observed.

"Whyever should you think that?" she asked, rubbing her nose with her small white handkerchief.

"For one thing, your eyeballs are usually white, not red."

"Gave it all away, I suppose."

"Quite." Jane nodded.

Horatia stood in the doorway a bit longer, sniffing loudly every now and then.

"What is the matter, Horatia?" Jane asked. "Would you care to discuss it?"

Horatia shook her head nonchalantly, then nodded, then said, "No," in a tiny little voice. Suddenly, she wailed, "Oh, Jane!" and threw herself into her cousin's arms.

Jane enfolded her in a comforting embrace. "Come, tell me what is wrong."

She guided the weeping girl to the bedside and seated her there. Jane sat beside her, still keeping a consoling arm wrapped about her quaking shoulders.

At length, Horatia stopped weeping enough to mumble,

"I can talk to you, can't I, Jane? You will understand. Sometimes I think you are the only one who *can* understand."

Jane decided that if she knew what her cousin were talking about, it would make the situation so much easier.

"You ran off with the highwayman," Horatia continued. "You know what it's like."

Jane suddenly had the horrible realization that she did indeed know precisely what her cousin was talking about, and no, it did *not* make it any easier.

"I have heard it is a wicked thing to do," Horatia said, then blew her nose into her handkerchief. "But it's very wonderful when it's with someone you love."

Jane stared at her cousin, mouth agape. She wished she knew what kind of response to make to Horatia's confession.

"There was nothing wrong with it! I love John. I thought he loved me. Now. . . ?"

Horatia disintegrated into a piteous wail and was unable to continue.

Jane wished she knew something to say to comfort her distraught cousin. All she could think of was the fact that if Aunt Olive and Uncle Horace discovered this, Horatia might as well lay out her shroud—and John Tipton his, too, if Uncle Horace left him in pieces large enough to warrant burial.

She herself was not feeling very calm right now, so it was even more difficult to think of something soothing to say to Horatia. If she knew any words of comfort, she would certainly be telling them to herself as well.

"Suddenly, he will have nothing to do with me—and I am still so in love with him. Oh, what shall I do?" she wailed, holding desperately onto Jane's hand.

"I wish I knew, Horatia."

"You've always been so clever, so wise. . . ."

"I? Wise?" Jane shook her head. " 'Tis a good deal easier to be wise regarding what to wear with which gown than it ever is to be wise regarding what to do with men."

After all the lies and deceit and exciting tales of adventure, how could Jane explain that she had been rejected, too? And that it hurt just as much.

Why had Dalton turned her away at the inn, yet said that

he wanted her now? He could not—or would not—explain why.

What hurt most was that, in spite of the rejection, in spite of their perplexing situation, she still loved him. Yet, she remained betrothed to Lord Scythe, a man she had never loved and never could.

Horatia laid her head on Jane's shoulder and quietly wept, with no sign of relenting. Jane reached out and placed both arms about Horatia. She began to rock her back and forth, as a mother would cradle a weeping child. There was nothing Jane could say or do to make the situation better. The least she could do was offer what comfort she could to salve Horatia's broken heart.

In whom could Jane confide? Who would comfort her? While Horatia quietly wept on her shoulder, Jane began weeping, too.

'Why can't the bloody highwayman make it easy on these old bones and just waylay my carriage?' Lord Scythe thought as they rumbled along. Then he wouldn't have to go out anymore, searching every highway, byway, and sheep trail for the wretched fellow and his blasted Green Horse Inn.

Suddenly, the carriage stopped.

"I think I've found what *used* to be a road." Attley said, pointing across the plowed field to a small opening in the trees.

Lord Scythe peered intently in that direction with a supremely satisfied grin.

The path had indeed once been a road. Saplings encroached on the borders, making it narrower than it originally was. Scythe and Attley left the carriage in the charge of the footman and proceeded on foot.

The path opened onto a dilapidated courtyard, full of all manner of discarded farming and coach equipment. Propped against the wall of the half-collapsed stable was a broken, weathered board. Barely discernible on the wood was the crudely painted image of a horse, now headless, but definitely green.

"Good day to you, innkeeper," Lord Scythe called pleasantly to the rotund man behind the tap. He seated himself at a table near the fire. "A bottle of your finest."

"Here, we all drink nothing but the finest," the innkeeper replied with a wry laugh. He supplied Lord Scythe with a mug of ale.

"In that case," Lord Scythe replied expansively, "I am pleased to be drinking with only the finest men. Full mugs for all, innkeeper."

Lord Scythe rose and lifted high his mug. "Gentlemen, to the King!"

"Here, here," the men responded and gulped down their ale.

Lord Scythe first peered cautiously at the contents of his mug. He merely sipped at his ale, then called for the men to be served more.

"Gentlemen, I give you peace and prosperity!"

As the others began to respond as before, one man called loudly, "I'll take your peace, but you can keep your prosperity, m'lord, for all the good it's done me!"

"You sound displeased, my good sir."

"A man has a right to be displeased without a decent roof over his head and without enough for his children to eat!"

"Are times that hard here, my good man?" Lord Scythe asked, trying his best to appear deeply concerned. "Have you no farming? No industry?"

"There were farms and shops here, once," the man answered as the rest of the men slowly began to drift away.

"What do you do to put bread on the table and clothes on your back?"

The man lifted his mug and threw back the last of his ale. "We waits 'til nobs like yourself come along to pay for the drinks!" he answered with a loud laugh. Then he, too, stalked from the inn.

Lord Scythe looked with bewilderment about the empty taproom. He had been friendly. He had spent money on them for drinks. Still, he hadn't learned a blasted thing. What in heaven's name had he done wrong?

"Looks like you're all alone, m'lord," the buxom wench said as she swayed her expansive hips provocatively in his direction. "Won't you let Nell keep you company?"

Lord Scythe drew in a deep breath. "Yes, indeed." He gestured to the seat beside him. "Won't you join me, Nell?"

She settled her ample buttocks on the bench beside him.

Lord Scythe blinked, the better to adjust his aging eyes to take in all of her. Her auburn hair tumbled down, only partially obscuring her bare shoulders and enormous breasts.

Suddenly, Lord Scythe frowned. He reached out to grab the ornament affixed to her bodice.

"See here, m'lord! What kind of a girl do you think I am?" she cried, slapping his hand away. "At least wait 'til I give you a by-your-leave."

"Where did you get this?" Lord Scythe asked softly, indicating the small garnet brooch pinned to her low-cut bodice.

Nell clapped her hand tightly over the brooch. " 'Tis mine," she asserted.

"The gift of a well-pleased lover, no doubt."

Nell blew a snorting laugh. Then she tossed back her auburn hair. "I found it."

"Indeed? Well then, where did you find it?"

When Nell eyed him suspiciously, his lordship whispered, "It could be very important."

"This little thing?" Nell asked, glancing down at the brooch. Then her eyes narrowed speculatively and she asked, "Is it valuable?"

Lord Scythe shook his head. "Not very. But it *is* important."

"How important?"

"That depends upon where you found it."

"Well. . . ." Nell hesitated. She fingered the brooch and grinned speculatively into his eyes. "Do you think . . . just perhaps, m'lord, that you could let me keep the brooch . . . if I tell you how I came by it?"

Lord Scythe silently regarded her for a few moments. She began to blink apprehensively. Let her worry, he decided. He didn't want to let the wench think she'd struck too good a bargain.

When his lordship refrained from making any response, Nell grudgingly offered, "After all, he does owe me this."

"He?"

"The highwayman," Nell answered cautiously. "That's why you're here after all, ain't it?"

Lord Scythe peered into his mug as he spun the contents round and round. No sense in letting the trollop know she'd hit upon a subject of keen interest to him. "You know of him. Would you perhaps know his name?"

"It was hers," Nell continued, apparently eager to tell her own story before she would answer Lord Scythe's questions. "She looked like such a fine lady in spite of her awful clothes. She dropped it under the bed. When I found it the next day, I said to myself, he never gave you nothing, Nell. Why shouldn't you have it instead of her?"

"Indeed, Nell," Lord Scythe agreed most generously. "Why shouldn't you? Now, who brought the girl here?"

"You're going to try to trap him," Nell stated. She shook her head. "I won't tell you his name. I won't say too much, in case your plan goes foul. I won't have everyone here thinking *I'm* the traitor."

Nell's eyes hardened and her lips tightened. "But a gel can only stand being refused for so long, you understand. 'Twill serve him right for all the months I wanted him and he never wanted me."

Chapter 21

BLACKFRIARS WAS NOT the worst neighborhood. Still and all, Jane made her way to her destination with a certain trepidation.

Why in heavens name was Dalton St. Clair, heir-presumptive of the Marquess of Milburton, living here? She had heard rumors as she circulated about now in society that the Marquess of Milburton and his nephew had never rubbed well together. Still, she had not supposed that his lordship would leave his own heir in such dire straits. Apparently, she had supposed wrong.

Was his uncle's parsimony the reason Dalton disguised himself as a highwayman and robbed travelers—to finance his London sojourn? If that were the reason, Jane thought the man certainly could afford better accommodations than these.

She sighed. Deep inside, she knew that Dalton was not the kind of man who would terrorize travelers just so he could gamble away the night at Boodle's. She wished she knew what he was about.

'I most surely would not be doing this if it were not for Horatia,' Jane thought as she sought his lodgings.

Horatia had continued her strange behavior. Jane wondered if John were still behaving just as strangely. She could not be sure, as no one had seen him for days.

Even Lady Balford could not help her on this matter. Her ladyship reported that she had attempted to see him, but John had sequestered himself in his rooms at his club and refused to go anywhere which might bring him into even remote contact with Horatia, the Manleys, or even with his own beloved step-grandmama.

If he would not speak with Lady Balford, he most assuredly would not listen to her, Jane reasoned. By no means would he welcome a visit from Sir Horace!

Jane shuddered with a mixture of reluctance and fear at the very thought of attempting to explain to Sir Horace why he should *need* to speak to John Tipton!

There was only one other gentleman to whom Jane could turn for help. At the moment, the puzzling, infuriating Dalton St. Clair was her only recourse.

Instructing the maid to wait outside, Jane tapped at the door. She was admitted by a wiry little man with a pair of spectacles perched precariously on the end of his nose. The man, apparently the valet, disappeared into the other room.

"Jane!" Dalton greeted her, a wide smile lighting his eyes. He held out his hand to welcome her into the small sitting room.

Pride be damned, she almost said. Seeing him again, she wanted more than anything to fall into his strong arms and lose herself in the blue-green ocean of his gaze.

Yet, she held herself back from him and entered the room without taking his hand. She did have a certain amount of self-respect and stubborn pride, after all. If Dalton St. Clair did not want her, she was not about to go throwing herself at the man.

"Miss Manley," he corrected himself, assuming her own cool demeanor.

Jane's heart twisted as she watched the light fade from his eyes and the crooked smile disappear from his lips.

"To what do I owe the honor of this visit?"

"If you please," she said, her voice very small and quiet. "I would detain you only a moment."

"I shall always be able to spare at least a moment for you."

His voice was so warmly reassuring that Jane dared not look up into his eyes for fear of seeing again the intense desire that once was there. Then, surely, she should be completely lost to all her good intentions of avoiding the man.

"Come, be seated," Dalton invited, gesturing to the shabby little sofa by one tiny window.

Jane tried to calm her nervousness by smoothing out her skirt upon the cushions. She would have succeeded had not Dalton decided to sit beside her. She could see each dark lash that surrounded those sea-blue eyes. She could not meet his intense gaze. She dropped her eyes to stare at the reticule which she clutched in her hands. She could smell the vetiver which he habitually wore. Did the blasted man *have* to sit *so* disturbingly close?

"I am very sorry to bother you, but . . ." Jane began. She fidgeted with her reticule.

"'Tis no bother," Dalton quickly reassured her.

"There is no one else to whom I might turn with this problem," she tried to explain.

"I am gratified that you thought of me in your hour of need," Dalton replied softly.

Thought of him in her hour of need? He was all she ever thought about. Even when confronted with Horatia's predicament, when in need of someone to effect yet another rescue of a sort, he was the one who immediately came to her mind.

Jane took a deep breath. How would she ever find the words to explain to this man the distressingly intimate problem between John and Horatia?

Very slowly, without daring to look up from her reticule into the man's dangerously blue eyes, Jane explained the delicate dilemma.

"'Tis quite a difficult situation," Dalton agreed, stroking his squared chin. "How do you think I may help you . . . and Horatia?"

"We have no one else in whom to confide who might be admitted to the club to speak to John. Please say you will go," Jane pleaded. Inadvertently, she grasped his hand in desperation.

Dalton reached out, covering her hand with his own broad palm. His strong fingers wrapped gently about hers. The mere touch of his hand was warm and reassuring to her.

At last daring to lift her eyes, she smiled at him with shy gratitude.

Dalton drew in a deep, ragged breath. He broke their gaze

and quickly rose from the sofa. He strode to the far end of the room.

"I will do what I can to talk or, if necessary, shake some sense into Mr. Tipton's head, for poor Horatia's sake."

However Mr. St. Clair managed to fund his activities, he was not merely the spoiled heir-presumptive of the Marquess of Milburton out for a lark. He was an honorable man, Jane decided. But he was willing to assist her in the matter of Horatia and John because it was the proper thing to do, not because he held any concern or affection for her.

Ah well, she thought with a silent sigh, she knew as much when she came here.

"I thank you for your assistance, Mr. St. Clair," she said softly as she rose to leave, "whatever the results may be."

Dalton did not want to stand there watching her slender figure walking away from him. He wanted to go after her, sweep her up in his arms, and tell her that he would move heaven and earth to make her—or anyone she cared about—happy.

What would she do if he fulfilled his desires? She had made it quite clear that she suspected his every motive—and rightly so. How could he explain to her why he robbed wealthy travelers? He feared that the very fact she knew his identity involved her in the deception in such a way that she might be endangered.

Reluctantly, Dalton escorted Jane to the door.

"Begging your pardon, sir," Thompson asked from the doorway to the bedchamber. "Will you be wanting everything packed or do you intend to return shortly?"

"You are leaving?" she cried. Quickly, she tried to recover her cool demeanor. Even though they had argued, she dreaded the thought that, once more, she might never again see her highwayman. However, it simply would not do to have Mr. St. Clair see her so-transparent disappointment.

"I depart within the hour for . . . urgent business to the north," Dalton explained hesitantly.

Only one kind of business to the north came to Jane's mind. Had Dalton run short of funds and found it necessary to return to the Green Horse Inn to replenish his pockets? she wondered and worried.

'The Green Horse Inn!' she startled with the realization

and suppressed a shudder of fear. Also in the north was Lord Scythe and his diabolical plans for the bandit on the black horse.

She must warn him! He must not go to the Green Horse Inn.

"Oh, Dalton, don't go!" she managed to stammer.

He smiled his crooked smile down upon her, his eyes rekindling with warmth. "I would stay if you wanted. . . ."

"Don't go to the. . . ."

"Begging yer pardon, miss," the voice behind her intruded. "Yer hack be awaiting, sir."

He was leaving *now!* Jane realized with rising panic.

"Everything is ready, sir," Thompson said, emerging from the bedchamber lugging a worn valise.

"Best hurry, sir," he advised as he took the valise from Thompson and shouldered the heavy burden. "'Twill be dark before we're halfway there, as it is."

The hackman turned toward the stairs. Thompson bustled after him.

"Dalton, I must speak to you," Jane tried to tell him. But Dalton had taken her arm and was gently guiding her out the door.

"If I am to address the other matter of which we spoke, I must leave now," he explained as they descended the stairs. "You do understand."

Jane shook her head. She did not understand why he must leave in such a rush.

"Please, Dalton, do not go. 'Tis dangerous. . . ."

Dalton chuckled as he and Thompson entered the hack. "Oh, I doubt that Mr. Tipton will do me much of a damage."

With that, the hackman closed the door, swung up into his seat, and took off.

"Don't go. . . ." Jane fairly screamed after him in her frustration. Why could he not stop a moment to listen? Why had she not been able to speak faster to warn him? Her own fears caused a deep sigh to quiver from her.

"You will see this Mr. Tipton, sir?" Thompson asked as they rode along. "There's precious little time remaining. . . ."

"I must."

"For the lady, sir?"

"For a friend of hers."

Thompson regarded Dalton with a wry smile. "No need to dissemble with me, sir. I have served you for many years, and have never seen that particular look in your eyes before."

"I have no idea what you mean, Thompson."

"Whoever loved that loved not at first sight?" Thompson quoted.

"Ha! I have you now, Thompson," Dalton exclaimed, grateful for the chance to distract his valet. "'Tis from *As You Like It.*"

"Actually, 'tis originally from Christopher Marlowe, sir," Thompson admitted.

"Unfair, Thompson!" he exclaimed, shaking his head. "Not fair at all."

Indeed, Dalton pondered, it was unfair that he should love the lady so, from his very first sight of her, and not be able to do anything about it.

It certainly was not White's, Dalton decided as he regarded the modest brick-fronted edifice, but it was the kind of unassuming club to which Mr. Tipton would belong. The aging butler admitted him to a small sitting room, where Dalton, alone, awaited John's appearance.

The man's appearance was hardly worth the wait. Mr. Tipton had neither shaved nor changed his clothing in at least a week. Dalton sincerely hoped the unkempt man did not come too near.

"Mr. St. Clair. I do not believe I have had the pleasure of making your acquaintance heretofore."

"We have a mutual friend," Dalton explained. "Miss Horatia Manley."

"I beg your pardon, sir," John said, drawing himself erect. "You must be mistaken."

If Dalton had known the man better, he would have grabbed him by the throat and throttled him. After what he had done to the lady in question, how dare the man have the audacity to deny any knowledge of her!

Restraining his initial impulse, Dalton merely gestured to two chairs drawn close to the fireside.

"No, Mr. Tipton," he said. "*You* are the one who has been mistaken. That is precisely what I am here to talk to you about."

John stood his ground. His dark eyes narrowed with anger and something which Dalton might have labeled pain.

"I respectfully suggest that you attend to your own business, Mr. St. Clair," John said through tightly compressed lips.

"Your business is no longer solely *your* business, Mr. Tipton. You have involved someone who is dear to someone whom I hold. . . ." Dalton paused. The business at hand concerned Horatia and John. No need to go into lengthy explanations concerning his own romantic difficulties.

"I am a friend of the family, here on their behalf," Dalton decided to offer by way of explanation. "I suggest you listen to me. It is either that or meet Sir Horace with pistols at dawn."

"I have nothing to fear from *him!* Sir Horace could not hit my Aunt Fanny with a custard tart, even if she were standing directly in front of him," John asserted with a derisive laugh.

Dalton shot him a skeptical look.

"Very well, neither could I," John conceded.

"In that case, I submit that you have very little alternative but to listen to me," Dalton said, again indicating one of the two chairs.

This time John sat.

"Why, John?" Dalton asked quietly, as he took the chair opposite. "You do not appear to me to be the type of man who would seduce a young lady merely for sport."

"Indeed, I am not!" John declared, half-rising from his seat in protest.

Dalton motioned with his hand for John to settle himself again.

John sat in the chair, his hands clasped before him. He twiddled his thumbs. He studied the tips of his scuffed boots.

"I love the lady, sir," John explained very slowly. "Her parents are set against my suit, as I have nothing to offer her but my love. Still, shamelessly, I could not contain my ardor."

John hung his head and paused.

Dalton waited until John again raised his head.

"I have compromised her honor. How can I face her again?" he asked. "It will be better for her to forget about me, to find a better life than the poor existence I could offer." John breathed a heavy sigh. "And perhaps some day I shall be able to forget her."

"You cannot resolve your problems by hiding from them."

John looked up, frowning angrily. "What right have you to speak to me of resolving problems? What problems have you?"

Dalton grimaced and shrugged his shoulders. Now was not the time to be delving into his sorry tale.

"You say you love her. Now you must do the honorable thing."

John shook his head. "Sometimes, Mr. St. Clair, love can best be shown by releasing the one you love—no matter how much it may hurt."

"More often, love can best be shown by fighting for the one you love, no matter how much it may hurt—if you want her badly enough."

"I cannot face her."

"You must," Dalton insisted. "And you must explain to her why you behaved the way you did. And if she loves you, as you say she does, she will listen."

John still looked at Dalton, but Dalton could see that the man was truly looking inward for the answer to the decision he must make. Suddenly, Dalton realized that he, too, had some explaining to do to Miss Jane Manley, because he truly loved the lady. And he would tell her so, regardless of the consequences, just as soon as he returned.

"I will do it," John announced, springing to his feet. "How can I thank you for the good advice, Dalton?"

"Think nothing of it, John. Indeed, you have been invaluable to me as well."

Dalton met John's puzzled glance with a wry twist of his lips and an enigmatic shrug.

*   *   *

"Under Lady Manley's express orders, sir, Miss Manley is not receiving *you*—today or any day," Jane heard Snodderly telling the caller. She had a good idea who was calling.

"You must be mistaken, Snodderly," she said, approaching the door. "Miss Manley most certainly *is* accepting callers today."

"Begging your pardon, miss. . . ."

"You will remember, Snodderly, *I* am Miss Manley, too."

Snodderly raised his bushy eyebrow, yet nevertheless backed up, allowing John to enter.

Jane was relieved to see that he had bathed, shaved, and donned a clean set of clothing. She wished she could say the same for Horatia.

"Snodderly will provide you with some refreshment, Mr. Tipton," Jane told him. "I will bring to you what I believe you truly came for."

"I could not eat," he protested, shaking his head.

Well, in that, he is still suffering the same as Horatia, Jane observed.

Horatia planted herself firmly on the edge of her bed, arms clasped tightly over her breasts. "I refuse to go down."

"Do not be an idiot!" Jane scolded, seizing her cousin's hand and pulling her up from the bed.

"How can I ever face him again?"

"The man appears to have come to his senses. Do not spoil your chances for a happy life by rejecting his overtures."

"If I had rejected his overtures in the beginning, I would not be in this fix right now," Horatia mumbled crossly. Still, she allowed Jane to push her to the mirror.

Jane did her utmost to salvage what she could of Horatia's once-lovely appearance. Standing back to view her handiwork, Jane considered that she had done an acceptable job.

Horatia hung back at the doorway to the drawing room. "Good afternoon, Mr. Tipton," she said shyly.

John sprang from his seat. He quickly took two long steps toward her, but when she backed away from him, he halted in mid-stride. Without taking his eyes from her, he slowly moved away, placing the bulk of the sofa between them.

Horatia merely watched him as she slowly slipped into the room and closed the door behind her.

How she had missed him! How glad she was to see him—to look up into his soft brown eyes, to see him smile at her. Oh, why hadn't she changed into that new pink frock? Why hadn't she insisted Jane arrange her hair in a more becoming style?

"Miss Manley. Horatia. I have come to apologize. I should never have taken such unfair advantage of your affection for me."

"The fault was not yours alone, John," she admitted. "I, too, allowed the passionate side of my nature to take the upper hand."

"Since then 'tis I who have behaved abominably."

Horatia nodded. She readily conceded him that point.

"I never meant to treat you badly," he continued. "I was so ashamed that I simply could not bear to face you again."

She could not look into his eyes. Studying her slippers as she ground the toe into the carpet, she quietly told him, "I was afraid you had lost all respect for me."

"Horatia, I *love* you! I do not have to respect you."

Horatia stared at him, mouth gaping open.

"No, no!" John waved his hand before him, as if trying to wipe away what he had just said. He drew in a deep breath and tried again. "My love for you outweighs my respect . . . No, no, no! That is not right either. Blast! Why can I not say what I mean?"

Horatia smiled and shook her head. She advanced the rest of the way across the room toward him.

"It does not signify, John," she said, taking both his hands in hers. "I know precisely what you mean. Love and respect go hand in hand."

John enveloped her in his arms. Horatia had not felt this happy for a long, long time.

"I want to marry you, Horatia, but I fear I haven't the courage to ask your parents' permission."

"We do not need their permission," she declared, a defiant gleam lighting her pale blue eyes. "I *will* marry you, John!"

"You most certainly shall not!" Lady Manley's shrill voice cut across the room. She stood, her arms outspread between the doors to the drawing room, rather like Samson prepared to devastate the temple of the Philistines.

Horatia quite believed her mother capable of wreaking equal havoc upon her own hopes for happiness.

Sir Horace stood behind Lady Manley, longingly eyeing the liquor cabinet.

John disengaged himself from Horatia's embrace.

'Oh, no,' she wailed inwardly. 'Mama has succeeded in scaring off my shy John. I shall forever be miserably alone!'

Yet Horatia saw John bravely striding across the room to stand before her formidable parents.

"Begging your pardon, sir, my lady, I *will* marry your daughter," John asserted quite forcefully. "With or without your permission!"

Horatia blinked in surprise. Lady Manley blinked, too. Sir Horace elbowed his way past them both to make his way to the liquor cabinet.

"I have no fortune, no prospects, 'tis true," John conceded. "But I love your daughter, and with that and that alone I will be able to offer her a better life than any mere duke you may ever find for her."

John walked to where Horatia was standing. He placed his arm about her waist. "I would appreciate your permission," he told them gently now. "But, with or without it, I *will* marry Horatia!"

It took Lady Manley a few moments to gather her wits about her after such a confrontation from the usually timid Mr. Tipton.

"You most certainly shall not," Lady Manley declared, drawing herself up.

Rather like a puffed-up little pigeon, Horatia thought. And this time, her mother appeared just about as frightening, too.

John continued, undaunted. "I have never been able to obtain anything to which I aspired. I am quite determined to change all that regarding my marriage to Horatia."

"I am quite determined on this matter, too," Horatia warned her parents.

"You shall not marry!" Lady Manley declared, stamping her foot ineffectually. "I shall . . . I shall. . . ."

"You are not dealing with poor, little Jane now, Mama. You shan't lock *me* in the attic! John and I *will* be wed!"

Lady Manley, still gaping, stumbled to the sofa and collapsed upon it. Sir Horace, bottle in hand, collapsed beside her.

"Horace," Lady Manley said with resignation, "we appear to have no alternative. I suppose we must simply make the best of it." She laid her hand upon her husband's and heaved a deep sigh.

Sir Horace stretched his neck to look all about him, examining the drawing room of the town house they had gone to so much expense to let for the Season. Then he turned to Lady Manley and said, "All this, and for what?"

"What, indeed?"

"He has no title," Sir Horace lamented. "No fortune."

Lady Manley glanced up to John, then back to Sir Horace. "He *does* appear to have a great deal of determination."

"No prospects," Sir Horace continued to bemoan his daughter's choice of suitor.

"Well, Horace, all is not lost," Lady Manley mused with a bit more lightening of her spirits. "There is still old age, disease, and the occasional duel. Uncles, cousins, and older brothers are dropping off every day from some such things. Perhaps some day John may succeed to the earldom after all."

Sir Horace shrugged. "I suppose there is always hope," he conceded.

Lady Manley rose from the sofa. "We may as well make the best of the situation. We will simply convert the ball we were planning for Horatia into a celebration of the announcement of her betrothal."

"Good," Sir Horace pronounced. "Then we shan't have to expend any more money."

Chapter 22

HORATIA FLITTED ABOUT the town house, as chipper as a little sparrow, joyously overseeing the final preparations for her ball. Everything must be perfect, she insisted, right down to the very last detail.

Jane debated whether or not this was an improvement over the way she had been acting only a week ago. She was beginning to find both her cousin and her enthusiasm rather irritating. In all fairness, however, Jane had to admit that her jaundiced view of Horatia's zeal might be due to the fact that the impending ball did not hold nearly the same interest for her.

Well, at least Horatia was happy, Jane mused. Horatia had come to London fully expecting to be happy and had not been disappointed. Jane had come to London with every expectation of leaving there unhappy, and she had not been disappointed in that, either.

Jane released a deep sigh. In no small measure, John and Horatia owed their happiness to the efforts of Dalton St. Clair. She wished she had been able to see him once more, to thank him for all he had done.

Where was he now? She closed her eyes and felt her heart contract with fear each time she envisioned him prowling some dark highway in search of wealthy victims. If anything happened to Dalton, she knew that she should never be able to forgive herself for not warning him away from the Green Horse Inn.

How she wished she could know that he was safe in spite of all Lord Scythe's efforts to capture the highwayman. Perhaps Lady Milburton would have some news. Dare she make inquiries of her ladyship?

Well, she had dared to jump onto the back of Dalton's horse. She had dared to seek his help in the matter of John and Horatia. As far as approaching his aunt to inquire after him? She supposed she might as well dare that, too.

"By the bye, how is your nephew, Mr. St. Clair?" Jane asked in as offhanded a manner as she could. She hoped the teacup would not rattle in her hand from the anxiety she felt awaiting her ladyship's answer.

"I have had no communication from Dalton since he left," Lady Milburton told her.

For the briefest moment, a look of deep concern flickered in those cool, gray eyes. Jane wished she could conceal her own worry nearly as well.

"I am not overly concerned," Lady Milburton said lightly. "He may communicate with you soon. Dalton has ever been a notoriously poor correspondent."

"Why should Dalton communicate with me?" Jane asked quietly. "We are . . . just friends."

The look in Lady Milburton's eyes let Jane know that she did not believe her for a minute.

Jane grimaced. For everyone's sake, she had tried so hard not to allow her affection for Dalton to show.

"One would have to be blind not to see that you care for Dalton a great deal . . . even more than you care for Lord Scythe," Lady Milburton said. "How unfortunate . . . for all three of you."

Unable to deny her ladyship's assertions, Jane said nothing.

"I have known Derwood Marchant for many years," Lady Milburton continued. "Forgive me for saying this, my dear, but he does not care for you. All he cares for is to possess you, just like every other ornament which caught his eye as he passed the shops."

Jane hung her head. "I knew that from the very beginning, Lady Milburton. It did not seem to matter much at first. . . ." She found the courage to add, "Until I met Dalton."

"I can see that Dalton cares a great deal for you, too," her ladyship said.

"It does not signify now," Jane continued sadly. "Dalton and I have had a fearful row."

"Ah," Lady Milburton said, nodding. "And you feel that you are the cause of his rapid departure?"

They had now come to the point in their desultory conversation to which Jane had been leading all the while. She swallowed hard and answered, "No, Lady Milburton. I believe Dalton had another reason. I . . . I thought you might know. . . ."

Lady Milburton avoided Jane's eyes. "Oh, Dalton has reasons of his own . . . of which he usually prefers to keep me unaware."

Jane had no wish to disturb this gentle lady, but if she was to discover what had happened to Dalton, she must begin. "Lady Milburton, I am *very* concerned for Dalton's safety."

"Whatever could Dalton do that would cause one to worry for his safety?" Lady Milburton asked with a nervous little laugh.

"Lord Scythe has sworn to kill the highwayman."

"Yes. Well, Derwood always was a one to overestimate greatly his capabilities," Lady Milburton replied.

"In order to accomplish that very deed, not long ago he left for the Green Horse Inn."

Lady Milburton drew in a sharp breath. Then she raised her thin brows and inquired quite coolly, "Why, Jane, whatever does that have to do with Dalton?"

Jane studied her tightly clasped hands resting in her lap. "I . . . I know Dalton is my highwayman. . . ."

Lady Milburton smiled blankly. "Oh, my dear. What makes you so certain?"

"Even behind a mask, how could I not recognize the face of the man I love?" Jane confessed.

Lady Milburton looked at Jane intently. "How long have you known?"

"I have been suspicious since I first saw him again at Great-Aunt Georgina's," Jane replied. "I was not certain until I saw him in the park at sunset upon his coal-black horse."

Lady Milburton slowly nodded.

"I still cannot fathom why on earth he would rob people. He surely is not mad."

"If he is, my dear, he certainly has good reason to be. Lord Milburton is a most impossible man, obsessed with drink and gambling—not to mention other vices. He gives little thought—and even less money—to the family estates, estates which Dalton loves. Therefore, in order to help support the families and to maintain. . . ."

"Oh, merciful heavens! So that is why he does it," Jane exclaimed. She seized Lady Milburton's hand and smiled up into her face. "Oh, I am so relieved to know he is not mad."

"No, my dear, he is quite astute about his banditry." Lady Milburton continued to explain. "For almost a year now, he has very carefully been robbing only the wealthy, giving the money to those families in desperate need of food and shelter."

"What of the stories others tell, of a highwayman who abducts and kills people?" Jane asked. "That cannot be Dalton!"

"Most assuredly not! I can only suppose the tale grows as it is told, just as yours did."

Jane suddenly released Lady Milburton and covered her cheeks with her hands.

"If only I had known!" she wailed. "If only he had explained to me. I could have apologized. Oh, we would never have argued in the first place."

She began babbling to herself with sudden realization. "'Tis no wonder he was so irate. To think how it could have endangered him and his men if Aunt Olive and Uncle Horace had set the authorities upon him when I ran off with. . . ."

"Ran off with him?" Lady Milburton completed. She began to chuckle.

Jane grinned guiltily up at her. Lady Milburton laughed aloud.

"I never did believe Dalton capable of carrying off a young lady, even one as charming as yourself." Lady Milburton reached out and patted Jane's hand. "Not to worry, my dear. I think I have proven that I can keep a confidence as well as—indeed better than—most people."

Jane breathed a sigh of relief. Then she shook her head. "That still does not keep him safe from Lord Scythe. Oh, why could I not have warned him. . . ?"

Lady Milburton's slim fingers wrapped about Jane's. "The first I hear from him, I will notify you immediately."

For John and Horatia's sake, Jane did her best to appear to be enjoying their ball. Inside, she was wretched with anxiety. Neither she nor Lady Milburton had received any communication from Dalton in nearly two weeks. Fortunately, she had no word from Lord Scythe either.

Jane was listlessly following Mr. Peters as he tried to lead her in a quadrille.

"Oh, I do beg your pardon," she repeated as she trod upon his toes for the fourth or fifth time.

"You appear extraordinarily preoccupied tonight, Miss Manley," Mr. Peters said. "Whatever could worry a lady as lovely as yourself?"

"Lord Scythe," Jane replied before she could actually think about what she was saying.

"Ah, yes," Mr. Peters replied, nodding his head. "I suppose you would miss your betrothed."

"One would suppose so," she remarked.

"Especially when you know that he has gone off in search of an extraordinarily dangerous highwayman."

Jane nodded. "Indeed, I am very concerned about his search for the highwayman."

"Ah, then you may quiet your worries," he said, stretching his neck so that he could peer toward the doorway. "His lordship has arrived."

Jane faltered in midstep, once again treading upon the unfortunate Mr. Peters' much-abused toes. With every ounce of self-control she could summon, she forced herself to turn around.

"I have done it!" Lord Scythe announced to the assembled company. He stood in the doorway, flailing his thin arms high above his head. "Where others failed, *I* have succeeded, just as I said I would. *I* have killed the highwayman!"

The last thing Jane heard was Mr. Peters calling her name as she collapsed at his feet.

The next thing Jane saw was Lord Scythe kneeling over her.

"She is overcome with joy at my return, no doubt," his lordship said.

"No doubt," Lady Milburton commented wryly. She tapped him on the shoulder. "Begging your pardon. Allow me to reach her with the vinaigrette."

Lady Milburton waved the small vial back and forth under Jane's nose. Jane sat up with a start.

"Oh, Lady Milburton, he's dead!" Jane wailed when she saw the lady's face appear above her.

"Hush, child," Lady Milburton said, laying a slender finger over Jane's lips to quiet any further imprudent outbursts.

Jane marvelled that her ladyship could contain behind such a cool veneer the pain which was so evident in her eyes.

"Later we may talk alone together," her ladyship told her, then quietly backed away to disappear into her own private hell.

"Ah, my Jane, quite fine after all. Must be the excessive heat in this room." Lord Scythe extended his hand to assist Jane to rise from the floor.

Jane stared at his hand. This was the hand that had killed the man she loved. She did not want to touch it!

But in her befuddled state of mind, Jane was helpless to draw back, powerless to rise and flee. His lordship lifted her to her feet and drew her closer to him.

"My dear Jane," Lord Scythe said, "*Now* we can be wed!"

Once more Jane's knees quivered beneath her. This time there was no Dalton St. Clair standing behind her, ready to offer his support. Never again would there be, she realized with a horrible sick feeling in the pit of her stomach. She knew she must stand all alone. She began to cry.

"Tears of joy, my Jane?" Lord Scythe asked.

Numb with pain, Jane was unable even to raise her hand to wipe away her falling tears.

"How did you manage the incredible feat, Scythe?" one gentleman called. The group that had gathered about them clamored for the answer.

Lord Scythe smiled broadly. "'Tis quite fitting that I tell the end of the tale my Jane began."

'Not a fitting end at all!' Jane protested, although she was too numb to say a word aloud. Certainly not a fate which Dalton deserved when he was only attempting to rectify his uncle's wrongs.

Her stomach churned within her. If she had been able to warn him, her love would be alive still!

"I had determined by information which certain parties obtained for me," Lord Scythe began to recount to the crowd which had formed about them, "that the highwayman might be encountered at a place known as the Green Horse Inn."

'A curse upon that green horse,' Jane pronounced. 'And upon the man who found it,' She quite visibly contracted with the pain of her knowledge. 'And upon the girl who was too incredibly slow to warn Dalton about that infernal green horse.'

Suddenly, the thought struck her.

"What color was his horse?" she demanded.

Lord Scythe turned to her, his bushy eyebrows raised in surprise. "I beg your pardon."

"Was the highwayman's horse a black or a roan?"

"Why, all horses are black at night," his lordship answered.

"Oh, *please*, Miss Manley," a tall young woman from the center of the crowd scolded, "do not interrupt his lordship's stirring tale."

"I instructed my coachman to patrol the roads," his lordship continued. "I waited inside, curtains drawn, pistols loaded, primed and at the ready, until the villain should make an appearance."

"Was that not frightfully tiring?" asked a plump young lady in an extraordinarily low-cut gown as she elbowed her way through the crowd to stand at Lord Scythe's side, opposite Jane.

"Indeed, miss," Lord Scythe answered, turning to her. He flexed the fingers of his right hand. "A lesser man might have found it so."

"I'm sure you were exceptionally brave," the lady said,

smiling with undisguised admiration into his lordship's eyes.

Jane could not help but marvel that the same ladies who had thought the highwayman so handsome and romantic when she had told the tale of her kidnapping should now so avidly await the account of his death.

"At length, the rogue and his band stopped my carriage. When the scoundrel opened the door, I was quite prepared. I shot the monstrous villain directly through the heart," his lordship boasted. "Toppling from his horse, he was dead before he struck the ground. I have done my modest best to deliver the good people of England from another scurvy scum and have made her highways just a bit safer for honest folk to travel. My only regret is that I did not have the immense satisfaction of seeing the miserable fellow swing."

"Oh, Lord Scythe," a lady with flaming red curls said as she pushed her way through the crowd.

The brazen vixen did not stop there, Jane observed. She deftly managed to insinuate herself between Jane and Lord Scythe.

"I am so disappointed, my lord," she said, swinging those flamboyant tresses under his lordship's nose. "I missed the first part of your exciting recitation. Would you please be a dear and retell it again, just for me?"

"Oh, and me, too," another young lady pleaded. Additional feminine pleas echoed through the crowd.

"Why, certainly my dears," Lord Scythe answered, a wide smile renovating his usually sagging face. "Now, where was I? Ah, yes."

The people who had at first gathered about them drifted away, to be replaced by other interested observers, most of whom were female. The listening ladies were increasingly impressed as Lord Scythe added detail upon fantastic detail to his account. And Jane had thought *she* had an extremely fertile imagination!

Pressed in by the constantly changing crowd, Jane was unable to slip away. She was forced again and again, to endure his lordship's lurid account. Again and again she was confronted with the reality that it was not only Lord Scythe's action, but *her* own omission which had killed her dashing highwayman. For the rest of her life she would be forced to live with the knowledge that she herself was as responsible as Lord Scythe for the death of the only man she would ever love.

A thousand tiny stars twinkled at the periphery of her vision, threatening to engulf her. The candlelight shimmered before her eyes as she struggled to hold back her tears. Each time his lordship told the tale, she died a little more inside.

If only she had not told such a fantastic story about her highwayman, Lord Scythe would never have taken it into his head to hunt down and kill him. If only she had stayed in the carriage in the first place, she would never have met Dalton—would never have fallen in love with him. But, she lamented, at least he would still be alive.

Everything had gone so wrong! She was doomed to spend the remainder of her life married to a man she did not love and who did not love her, caring for his six obstreperous children, walking though all her social responsibilities as a viscountess—and all the while being ever alone and empty inside.

"My congratulations, Lord Scythe, upon your most astounding accomplishment," the rich, deep voice smoothed like honey across the room.

Jane looked up, furiously blinking back those blasted tears—tears which prevented her from seeing and believing what she could hear but still could not believe.

Now, even though she saw him, she could scarcely believe it. Dalton St. Clair stood before her. Here! Alive!

He was alive! The abject misery which had kept her immobilized vanished. The immense relief she felt at once again seeing him compelled her forward. She quite heedlessly pushed her way through the shocked group of ladies.

Drawing up abruptly before him, she breathlessly exclaimed, "I thought you were dead!"

"I? Dead?" he answered, surprised. "Why, I'm far too busy to take the time to be dead."

She did not want merely to stand there, staring into his fathomless sea-blue eyes and watching him smile that beloved crooked grin. She wanted him to hold her in his arms the way he had in the garden that night. She wanted to kiss his warm lips once again.

The best she decided she could do, considering the situation, was to seize his hand. Dalton lifted her hand and enfolded it in both of his large hands. He smiled down upon her.

"Come, let us talk," he said. He led her past a beaming Lady Milburton and out to the moonlit porch.

He looked down upon her, the soft creases around his sea-blue eyes deepening with his smile.

"I was never in any peril. I merely returned to Milbury Hall to supervise some minor repairs to the house after a small fire."

"But Lord Scythe killed the highwayman. . . ." Jane protested.

"There was another, very dangerous highwayman working in the same area," Dalton explained. "I have known of him for some time and have detested him for his cruelty and violence. Lord Scythe, in ridding us of him, truly has become a hero."

"I thought it was you. . . ."

"You should have known it was not I that he killed," he told her. "Lord Scythe is simply not the class of person I would rob."

She grinned, the smile widening across her face, until she laughed aloud at the sheer joy of seeing him alive, of being with him again.

Chapter 23

"SEE HERE, JANE." Lady Manley scolded.

"Yes, see here, St. Clair," Lord Scythe called as he, too, shouldered his way through the crowd to follow them outside. He stood beside Sir Horace and Lady Manley. "I demand an explanation."

Jane noticed that the plump young lady and the lady with the masses of red hair had not detached themselves from either of Lord Scythe's arms. Nor did it appear that his lordship was making any effort to disengage himself from the ladies.

"This simply will not do!" Lady Manley insisted.

"Indeed not!" Lord Scythe agreed.

"This *is* Horatia's ball, after all," Lady Manley continued to scold. "It was bad enough when Lord Scythe had to come back tonight, of all nights, and steal all the attention away from Horatia with his lurid tales. Must *you* comport yourself in such a scandalous manner and contribute to our embarrassment?"

"Indeed, she must, Lady Manley," Dalton answered.

Quite shamelessly disregarding all convention, he enfolded Jane in his long, strong arms. Jane, with just as much shameless disregard for convention, pressed closer to him. Directly in front of everyone there assembled, he kissed her.

"You see, Lady Manley, I intend to marry Jane, just as soon as possible."

"We shall continue this most unusual discussion elsewhere," Lady Manley commanded. "Somewhere private."

Sir Horace gulped down in one huge swallow the entire contents of his large glass of rack punch.

"There's whiskey in the library," he suggested, moving in that direction.

Lord Scythe excused himself from the pouting ladies, who vowed that they would eagerly await his return.

As Dalton closed the library doors tightly behind them, Jane slowly turned to face Lord Scythe.

She wished she had been able to say in the very beginning what she was about to say now. If she had been possessed of adequate courage then, she would have been able to spare everyone a good deal of trouble.

Jane groped for Dalton's hand. The mere touch of him gave her strength. She drew in a deep breath and began.

"Lord Scythe, under the circumstances, I feel it wise that we should cry off our betrothal."

She hesitated. Lord Scythe was still just watching her, waiting perhaps for more explanation. He was right. She supposed she owed the gentleman some sort of plausible reason for her actions.

"There is a . . . not inconsiderable difference in our ages."

Lord Scythe merely nodded.

"There is a great disparity in our rank and fortunes."

Lord Scythe nodded again.

"We share few common interests. . . ."

Lord Scythe quickly conceded that point, too.

"We . . . we. . . ." Jane scoured her brain for some definitive reason for crying off this betrothal, but in the long run there truly was only one.

"I am not in love with you, nor you with me. Therefore, I . . . I. . . ." Jane had said it all. She could think of nothing more to say.

She held her breath, fully expecting the overpossessive and highly excitable Lord Scythe to make an inordinate amount of fuss.

"Jane," his lordship stated.

Not '*my* Jane'? she noted with surprise.

"I think that a very good idea," he agreed.

Jane's mouth dropped open.

"Since I dispatched the wicked highwayman, I have received a great deal of attention from a great many ladies who, heretofore, would not have bothered to pass the time of day with me. They . . . they think I'm a hero," he admitted with a great deal of delight. "I find I rather enjoy it!"

Jane could not help but smile.

"I should like for it to continue for a good while longer yet," he concluded.

"My lord," Jane told him, "I would never wish to spoil your fun."

She extended her hand to him. "While I have never been in love with you, nor you with me, I do hope we may hereafter be friends."

Lord Scythe held her offered hand. For the first time, Jane felt no desire to draw away with aversion. She supposed that she could accept him as long as she knew that it was only her hand he would ever be holding.

"I see now that we do not agree on what the best is, but I have always only wanted the best for you," Lord Scythe said.

"I understand that now, and I wish the same for you," Jane answered. She decided that she truly did, too.

Lord Scythe left the library, no doubt to resume his stimulating discussions with the eager ladies awaiting him.

Dalton placed his hand lightly on Jane's waist and faced the Manleys.

"Sir Horace, I ask your permission to marry Jane," he said.

Sir Horace and Lady Manley stared blankly back at him.

"However, I tell you now, with or without your permission, we *shall* be wed."

Sir Horace and Lady Manley stared blankly at each other.

"Why do you two hesitate?" Jane demanded. "You were not so particular in your choice of suitor when you decided to marry me off to Lord Scythe."

"Well. . . ." Sir Horace mumbled to Lady Manley, "he *is* the heir of the Marquess of Milburton."

Lady Manley shook her head in resignation. "'Tis just as I had dreaded. I so detest the fact that Jane will outrank Horatia."

"We must face the sad truth, Olive," Sir Horace said. "Almost *anyone* will outrank Horatia."

"Very little we can do about it, I suppose," Lady Manley

commented. "Come, Horace. We may as well attend to our guests."

As the door closed behind her aunt and uncle, Jane turned to face Dalton.

"How soon can you have your wedding dress prepared?" Dalton asked.

"You do want to marry me," Jane stated, half in disbelief. "You do love me?"

"I have loved you since I first saw you," Dalton said, drawing her even closer to him.

Jane sighed and shook her head. "Then you *must* tell me, why did you not want me. . . ."

"Oh, but I *did* want you," he corrected her.

"Then *why*," Jane cried in exasperation.

"You know perfectly well why. How could I risk endangering you by involving you with my problems?" he asked. "How could I take you into my life when, at that point, I had nothing to offer you?"

Jane nodded her comprehension.

"Now, I have more to offer you, Jane," he told her. "In his remaining time, my uncle has become reconciled to me, for which I am heartily grateful. He not only has allotted me the funds to renovate the Milburton estates, but has increased my own allowance to the point where I can now offer quite a pleasant life for my future wife. And one day, I will be the Marquess of Milburton."

"I am glad to hear that," Jane said. "Now you will be able to pursue a more reputable and certainly a much less dangerous pastime."

"On the contrary," Dalton protested. "As a matter of fact, I intend to take on an accomplice—a young lady who once showed a great deal of promise for becoming an accomplished highwayman. I also intend to make her my wife," he added, drawing her into his arms. "If you will have me."

"Of course I shall," she responded, gazing into his sea-blue eyes. "And this time, you will not even have to kidnap me."

Dalton lowered his face to hers, caressing her lips and cheeks, then he drew back slowly.

"You see, sometimes love is making love. . . ."

"Like John and Horatia?"

"Precisely," Dalton agreed, reaching up to stroke her hair. "And sometimes love is knowing when to wait."

"Like us? Like then and now?"

"Precisely." He drew her closer to him. "Jane, my dear, lovely Jane, I am tired of waiting."

She touched his face gently. Slowly, she ran her finger from the soft crease of his eyelid, through the hollow of his cheek, down his firm jawline to the tiny cleft in his chin. "I, too, am rather weary of waiting," she shyly admitted.

"However, I shall continue to wait precisely long enough for us to obtain a special license and have a proper ceremony with proper guests in a proper church. . . ."

He kissed her slowly and firmly, first upon the lips, then across her cheek and down her throat to the place where her cream-colored gown exposed the tops of her breasts. His lips meandered up her throat and about her ear.

Pulling her even more closely to him, he whispered hoarsely, "And not a moment longer!"